THE
GUEST
ROOM

BOOKS BY RONA HALSALL

Keep You Safe

Love You Gone

The Honeymoon

Her Mother's Lies

One Mistake

The Ex-Boyfriend

The Liar's Daughter

RONA HALSALL

THE GUEST ROOM

bookouture

Published by Bookouture in 2022

An imprint of Storyfire Ltd.
Carmelite House
50 Victoria Embankment
London EC4Y 0DZ

www.bookouture.com

Paperback ISBN: 978-1-80019-296-6
eBook ISBN: 978-1-80019-295-9

This book is for everyone who works with homeless people, helping them to find food, shelter, and the support they need to get their lives back on track.

CHAPTER ONE

Steph woke early, the contents of the solicitor's letter prowling through her thoughts, a sense of uneasiness making her stomach gripe. The sun was already shining through a crack in the curtains, the room humid. She threw back the covers, ready to face the day. And the decision.

Morning was her favourite time. Always had been, especially when Max and Bea were small, and she'd have a magic half hour to herself before they woke up and the messy turmoil of family life began.

Now the house was empty, her family gone, even her husband. But at least she could take her time in the shower, instead of being interrupted by someone else wanting to use the bathroom; just one of the simple pleasures she was learning to enjoy.

Another simple pleasure was the first coffee of the day, and she savoured every sip as she sat in the kitchen listening to the chatter of the radio, ignoring the chatter of her thoughts, and her husband's demands through his solicitor. She gazed around the kitchen, a space they'd decorated many times over the years. She liked its current look the best, though, maybe because this time it had been her choice. A job for her to get stuck into when she'd first been left on her own.

She'd painted the units a pale olive, the floorboards a soft grey, the walls white. It was fresh and clean and homely, with her favourite pictures, drawn by the kids when they were little, framed on the walls. *Cheerful.* Like the radio. Having it on in the morning was a new habit, ironic really because she'd always enjoyed a bit of quiet in the mornings in the past. *Funny how things change.* At least with the radio on it felt like they were talking to her, like she had company, a voice to greet her at the start of the day.

A tendency to gulp food down while she got on with jobs for the family had been replaced with leisurely breakfasts, because she had nobody to run around after anymore. All this spare time was something she'd decided to luxuriate in, like a lovely hot bath. Hadn't she yearned for this very thing ever since she'd first had children? There had to be positives with her newly single situation, and she'd decided that this was one of them, to be enjoyed rather than scurried through with guilt sitting on her shoulder telling her she had things to do.

'You know your problem?' Cara, her friend at work, had said while she watched her bolt down a sandwich in three mouthfuls. 'You don't chew. How do expect your stomach to digest things if you don't chew them up first?' She shook her head. 'Honestly, you have to understand the digestive process. Give your body a chance to prepare itself before you expect it to get to work. It's like oiling an engine.'

Steph had laughed. Cara had been seeing a nutritionist and she was getting used to having her diet questioned but this was a new one.

Even though Cara was almost a decade younger, they'd hit it off straight away. She was a real chatterbox, her mouth always busy, while the rest of her was all neat and tidy; hair scraped back into a short ponytail at the nape of her neck, always dressed in dark trousers and white tops. She looked like a funeral director, talked like a barmaid and had a warm heart.

She gave Steph one of her stern looks. 'Look, I know these things because I used to be just like you. Never giving myself time to just rest for ten minutes and concentrate on refuelling my body properly. Then I ended up with a stomach ulcer and I'm telling you, love, you really don't want one of those.' She grimaced, her hand instinctively going to her stomach. 'The nutritionist explained it all to me. So now I eat mindfully.'

'Mindfully?' Steph picked up the second sandwich, took a smaller bite, the burn of indigestion already present. 'Honestly, Cara, I've no idea what you're talking about.'

'So first you spend a moment just looking at your food, letting your body get ready for eating. Then you take little bites and chew twenty times, focusing all your thoughts on eating and nothing else.'

'Flippin' heck, twenty times? You've got to be kidding. I'd be here all day if I did that.'

'Well, even ten times would be better than no times.' Cara wagged a finger at her. 'You are your own worst enemy, you know. And chewing your way through packets of those indigestion tablets is not the answer.' She put a hand on Steph's arm. 'I'm telling you, in times of stress, the important thing is to look after yourself.'

After that little lecture, and an acceptance that perhaps she was consuming way too many indigestion remedies, she'd tried to follow Cara's advice.

However, even eating at a snail's pace didn't fill the time before she needed to leave and catch her bus to work. She remembered the film of dust she'd noticed on everything in the lounge the night before, when the evening light shone through the bay window. She grabbed a cleaning cloth, thinking she'd have time to have a quick whizz round and go to work feeling she'd already accomplished something.

She sang along to the radio, letting her voice swoop and soar. There was nobody to tell her to shut up because she was giving them a headache, nor the need to creep around lest she wake someone too early. Having the house to herself could feel quite liberating at times. At other times, she'd hear every creak and groan of the floorboards, every rustle of the wind moving the curtains when a window was open, every murmur and hum of the fridge. Voices from people passing outside, sounding like they might be inside.

She sang louder. It was time to enjoy her independence, time to find out who she really was. An adventure, that's what Cara had called it. Something to embrace and enjoy rather than being all melancholy about things she couldn't change. She had to celebrate a new beginning rather than let herself be dragged down by the sadness of an ending.

She polished the mirror which had belonged to her mother, a lovely round art deco piece with mother of pearl set like a starburst round the edges. She smiled at her reflection, admiring her new haircut. It had been her daughter, Bea's, treat, something to cheer her up. She'd paid for Steph's appointment at a swanky hairdressers. It had taken for ever for the cut and colour, but she loved the result. A short pixie cut, which made her grey eyes look huge and accentuated her high cheekbones. Amazing what a good haircut could do for self-esteem, she thought, as she moved on to dust the sideboard.

She reached the mantelpiece where she kept her favourite pictures, all in matching frames now – silver, to go with the newly decorated walls. She'd kept the dusky theme from the kitchen, but in here she'd gone for a turquoise feature wall where the fireplace was. She picked up the first picture. Max as a baby. What chubby little cheeks, a mop of dark hair. He'd been a gorgeous child. Who knew he'd grow into such a lanky, difficult young man? She kissed the baby in the picture, put it back on the shelf. How proud they'd been when they brought him back here from the hospital. A baby boy, exactly what her husband, Andy, had hoped for. Of course he'd said he wouldn't mind if it was a girl, but what man doesn't want a son?

The next picture was Bea, a golden-haired toddler with her favourite teddy clasped in her arms, looking like butter wouldn't melt in her mouth. Steph cleaned the picture, gave her daughter a kiss too. What a blessing she'd been over the years. And now, even though she'd been devastated by her parents splitting up, she'd tried not to take sides and had been so good at coming over to check Steph was okay, bringing her little treats, taking her out for meals and shopping trips. They'd had more fun together than they'd had for years. One of the silver linings of the cloud she'd been under.

She paused at the next picture, wondering if it should even be on the mantelpiece anymore. A family shot taken on a holiday in Cornwall, the kids still in primary school. They'd got on then, the two of them, before they grew into very different people. Andy was holding up a huge crab, the kids each holding a smaller version. Their tanned legs were dusted with sand, feet bare, hair all matted from swimming in the sea, the three of them perched on barnacle-covered rocks. It had been a perfect holiday, a memory she cherished because it was probably the peak of her happiness.

Everything got a little harder after that. Problems with Andy being made redundant. That was an anxious time until he got his new job. Then Max having trouble at school. Then... She stopped her train of thought, not wanting to dwell on the negatives, dusted the picture and put it back. Andy was the father of her children, nothing was going to change that and although all the wedding pictures had been taken down, along with photos of them as a couple, this one could stay. There was love in his eyes, laughter on his face. This was the Andy she was happy to remember, a time in their lives when they'd been strong together.

The last picture was Steph with the a cappella group, Song-birds. The six of them were laughing, their arms round each other's shoulders. They'd started it when she worked in the bank and there was a programme on TV about workplace choirs. Management decided to give it a go and a weekly practice started, which she found she thoroughly enjoyed. Not only did it give her a new hobby, but she developed new friendships and when the bank had made most of the members of the choir redundant, they'd decided to carry on practising anyway.

She smiled as she dusted the picture, put it back in its place and picked up the card next to it. 'We Miss You' it said on the front and inside it said, 'Please come back, we sound rubbish without you!' Signed by all the girls. It had been sent with a bunch of flowers; such a lovely thought, it had made her burst into tears. Was she ready? Could she go back after she'd let them all down so badly?

She put the card back, finished dusting the room. Time for work. She hummed as she put the cleaning cloth away and picked up her bag and jacket, just in case it rained. It was looking a bit ominous out there now, with thunderstorms fore-cast for the next couple of days.

The door closed behind her with a satisfying clunk, and she gave it a push to make sure it was locked. You had to be careful these days. She stood back for a moment, admiring the glossy red of the front door. She'd been wanting to paint it that colour for years, but Andy always wanted racing green. Said it was more practical. She'd wanted cheerful, so that's what she had now, and it looked good against the white paintwork. *Smart.* She looked along the terrace, all the bay windows, the different hedges, some well looked after, some growing wild. It had always felt like home, from the minute she'd stepped foot in the place when they came to view it with the estate agent, excited that they could afford it. She liked having neighbours, found comfort in their comings and goings. For years, Andy had been on at her to move out to the suburbs, but she'd resisted and now she was glad.

Whatever Andy said, whatever he wanted, this was her home and had been for most of her adult life. This was the house where their children had been conceived, where those young lives had begun and been nurtured. Bea had been born on the rug by the fire in the lounge. This had been their sanctuary for thirty years, her home from the age of twenty-two. She could hear her teeth grinding and relaxed her jaw, knowing exactly what answer she would give to that solicitor's letter. Andy had a fight on his hands if he thought she was just going to leave.

CHAPTER TWO

Steph sniffed the air as she opened the front door, shaking raindrops from her hair.

Cigarette smoke?

She stopped and sniffed again. This time she was sure, the hairs rising on the back of her neck, goosebumps prickling her arms. She lived alone and didn't smoke. Nobody in the family smoked.

Is there somebody in the house?

She picked up one of the metal crutches she'd propped by the door, ready to take back to the hospital now that her broken ankle had healed. Her heart thundered in her chest as she stood still, holding her breath as she listened. The ticking of the carriage clock, a wedding present, was the only sound she could hear.

Hardly daring to breathe, she inched down the hall and peered into the front room. Empty. Then a new thought lit up her brain.

She dashed down the hall and into the kitchen. 'Max!' she called, frantically looking for signs of her son. 'Max, are you here?' He probably smoked. Being in the forces, going on tour to all those war zones. So stressful they probably all smoked.

'Stupid woman,' she scolded herself aloud, as she scanned the empty kitchen, the smell stronger in here. 'If he's not been home for ten years, why would he suddenly turn up now?' *Because... he's injured. He's missing me. He's decided to forgive me for not taking his side.*

She sighed and put the crutch back in the hall, went and filled the kettle, then watched the rain trickling down the windowpane while she waited for it to boil. She forgot for a moment about the smell and what that might mean, her thoughts fixed on her absent son, her eyes staring into the back garden, her gaze unfocused. Until she noticed a bin bag of rubbish, which had been thrown over the back wall into her garden and burst, littering the contents all over the path.

She cursed under her breath. The area where she lived wasn't what it used to be. A lot of the houses in the row had been bought up by landlords and rented to students, with just her and Mr Roberts next door left as live-in property owners. It hadn't really bothered her when Andy was still at home. In fact, she enjoyed living amongst all those young people with their futures ahead of them. It felt optimistic.

A bunch of girls had lived in the house next door for the past three years, all of them nurses. They were always popping round to borrow milk or tea bags or bread when they hadn't had time to go shopping. She let them use her shower when they ran out of money on the meter, enjoyed sitting down for a coffee and a chat, helping them sort through whatever was bothering them at the time. Since Andy had gone, she'd even been invited round for a girls' night in with them, watching Netflix and eating popcorn.

'We wanted to say thank you for looking out for us,' Sian had said, presenting her with a box of Belgian chocolates. 'We've just got a couple more exams then we'll be finished.'

Nia, who was sitting beside her, gave her a hug. 'You've been the best neighbour. Honestly, what would we have done without all your tea bags?'

She'd blushed and laughed when Jess had handed her an enormous box of tea bags, tied with a pink bow. 'With love from all of us.'

It had taken her a moment to swallow down the knot of emotion lodged in her throat. 'I'll miss you all.' She'd looked at each in turn. 'I can't believe you'll be gone. None of you thinking of staying around?'

'We're going back home to Wales,' Sian had said, glancing at Nia. They were friends from school who'd come to Leeds to study nursing together, wanting the excitement of the big city before they went back to their rural roots. 'Jess might stay on a bit.'

Jess shrugged. 'If I can find some people to share with, I'll stay here.'

The other two laughed. 'Don't be daft. You're moving in with Aaron. You know you are. He'll win you round, he always does.'

Steph had left the house feeling a little lost, wondering who she might get next door after the girls had moved out, hoping it wouldn't be empty for too long.

Bea had a different perspective.

'It's not safe, Mum. Not with the park opposite and all those losers hanging around, doing drugs and whatever else they get up to. And that little group of tents that keeps popping up, full of homeless people.' Bea had scowled. 'I honestly don't understand your logic for staying.'

'This is my home, love.' She'd looked at her daughter, wondering how best to explain. 'It's like a cosy old jumper; you know, the sort you snuggle up in when you're under the weather. Nothing fancy, well worn, but comfortable.' She ran a hand through her hair, aware that Bea still didn't understand.

'This is where all my happy memories are. I'm not ready to move.'

Now, as she remembered the cigarette smoke, she was wondering if Bea had a point.

A crash from upstairs had her jumping out of her seat as if she'd been electrocuted, her heart leaping up her throat. She stood still, body rigid, ears straining for sounds of movement, but it was quiet, no creaking floorboards. Nothing.

There's nobody there. You're imagining things again.

Several times since she'd been living on her own, she could have sworn she'd heard someone in the house. She'd even called the police, but when they came there was nobody there and no sign of forced entry. *I can't go ringing them again.* She'd be getting herself cautioned for wasting police time if she wasn't careful. She swallowed, her pulse still racing.

It's probably nothing.

But she wasn't convinced, all her instincts yelling at her that she wasn't alone.

She took a deep breath, sweat inching down her back as she crept down the hallway, grabbing the crutch as she went past, holding it out in front of her as she climbed the stairs. *What would I do if I did find an intruder?* She stopped for a moment and considered, her scalp tightening. It was almost too scary to contemplate. *What if they're armed? With a knife or something?* Her breath hitched in her throat, and she looked back down the stairs, wondering if that was a better option. Then she remembered the false alarms, the three times the police had been called out for nothing. Her hand folded round her phone in her back pocket, and she pulled it out, dialled the emergency services, her finger hovering over the call button as she inched forwards.

When she neared the top of the stairs, a blast of cool air hit her in the face. It was coming from her bedroom, which was to the right and ran from the front to the back of the house.

'I'm armed!' she shouted, watching the door moving backwards and forwards in the breeze.

The window must be open. Or is somebody behind the door?

She darted forwards, pushing the door so hard, it slammed against the wall, bouncing back and almost hitting her in the face. Listening for a moment, she could hear the curtains rustling, the patter of rain, but nothing else. Gingerly, she peeked into the room, letting out a relieved breath when she saw it was empty. Her eyes settled on the remnants of a favourite vase, which lay in pieces on the floor in front of the fireplace. That's what she'd heard, the crash. *It must have been blown off the mantelpiece by the wind.*

The back window was half open. *Did I leave it open?* It had been a hot and humid night, not a breath of wind, and she could easily have forgotten to close it this morning before going to work.

Despite the heavy downpour, she pushed it up and poked her head out, looking for signs of an intruder running away.

Her gaze swung over the muddle of back gardens, most of them unkempt, or paved over. Mr Parker's garden next door was spick and span, as usual. Steph's little patch wasn't looking so great at the moment, the garden having been Andy's domain.

Something caught her eye, a movement below. Her heart skipped, but it was only Nia next door, scrabbling to take the washing off the line. The chill of the breeze and the splatter of the rain made her retreat, closing the window, making sure she secured it.

Her eyes travelled round the room, noticing the indent on the bed, like someone had been sitting there, and when she went over to take a closer look, she caught the smell of cigarettes in the air again. She swallowed. Someone had definitely been in her house. In her bedroom. She tensed, her heart flipping in her chest.

Her hand grabbed for the crutch again. If someone was still

here, they would have heard her coming up the stairs, banging the door open. They'd know to be quiet until they could make their escape.

She swallowed her fear and crept onto the landing, pushing open the bathroom door with the end of the crutch while her muscles bunched ready for action. Empty. Her breath was fast and shallow as she tiptoed down the landing to the bedroom at the front. Max's bedroom. That aroma of cigarettes again and for a wild moment she imagined her son, lying on his bed, giving her that lazy smile of his when he saw her in the doorway. But that room was empty too.

She glanced up the stairs to the attic, Bea's bedroom, and the only other place an intruder could be. The door was shut. Her heart was beating so fast she thought she might be sick. *Calm down.* She took a few deeper breaths and listened. Frowned at a new sound, the steady drip, drip, drip of water, a cold breeze filtering down the stairs from under the bedroom door.

Suddenly she understood what the noise was and dashed up the stairs, pushing the door open to see the skylight was wide open, water streaming down the glass and into the room, splashing in the puddle that was creeping outwards on the floor. She grabbed the latch, squinting against the pounding rain, and slammed the window shut. Her feet squelched on the sodden carpet. *I know I didn't leave this window open.*

She rarely came up here now Bea had left home, but she always tidied round after one of her sleepovers, which happened more often since Andy had gone.

She shivered, not just with the chill of the rain, but with the knowledge that she'd had an intruder. There was no doubt about it this time. She called the police.

'We've had quite a spate of robberies in your area,' the police offer said. 'We'll send someone round to take details.'

'But I don't think it was a robbery,' Steph insisted. 'I can't see that anything has been taken, but someone's been in the house, sat on my bed and two windows were left open in the pouring rain. The carpet in the attic is ruined – I'm going to have to claim for that.' She sighed, reminded of the hassle it had been when she'd last made an insurance claim. That was when she'd broken her ankle at the shopping centre, and it still wasn't settled.

The fall was a bit of a blur, if she was being honest. Each time she tried to recall exactly what happened she felt less sure. She'd called in at the shopping centre after work and the place was practically empty, about to close. One minute she'd been messaging Bea on her phone to tell her about the summer sale in Superdry, the next minute a skateboarder had clipped her, sending her tumbling down the escalator.

She squinted at the damp patch inching its way down the attic wall, trying to remember. *Did I feel hands on my back?* Or had she imagined that? Her mind making up excuses for her clumsiness.

There was no doubt she'd been distracted. Anyway, skateboards weren't allowed in the shopping centre, and it was on CCTV, so they'd had to admit liability. Not that they caught the skateboarder. 'A constant problem,' the security guard who'd tended to her and called the ambulance had said. 'Use it as a short cut, don't they? Nothing we can do to stop them. Some of them do it as a dare, I'm sure of it.'

'Can't you just admit that you should have been looking where you were going?' Bea had asked when she picked her up from A&E and took her home. 'Why would anyone want to push you down an escalator? Honestly, Mum...' She'd tutted and shaken her head.

Steph sighed. Bea was probably right. If she'd been paying attention she probably could have dodged out of the way. But the skylight being open definitely wasn't her doing. A bead of fear lodged in her chest, and she sank onto the bed, shivering uncontrollably now.

Was I right those other times when the police found nobody here?

More concerning, though... Would they do it again?

CHAPTER THREE

She sat with the phone still clasped in her hand, gazing around the attic room. Nothing had been touched, everything was just as Bea would have left it – immaculately tidy. Could it be that the window latch had not caught properly, and the force of the rain had pushed the tilt and turn mechanism open? It was a possibility she had to consider instead of all the melodrama of an intruder.

She stood, her feet squelching on the soggy carpet as she headed back downstairs, her teeth clamped tight. Now she'd have to ring the insurance company and have all that palaver to sort out.

She locked the front door on her way past and put the chain on, then checked all the windows and the back door. As far as she could see, nothing had been disturbed or taken and she couldn't think of a logical explanation for someone to come in and just leave windows open. Then she remembered the smell of cigarette smoke. The dent on her bed where it looked like somebody had sat, and a prickle of unease worked down her spine.

The kitchen was a single-storey extension, and it would be

easy enough to clamber onto the roof and in through her window if she'd forgotten to close it. It seemed the most likely scenario. Or had she sat on the bed this morning after she'd made it? She shook her head, confused now about what was an actual memory and what was a possibility.

I'm probably imagining things again. Living on her own was taking a bit of getting used to and despite the things about it she quite enjoyed, it was a little scary at times.

Bea's words echoed in her ears. *It's not safe round here anymore.* Perhaps she was right about that. She gave a wry smile. Bea had an old head on young shoulders and an innate ability to point out truths that Steph was trying not to see. It was a quality that impressed and annoyed her in equal measure.

She opened the fridge, and gazed at the meagre contents, deciding she'd make do with a sandwich for her supper. She used to love cooking when she'd had a family to feed. It was her thing, the kitchen her domain, but now it felt empty, lacking the essential ingredients of family life.

Tears pricked at her eyes. *Pull yourself together*, she warned, not wanting to wallow in self-pity. Something she'd managed to keep at bay most of the time. *Look at all the positives of being single.* She'd had this very conversation with Cara only the other night when they'd popped out to the wine bar after work.

'You wouldn't be doing this if Andy was still at home,' Cara said with a knowing nod as she sipped her G&T.

Steph raised her glass. 'To all the single ladies,' she said as they clinked glasses. It was the first time she'd really considered herself in this light. *Single.* It was such a big thing to get her head around after being part of a couple for so long. 'And you're right. For some reason I was always scurrying home, wasn't I?'

'Like a good little wife,' Cara agreed. 'Programmed to get home and make his tea.'

Steph laughed. 'It sounds ridiculous, but that's what I've

been doing all my married life.' She took another sip. 'Thirty years of scurrying.'

'Scurry no more.' Cara winked at her and took another sip of her drink. 'Now you have time to be yourself. Decide how *you* want to run your life, with nobody doing that for you.'

Steph stared at her drink, watched the bubbles rising to the surface, wiped at the condensation on the side of the glass with her finger. She looked across at Cara. 'The weird thing is... And this is going to sound stupid... But I've no idea what I want my life to be like. There's nothing I've yearned for. Nothing I wished was any different.' She sighed. 'I liked being married. It was... comfortable.'

Cara leaned across the table and rubbed her arm. 'You don't sound stupid at all. It's a big change for you. But once you embrace it, I'm pretty sure you'll find all sorts of things you fancy doing that you wouldn't have even considered if you were still with Andy.'

Steph was silent for a moment, then grinned. 'You mean like going skydiving? I've always fancied that.' She glanced at Cara. 'Or riding across the desert on a camel. Or... um... I don't know, maybe going down in one of the cages to see the great white sharks.'

Cara spluttered on her drink, dabbing at her mouth with a napkin. 'Sort of. Except I can't see you doing any of those things. But I do think we could go on a wine tasting weekend in France. Or in the UK if you don't fancy going that far.'

Steph's eyes widened. A wine tasting weekend. Now that sounded like fun. And something Andy wouldn't have been interested in. He was more of a real ale fanatic.

She raised her glass. 'Now that's a bloody brilliant idea.'

'Let's do it!' Cara's eyes sparkled. 'Let's have a look and see when we could get the time off together.'

They clinked glasses and Steph had gone home feeling quite excited about the possibilities of the future. A little holiday away with Cara was exactly what she needed to launch herself into single life. She'd spent a couple of happy hours researching on the internet, narrowing it down to five options. They still hadn't decided which one to go for, and hadn't been able to speak to their boss about a time when they could both be off together, but it had certainly given them something to look forward to.

Now she reminded herself of the other benefits of being single. At least she didn't have Andy going on at her in a jealous rant anymore. And she had to admit that was a relief. Those weeks had been exhausting. She still had no idea why he'd been so convinced she was having an affair. Even when she'd brought Cara round to help explain that the pictures he'd been sent were deceiving, he wouldn't believe her.

Yes, she'd been talking to her boss. Yes, they'd been close, their heads almost touching, but that was because they were looking at figures, trying to work out how much of a grant they should be requesting in the application. Of course she'd have his phone number in her contacts list on her phone. And yes, she did sometimes need to ring him out of work hours, when she needed to remind him about things, or had an idea she wanted to discuss. But those things did not add up to what Andy claimed they did, before he'd left for good twelve weeks and three days ago.

Was I out of order? Flirting? Her cheeks burned at the thought. It hadn't been her intention, but she could see how things could be taken out of context. Andy's reaction had been a clear demonstration of how a few phone calls out-of-hours could be construed as something they definitely weren't.

Steph worked at a homeless shelter run by a local charity, a job she'd taken up when she was made redundant from the bank almost a year ago. It was the perfect role for her, helping residents to sort out their finances, filling in all the forms with them to claim benefits, trying to find housing. Her boss, Bill, was a big, tactile man big brown eyes and an animated face that was never still under his mop of unruly grey curls. She remembered going for her interview, feeling quite intimidated by the size of him, the boom of his voice.

'Come in, come in,' he bellowed when she hovered at the door. He picked up a pile of files from the only chair she could see and dumped them on the floor, and waved her in. 'Come and have a seat.'

She sat, sweating profusely in the summer heat, all dressed up in her best navy-blue office suit. He was wearing a Hawaiian shirt, knee-length shorts and flip-flops. Her cheeks burned as she realised her first mistake, wishing she'd gone for the summer skirt and blouse instead. He grinned at her. 'I'm not that great at doing interviews.' He indicated his attire. 'As you can see, we're all casual here. Works best with the clients.' He sat on the other side of his cluttered desk and leaned back in his chair, eyes assessing her for a long moment. She shuffled in her seat, tucked a strand of hair behind her ear and smiled at him.

'Now let me give you a bit of background,' he said, elbows sticking out as he rested his head back in his hands.

Steph was mesmerised as he went through the story of how the charity had been set up, his role from the very start and how they'd grown in recent years. He spoke of the grant funding they'd secured for their latest project and how her job would fit in.

'Any questions?' he said when he finished.

Her mind was a blank, her whole being drawn into his narrative, the idea that he'd been homeless himself after a divorce and had somehow found the will to turn his life around and devote himself to helping others. He'd even taken youngsters into his own home on a few occasions before their new unit was ready, so desperate was he to save them from a life on the streets. She cleared her throat. 'No, not really. I think it's all very clear.'

He jumped up, the office seeming so much smaller when he was standing. He squeezed round the side of the desk, opened the door, and beckoned her to follow. 'Let me show you around.'

She tagged along behind, watching him greet every person they met with a kind word, a hand on the shoulder, a fist bump, or a joke. It was obvious he was the heart and soul of the place, the motor that kept the machine working. She admired what he had achieved, his total commitment to the cause. This wasn't just a job, this was his life. At the end of the tour, he asked a couple of questions about her CV, then sat for a moment looking at her.

She smiled at him, feeling a need to break the silence. 'What a great place you've created.' She blushed. 'Honestly, it's... well, it's inspirational. I'd love to be involved.'

He laughed. 'You mean I haven't put you off? You still want the job?' He leaned forwards, raised an eyebrow. 'Do you think you can work with someone as organised as me?' He swept an arm round the office, indicating the chaos.

'I'd love the job,' she confirmed, with genuine enthusiasm, completely sold on the whole ethos of the place. Now she could do work which felt worthwhile, and even if the contract was only short-term – it wasn't permanent because it was grant funded – at least it was something to keep her going for the next eighteen months. It was the start of something new. Something exciting. She grinned at him. 'And the first thing I'll do is get you a PA.'

Two weeks after she started work, Cara had been appointed as his assistant and had quickly got him organised. Together, they kept the place going, a tight little team. There were a few more staff, including Phil in the kitchen with his group of volunteers and a team of support workers who ran the accommodation blocks.

Steph took to it so well the place felt like a second home, Bill and Cara becoming good friends as well as work colleagues.

Her customer service skills had seen her through a few tricky moments and that training course on how to deal with difficult people had been a lifesaver on occasion.

Steph had never worked for such an awe-inspiring man as Bill. His passionate desire to provide proper, constructive help for the homeless rubbed off on all his staff and she found working for him energised her in a way that twenty-five years working for a bank never had.

She sat and thought about it now. Okay, perhaps she *had* been over-enthusiastic. Maybe she'd allowed boundaries to be blurred. But an affair? No, never.

Anyway, the whole thing had been blown out of proportion. After weeks of arguments, going round in circles, Andy moved out. Just like that. After twenty-nine years of marriage, he left her. Currently, he was staying with Charlie, a workmate, who lived in a swanky apartment in the city centre. A new development by the river. She was sure he'd be drowning his sorrows in one of the numerous wine bars located nearby. Eating in one of the lovely restaurants on his doorstep.

She could hear Cara's voice: 'Very convenient to have this accusation to throw at you as an excuse to leave, don't you think? Men always want to make it your fault. My ex was exactly the same.' Steph was inclined to agree, wondering if Andy had just got bored with her and wanted a different sort of life.

Bea was exasperated with the pair of them. She thought it was a storm in a teacup, her dad having a mid-life crisis and they should be adult enough to sort it out.

Adult enough. Steph huffed. It was Andy who was behaving like a jealous teenager. There was no reasoning with him and, at the moment, every conversation degenerated into an argument. She'd never been in this situation before, had no clue what to do to sort things out.

Is that what I want? To sort things out?

Cara's voice again, a different conversation. 'Don't you want to experiment? Just think, you've only ever been with one man, now you can have fun finding out what you've been missing.' She winked at her and laughed, pulling up a dating app on her phone. 'Come on, let's get you fixed up with some dates.'

'God, no.' She didn't want to date. The whole idea of it was far too scary, especially now she was hurtling towards the menopause. A part of her yearned for Andy's soft kisses and gentle caresses, his way of making her feel loved just for who she was, not what she looked like.

Cara gave her a playful tap on the arm. 'Oh, come on. It's just a bit of fun. We'll make an independent woman out of you yet.'

'I'm not dating through an app,' she said, firmly. 'You hear all sorts of horror stories.'

Cara pulled a disappointed face, then her eyes lit up. 'I know. Dev's brother! Then we could all go out together.' She cocked her head, waiting for an answer.

The idea of going out for cosy foursomes was even scarier than internet dating; her friend would be watching her all the time to see what her reaction to her latest boyfriend's brother would be. No thank you. And anyway, he'd be far too young for her.

She forced a laugh. 'I don't think he'd be interested in an old woman like me.' She shook her head. 'It's a lovely thought, but I'm not ready for any of that. Not yet.'

Cara's face dropped and Steph made her excuses and got back to work.

The truth was, her life had changed in a direction she hadn't wanted. She hated having to make all the decisions. It was daunting, uncomfortable and if she was being perfectly honest, she was a little anxious about living alone for the first time in her life.

They'd been comfortable together, her and Andy, like a pair

of old slippers. And what was wrong with comfortable? It had been lovely having someone to snuggle up to on the sofa on a Friday night, watching a film. Or coming home to find he'd ordered a takeaway. Or little excursions at the weekends into the Dales, out for a pub lunch, a nice walk, or a bit of shopping in one of the market towns. He was her best friend, someone she shared everything with. Now she spent a lot of time talking to herself.

Steph pulled the margarine out of the fridge, plastered it on a couple of slices of bread, slapped on a bit of ham and cheese. Added some pickle. She was about to take it into the lounge to watch a bit of TV, when her foot scuffed something on the floor. She bent to pick it up. A cigarette stub.

Snatching her hand back, she left it on the floor tiles. Staring at it while she pulled her phone out of her pocket.

There was no doubting it now. She hadn't been imagining the smell of cigarettes. Someone really had broken in, spent time in her bedroom, smashed her favourite vase, and left the window open to damage the loft.

She called the police again and spoke to the same officer, who tutted sympathetically. 'I'll pass this on. Let me give you a reference number and then you can expect an officer to call later this evening.'

Steph thanked him and disconnected, staring at the cigarette butt on the floor, a cold dread lodged in her chest. She couldn't work out what her intruder's motive could be, but if scaring her had been their objective, they'd succeeded.

CHAPTER FOUR

Steph rang Bea, her whole body trembling now as she stood in the lounge, peering out of the window. She didn't want to be alone, and Bea could often pop over at short notice.

'Hey, Mum. How are you doing? I was just going to ring you actually, see if you wanted me to bring us a treat for tonight?'

'Oh, sweetheart, you'll never guess what's happened now...' She gulped back a sob as she went through everything with Bea, her words flooding out in a rush. It seemed even more sinister now she was relating it to her daughter, and she sank onto the sofa, all the strength going from her legs.

'Oh God, that's awful! Look, I'm coming over. I'm not too far away, I've just been doing a bit of shopping. Should be fifteen minutes or so.' Steph sank back, relief fluttering in her chest. She could manage fifteen minutes. If she just sat here, quietly, the time would soon pass. She heard the roar as Bea started the car engine. 'I'll be there as fast as I can.'

Steph didn't doubt it. She could imagine her daughter in her white BMW convertible. Such a fancy car, she hadn't liked to ask how much it cost, but then money wasn't an issue for Bea.

She'd married a wealthy man and now lived a life of comfort, a life most people could only dream of. The funny thing was it hadn't affected Bea at all. Although she now wore designer clothes and always looked fabulous, she was still the sensible down-to-earth child she'd always been, even if her husband could be a bit too much at times.

Mark had been a professional footballer, playing for Leeds United until he'd wrecked his knee ligaments and his career had ended. He had a good business brain, though, had invested wisely while he was earning a footballer's wage, and had set himself up as a football agent. Now he spent his time travelling the world, matching up clubs and players, doing deals for enormous sums of money. Meanwhile, Bea could do as she pleased. She'd dabbled in an assortment of jobs when she was younger but settled in none of them. Now she supported her husband as and when he needed her, organising events at their newly built house in a village just outside Harrogate, but she had no work routine.

'Aren't you bored at home?' Steph had asked Bea recently, when they were having a spa weekend, Bea's treat for Steph for Mother's Day. Bea laughed. 'Why would I be bored? I'm always doing things. People to meet, you know. Networking. That's work, Mum, even if it doesn't look like it. And... well, I'm just looking after myself because I need to be in good shape if we're going to start a family.'

Steph couldn't stop her scream of delight. That was the best news. She was wondering what her daughter's plans were regarding children, not wanting to ask because it would feel like she was putting pressure on her. 'That's fantastic news.' She leaned over and gave Bea a hug. 'I can't wait to be a grandma. And you will be a fabulous mum.'

Bea laughed. 'It would be easier to get pregnant if Mark was actually home, but...' She turned away, settled back on her sun lounger. 'He's got loads of trips lined up, so you'll be seeing a bit more of me for the next few weeks.'

Steph could hear the catch in her throat and knew that Bea was a bit upset. 'I'm sure once you have a baby he won't be away so much.' She gave her arm a reassuring rub. 'It changes everything... you'll see.'

'Hmm,' Bea said, turning her head away. Steph wondered if she might be crying. She put a hand out to comfort her, but took it back. Bea was a private person when it came to sharing her emotions and Steph knew it wasn't the right time to press her. There'd be time over the weekend to try and get her to open up, because there was clearly a problem. The conversation never really took place, though, Bea bouncing back to being her usual upbeat self, insisting that she was just a bit hormonal.

The doorbell startled Steph out of her thoughts, and she hurried to open the door, sure it would be Bea. Her face fell when she saw Andy on the doorstep. He'd had his beard trimmed, and his hair – and she hated herself for noting that the grey at the temples suited him. In fact, he was ageing pretty well, his figure still trim due to his daily exercise routine, his skin firm, despite the fact he was fifty-four. His blue eyes met hers, then slid away. Funny how they couldn't do that anymore – look each other in the eye – when they'd spent years and years gazing at each other, sharing unspoken jokes when the kids were younger. She'd thought she knew him inside out. Her jaw tightened. *Apparently not.*

'I need to grab some of my things.' He didn't wait to be asked in but pushed past Steph and into the lounge. 'Whoa, splashing out a bit here, aren't we?' he said, looking at the new grey leather sofa dotted with mustard and aquamarine scatter cushions – all recent purchases which she couldn't afford. An impulse buy after she'd received the divorce papers. 'I thought you said you were skint.'

She gritted her teeth. 'Nought per cent finance if you must

know,' she said, all ruffled and snippy. 'Nothing to pay for a year. Not that it's any of your business now, is it?'

He turned to look at her, his eyebrows shooting up his forehead. 'Of course it's my bloody business. We've still got a divorce settlement to sort out, haven't we?'

Steph folded her arms across her chest, and bit back the rest of her response. She hadn't the energy to argue. 'Is that why you're here?' A surge of emotion swamped her, filling her chest and before she knew what was happening, she burst into tears.

Andy stood for a moment, flapping his arms at his sides before he came over and wrapped her in a hug. She hesitated, then laid her head on his chest. A place which had always been hers, ever since she was a teenager. They'd been together since the sixth form at school. Solid, she'd thought, and even with all the trouble with Max, they'd got through it together. He'd been her rock, someone she could always depend on, and he'd always treated her as an equal. As relationships went, she'd felt a little smug that hers had worked out so well.

And then... somewhere along the way something had changed.

It was around the time she'd lost her job at the bank. They were closing branches and she'd been shocked to find she'd been made redundant. After twenty-five years, that was it. 'Out you go, we don't need you anymore.' Thankfully, the blow had been cushioned by a nice redundancy payout, which she and Andy had used to pay off the last of the mortgage. But it wasn't easy finding a new job when you were in your fifties.

Finally, after being forced into a career change, she'd found the role at the homeless shelter. It was a job that gave her immense satisfaction and she wondered now why she'd spent so long at the bank. *Risk averse. That's me.* Plus the fact she'd had a discounted mortgage as a staff member. It had been safe, both financially and emotionally.

Andy had been pleased for her, initially. Then, when she'd

been there a few months, he started popping in at lunchtime and suggesting he take her to work and pick her up. Suddenly a bit possessive, seeming to be watching her and they started rowing about all sorts of things. He was tetchy and bad-tempered, and Steph found herself keeping out of his way.

She came down to breakfast one morning, and caught him scrolling through her phone.

Something broke then. That bond of trust between them. She'd said things she should never have said. And so did he, a whole marriage worth of resentment filling the space between them. He'd left and had never come back. Things had escalated and now they were halfway through divorce proceedings. Although she was finding things to enjoy about being single, she felt like a three-legged dog; able to get about but very aware that there was a part of her missing.

Now, as she leaned into him, it felt right being back in his arms. Comforting, and she allowed herself to imagine that the last few months hadn't happened. That he was still there for her when things went wrong.

'Hey, what's up, love?' he said, his chin resting on the top of her head. His voice rumbled through her, the vibrations familiar, his hand rubbing her back.

'Somebody broke in,' she hiccupped through her tears.

'What?' His hand stopped rubbing, his body stiffened, his voice taking on an annoyed edge. 'Why didn't you ring me? Have you called the police? What did they take? For God's sake, I—'

'Don't go on at me,' Steph snapped, back in reality where Andy was no longer even her friend.

She pulled away, putting distance between them and fumbled in her pocket for a tissue, blew her nose, scolding herself. He didn't want her anymore. She had to get that into her head. He was the one who'd started divorce proceedings. He was the one who didn't trust her. He was the one who wouldn't listen, wouldn't let her have a life of her own. She gave herself a mental shake, put on her brave face and tried to make her voice sound normal, matter of fact, like she had everything under control.

'Of course I've called the police. But nothing was taken. They just left a couple of windows open, caused some rain damage. The police said there'd been a spate of break-ins locally.'

Andy ran a finger over his beard, giving it a little tug. It was a habit she used to find endearing. If she was being honest, she still did. A yearning to be back in his arms engulfed her, back where she'd always been, safe and protected. Instead, she perched on the arm of the sofa, not wanting him to see the shaking in her legs.

'That's it?' He clearly didn't believe her, his eyes scanning the room. 'Are you sure there's nothing missing?'

Steph sighed, knowing that he wouldn't stop questioning her until he had all the facts, and she supposed half the house was still his. 'I came home, and it smelled of cigarette smoke. Then I heard a crash upstairs, went up to investigate and the bedroom window was open, a vase broken on the floor and it looked like someone had sat on the bed.' She fiddled with the tassels on one of the cushions. 'Then I found out they'd left the window open in the attic as well and it was pouring with rain. Basically flooded the place. They hadn't touched anything downstairs.'

Andy gave a derisive snort. 'Sounds like a homeless person to me. Wanting somewhere to keep dry.' She looked up, annoyed at his assumption. 'Are you sure it wasn't one of your clients? The ones you're all friendly with? Eh?' He took a step closer, his frown deepening. 'Do you think one of them might have followed you home? Been stalking you?'

Steph paused, the idea that she might have been followed home from the shelter never having entered her head. *Could that have happened?* It could well have, she realised now, but she wasn't going to admit it. She shook her head, trying to speak with a certainty she didn't feel. 'Don't be daft. They're not like that. None of them would break in and cause damage.' Her voice was wavering, not convincing herself, let alone Andy.

He ran a hand over his hair and leaned against the mantelpiece. 'Look, I know we've discussed this before and I know you don't like the idea, but don't you think—'

They both turned as the door opened and Bea walked in. She looked stunning, as usual, with her beautifully coloured blonde hair, hanging in glossy waves halfway down her back. Thick black eyelashes, cloaking her slate grey eyes. She looked at her dad, then her mum. 'What?'

'Good timing, love,' Andy said, going to give her a hug.

Bea kissed him on the cheek then pulled away and focused on Steph. 'Mum, are you okay? I came as fast as I could.'

Steph forced a quick smile, the tissue still balled in her hand. 'I'm fine, sweetheart. Honestly, just a bit shaken.'

Bea put an arm round her shoulders and leaned down to kiss the top of her head. 'I'll put the kettle on. Good that you're here, Dad.' Her gaze swung from one parent to the other. 'I think we've a few things to discuss now, haven't we?'

She bustled out of the lounge and down the hallway into the kitchen. Steph glanced at Andy who shrugged and followed his daughter, Steph, a few steps behind.

Bea had always been good in a crisis and by the time Steph reached the kitchen, she'd already filled the kettle and got the mugs out. 'You've got to listen to me now, Mum,' she said as she reached in the fridge for the milk. 'As I keep saying, this area is not what it used to be. I know you both stayed here because it was cheap, and you were worried about redundancy after what happened before.' She caught Steph's eye. 'Which was a good strategy at the time. But, honestly, Mum, you're not safe here on your own.'

'I *said* we should sell.' Andy sat at the kitchen table, leaning on his elbows, hands cupping his chin while his eyes settled on Steph. 'But your mum won't listen.'

Steph was about to pull out a chair when she decided she'd rather stand, not sure she wanted to be that close to him now he'd gone on the attack. *Well, two could play at that game and didn't they say that attack was the best form of defence?* She drew herself up to her full height, anger flaring through her body. 'I don't want to sell. This is where you were born, Bea. Where our family grew up. It's not just a house...' She threw up her hands, gave Andy a hard look. 'It's everything that has been good in my life. I feel comfortable here. Like I belong.'

Andy looked at the table, gave a shake of his head. 'That's not it, though, is it? That's not why you don't want to move. Come on, be honest.' His eyes met hers. 'This is all about Max.'

Bea stirred the tea with more clinking than was necessary. They'd never been close, Bea and Max, even though there was only a two-year age gap. Not surprising, given the tricks he used to play on his younger sister, the way he constantly tried to undermine her and get her into trouble.

Steph pulled a fresh tissue from the box on the worktop and blew her nose, unable to deny the accusation. In part he was right. But it wasn't the whole reason why she didn't want to move. There were practical considerations.

'Where would I go? This whole area has been home to me my entire adult life, more or less. And it's easy for work.' She returned Andy's glare. 'I have enough stress going on without having to think about moving.'

Bea put the mugs of tea on the table and put her arm round Steph, giving her a reassuring hug.

'We all love this house, Mum. And I know you've got lots of lovely memories here, but the problem is you being here on your own. This area is so tatty now all the houses are rentals. You don't know who you're living next door to anymore.' She laid her head on her mum's shoulder, took her hand. 'I get so worried about you. And now this happens. Surely this intruder has made you think again about not moving?'

'They're not all rentals,' Steph said, although she knew her daughter had a point. 'And I've got lovely neighbours with Mr Parker and the girls on either side.'

'Well, they're not much use, are they? Mr Parker must be eighty if he's a day and deaf as a door post and the girls work all sorts of shifts, so they're never here when you need them.' She moved away and sat down at the table, picking up her mug of tea, a frown putting a neat line between her perfectly drawn eyebrows. 'Didn't you say the nurses are moving out?'

Steph nodded, feeling the weight of Bea's arguments pressing on her chest.

'Who might you get instead? It could be a load of rowdy lads, having parties all the time.'

Steph felt hemmed in, cornered by arguments stronger than hers. Andy had been asking her to agree to sell the house ever since he'd moved out. In fact, he'd been wanting to move for years, but Steph had resisted, wedded to the idea that she needed to stay in case Max came back. It was her fervent hope that her family would become whole again, and she couldn't risk not being here when he did return.

'I've told you that you're welcome to come and live with us for a bit,' Bea said. 'Just until all the money's sorted out and you know what you can afford. Maybe then you could get a nice apartment in Harrogate?'

'I don't want to live in Harrogate,' Steph snapped, then her voice softened, aware that her daughter was only trying to help. 'It's very sweet of you to invite me to stay, but I have a job in Leeds.' She shrugged. 'This is where my friends are, where my life is and that's why I want to stay.'

'Stubborn as a bloody mule,' Andy muttered, taking a sip of

his tea. 'How are you going to pay me my share? Have you thought about that?'

Steph had thought about that. She'd spent many sleepless nights worrying about that very thing. But she wasn't going to let her husband throw her out of her home. That was not going to happen.

She sighed, thinking life had become so complicated she hardly knew which way was up anymore. If she wanted to stay in the house, she'd have to take out a mortgage to buy Andy out, something she couldn't afford on her current income. So that was the problem she had to solve. How to get a bit more money on a regular basis. She was staying, whatever the rest of her family thought. She'd just have to work out how to make it possible.

She glanced across at her husband, met his steady gaze. 'It's all very well being awkward about moving,' he said, 'but I worry about you. Doesn't the fact you've had an intruder change anything? How can you possibly feel safe here now?'

His hand reached for hers, but she snatched it away, moving back to lean against the worktop. She didn't know the answer to that question, having glossed over the threat, telling herself no harm had been done. Someone had been in the house. Could they get back in again? Now that was a genuinely scary thought. She chewed on a nail, keeping her eyes on the floor, aware that her husband and daughter were staring at her, waiting for an answer.

The awkward silence stretched for an eternity until Andy got up.

'There's no point trying to talk any sense into you, is there?' He went out of the kitchen and started rummaging in the hall cupboard, coming out with a couple of coats and a pair of shoes. 'Right, I'm off,' he said, slamming the front door behind him.

Bea stayed a bit longer, but she had an evening planned with friends, so she left too, promising to call later and check her mum was okay. Steph sank into a chair, her mug of tea cold and uninviting, her eyes gazing out of the back window, as the events of the day swirled before her.

The doorbell rang and she hurried to answer it, relieved to see two police officers on the doorstep. This was her answer. The police would find out who'd broken in, they'd help her make her house secure. Then she'd have nothing to worry about, would she?

CHAPTER FIVE

The next day, Steph got to work early, keen to have a chat with Cara before they started. She was already in the staff kitchen, filling the kettle at the sink.

'Morning!' she chirped, giving a broad smile. Steph noticed the dark rings under her bloodshot eyes. 'Are you okay?' She studied Cara's face, watched the smile fall from her lips.

'Couldn't sleep again.' Cara gave a heavy sigh. 'I was wandering about the house half the night.' She flicked the kettle on, stretched to get the mugs out of the cupboard. 'Honestly, I never used to have a problem sleeping.'

'Was it the neighbours again?'

'That's what started it. Yelling at each other as per usual.' She grimaced. 'I couldn't handle it so I had to get the police round in the end.' The kettle boiled and Cara poured the water into two mugs, the welcome aroma of coffee filling the air.

Steph put her bag on the table while she took off her coat. It was a familiar tale, poor Cara living next to a difficult family who seemed to argue day and night. 'Didn't the police come?'

'Oh yes, they came. The shouting calmed down. Then twenty minutes later, they were at it again.' Cara huffed and

stirred milk into the coffee. 'Waste of time. Anyway, it suddenly
went quiet and that got me even more worried than the shouting.' She brought the mugs over to the table. 'It's not like it's the
husband beating up the wife. Or the other way round even.
They just seem to like a good row. And then in the morning
they're all lovey-dovey like nothing happened. But when it
suddenly goes quiet, I think... what if something has happened?
And if something awful had happened and I'd done nothing
about it I'd never forgive myself.'

'Oh, you poor thing. But I know what you mean. We had a
noisy bunch of students next door before the nurses moved in.
Lots of shouting and doors banging. Anyway, one night I heard
a load of screaming. Honestly, I can still hear it in my head now.
Frightened the life out of me, so much so that Andy went
round.' She shook her head. 'They were playing a game, apparently.' She rolled her eyes, remembering how stupid she'd felt at
the time, making Andy get up at half two in the morning.
'Scared me to death, though.'

It reminded her that the nurses were moving out. New
neighbours would arrive in a few weeks, most likely another
group of students. Would they make her life hell, like the couple
next door to Cara? She pushed away the thought. Apart from
that one daft group of lads, they'd had no trouble at all, so why
would it be any different in the future?

'So... I was coming out this morning,' Cara continued as she
sat opposite. 'And the woman was getting into her car, says a
cheery hello, so I decide that I need to have a word, you know,
tell her that she's ruining my life by disturbing my sleep. Ask if
they'd mind keeping the noise down.' Her mouth twisted. 'She
told me to eff off and mind my own effing business. And if the
police came round again then I'd live to regret it.'

Steph tutted, appalled. 'She threatened you? Wow, she
sounds so awful.'

Cara nodded. 'Yep, she is. Anyway, I left her a little present, courtesy of the cat, on her doorstep. Hopefully they'll tread in it and spread cat poo all over the house.'

Steph blinked, unsure what to say. She wasn't a fan of revenge, believing that holding grudges did you more harm than the people you were angry with. But she understood that Cara was at the end of her tether and with all these sleepless nights, probably wasn't thinking straight. Things like this could escalate horribly but she wasn't about to voice her concerns. It was none of her business how Cara decided to deal with her neighbour.

'Hopefully they'll get the message,' she said, picking up her mug and taking a sip.

'No chance of that,' Cara laughed, 'but it made me feel better. Anyway, how are things with you this morning. You're sounding a little... distracted.'

Steph leaned towards her friend. 'You will not believe what happened yesterday. You weren't the only person who called the police last night. Somebody broke into my house.' Cara gasped, eyes wide. 'I know. Scary as hell. Thank God they'd gone before I got home. I think I must have left the bedroom window open. That's the only way they could have got in.'

'A burglar?'

Steph shook her head. 'Nope. That's the weird thing. They didn't take anything. As far as I can see, they sat on my bed, possibly broke a vase – but that could have been the wind blowing it off the mantelpiece. Then they went up into the attic and left the dormer window open. And you know what the weather was like yesterday. Well, it was like a waterfall pouring into the loft. The carpet's ruined.'

'Whoa. That's just weird. And vindictive.'

'Really weird.' She gave an involuntary shiver. 'Anyway, the police came and had a check round for me. They think it might have been a homeless person sheltering from the weather. You know there's a little encampment that keeps appearing in the park? Well, the police keep moving them on and every time they do that, apparently they get a spate of break-ins.'

Cara frowned, thumping her mug back down on the table, coffee spilling over the lip. 'It really makes me mad when they pin this stuff on homeless people. Where's the evidence? They're just jumping to conclusions. Adding two and two and making five.' She huffed. 'Meanwhile, they're not looking at other possibilities.'

Steph nodded. 'I know, that's what I told them. Anyway, they're going to get the community policing team to do regular checks, keep an eye out. And they've given me a talking to about security.' She rolled her eyes. 'So I'm going to have to change the locks, and make sure closing and securing all the windows is part of my morning and evening routine.'

'Sounds like a good plan.' Cara stood and got a cloth to wipe up the mess she'd made. 'You know you can always stay at mine if you get a bit freaked out.'

Steph laughed. 'That's so kind of you but after what you've told me about your neighbours, I'm not sure you're any better off than me.'

Cara gave a wry smile. 'True enough. But the offer's there. And they don't shout at each other every night. We can go weeks with it being fine, then we have a rough patch, then it's fine again.'

Steph reached over the table and squeezed her friend's hand. 'That's very thoughtful of you, but I'm trying to be independent here. I'm not going to let one weird incident scare me out of the house. I doubt they'll try it again. An opportunist. That's what the police said. A one-off.'

Cara sipped her coffee, looking a little disappointed and Steph felt bad about not taking up her offer. She drove the conversation on, hoping Cara would be distracted and forget all about it.

'To make matters worse, Andy turned up. And Bea – well, I

rang her. I didn't want to be on my own. But then I had the two of them ganging up against me telling me it wasn't safe to live there anymore.'

Cara tutted. 'Well, we both know why Andy would be saying that. But you stand your ground, love. He's out of order trying to force you out. In fact, he can't.'

Cara's words hit home then, and Steph squared her shoulders. 'You're right. He can't make me move, can he?'

'No, you can delay signing things for ages.' Cara shrugged. 'I did exactly that. Not because I wanted to stay in the house but just to teach the bastard a lesson. At some point, though, you'll have to buy him out, I suppose.'

Steph nodded. 'I've been thinking about that. And I did a bit of research with some mortgage companies.' She sighed. 'I need to be earning a bit more money really, if I'm going to borrow money to pay him off.' She puffed out her cheeks. 'I didn't think I'd have to worry about it so soon, but it seems like Andy wants to push everything along at twice the speed of light. God knows why.'

'Christ, he's turned into a right awkward bugger, hasn't he?'

She gave a little laugh. 'And then there's Bea trying to smooth everything over, saying I can stay with her. To be fair, she's been great since we split up, but I feel that would be like taking the easy option, you know? This is my chance to prove to myself that I can make a life on my own. If I go to Bea's, I won't have to lift a finger. It'll be like living in a hotel.' She frowned. 'I know that sounds ungrateful. But... it wouldn't be home.'

Cara finished her coffee, put her empty mug on the table. 'I wouldn't say no to staying in that swanky house of your daughter's.' She had a dreamy expression on her face. 'A swimming pool, sauna. Someone to cook and tidy up after you. You could just relax. And her bloke, well, he's easy on the eye, isn't he? It might be nice for you to have a bit of a rest after everything you've been through these last few months.' A smile lit up her face. 'And I could house-sit for you if you like. Make sure nothing happens while you're away.'

'That's a very kind offer and I will take you up on it if I change my mind, but the thing is, I don't want a rest. I like to be busy. And it might sound strange, but I want to work. You know how much I love this job. It's one of the best things I've ever done.' She tucked her hair behind her ears. 'I know Bea's only trying to help and she does love her mum-daughter time, but she can be a bit bossy. Especially when I'm at her house.'

Cara laughed. 'I suppose the grass is always greener. Other people's lives looking better than our own, when we don't really understand what's going on with them.'

Steph picked up her coffee, taking a large gulp. Cara always made strong coffee, but it was just what she needed this morning, and she could feel it zinging through her veins. Maybe she could find some evening work to fill the gap in her finances, that was always an option. She glanced across at her friend. 'Anyway, if you have any ideas about how I can earn some extra money, let me know.'

Cara thought for a moment. 'What about a lodger? That seems the most obvious solution. You've got three bedrooms, haven't you? It would give you a bit of company. You'd just have to be careful to choose someone you get on with.'

Steph's mouth dropped open, the idea seeming so obvious she wondered why she hadn't thought of it herself. A bit of company and some extra money. Perfect. 'And that is why you're my friend,' she said, with a smile. Cara laughed and gave a modest shrug. 'How much do you think I could charge?' Her mind raced ahead thinking about how it could work. 'They could have the attic. It's a big room and it's got an en suite. Christ yes, that's it! Bloody genius.'

Cara patted at her hair. 'That's me. Genius. Glad someone's recognised it at last.' She checked her watch and stood up. 'I'd better go. Bill's got a pile of work for me to do today. See you later.'

She gave Steph a little wave and left.

A lodger. That's the answer! Steph felt like singing with joy. Although she'd played down her worries with Andy, Bea and Cara, the intruder incident had really shaken her, and she'd hardly slept the previous night, imagining creaks, the pad of footsteps. She'd feel so much better with someone else in the house and it could be fun if she got the right person. As soon as the attic was sorted out she would start looking.

It couldn't be too hard to find the right person, could it? She finished her coffee and practically skipped to her office.

CHAPTER SIX

For the next couple of hours, Steph was busy with clients, helping them to fill in forms, discussing benefits, working through their finances, chasing up housing providers. Her work at the centre had made her very aware of what a struggle life could be when you'd got to the point of being homeless. Getting back to any semblance of normal life took a huge effort and lots of support and encouragement. Of course Bill was only too aware of this from his own experiences and he'd created a culture where every small step forward was a cause for celebration. Amidst the tragedy, there were plenty of success stories.

She watched her latest client leave her office, a man of fifty-five, who'd struggled after his divorce, lost his job because he couldn't get himself out of bed and ended up being evicted. He'd just had a haircut from the hairdresser who came to the shelter once a month, giving up a day of their time to tidy up whoever wanted their services. There was a definite bounce in the man's step now he knew there was a flat coming up for him the following week. She'd made it happen, helped him to move a step closer to a brighter future. *How can you put a price on the satisfaction of that?* she thought as she watched the man leave, sure he was standing taller than when he arrived.

Is that satisfaction worth my marriage, though?

The thought made her stop tidying the papers on her desk for a moment. She buried her hands in her hair, elbows on the desk as she let the events of the last few months fill her head.

Andy had forgiven her for the fictitious affair, and she'd been willing to stop correcting him about his misunderstanding and move on. He had wanted her to give up her job, move out of Leeds, and start again somewhere new. His job involved selling a range of engineering products to companies and it didn't really matter where he lived. 'A new beginning is what we need,' he'd said, eyes alight with the idea of a fresh adventure. 'We could go anywhere you liked. The seaside, maybe.' He beamed at her. 'You've always loved the seaside, haven't you?'

Steph had been tempted by the thought of walks on the beach, the sound of the sea, the taste of salt in the air, but she knew what a struggle it had been for her to find a job in the first place. She yearned for this tear in their relationship to be mended and it was looking like a possibility.

She remembered an evening – a reconciliation dinner – that had been going so well, until he'd mentioned moving again and then the air had become charged with the familiar crackle of tension. He glared at her as she finished off her wine.

'So you're telling me that your job is more important than our marriage? Is that what you're saying?'

She put her glass down carefully, trying not to catch his eye. 'No, no, that's not what I'm saying. It's just—'

'Just what?' Andy was so mad at her his eyes were almost hidden under the furrow of his brow.

She sighed, wondering why he couldn't understand. 'I finally feel like I've found somewhere I belong. You know I always felt a bit out of place at the bank. And I know I could have changed jobs sooner, but with the mortgage being with them and after that horrendous time we had when you lost your job, we decided not to take any risks, didn't we?'

He threw his napkin onto the table, an incredulous tone to his voice. 'You're blaming me for having to do a job you didn't like?'

'No, I'm not.' She was feeling flustered now, the conversation veering off on tangents she wasn't prepared for. 'All I'm saying is I have a job which I love, and I want to stay there. If we move, I'll have to give it up and who knows if I'll find something else?'

'Of course you'll find something else. There's always jobs going.'

'But not the right kind of jobs. And not for people my age. It's like we become invisible once we hit the big five-oh.'

His lips pressed together, the frown deepening. 'I get the feeling you're stalling.' Anger flashed in his eyes. 'Is this affair still going on? Is that what this is about? Can't bear to leave Bill?'

Steph pushed back her chair and stood, not able to contain her irritation. 'This has nothing to do with Bill. You know there never *was* an affair. I've told you so many times. It's all in your head.'

'Oh, so I'm imagining things now.' He gave a derisive snort. 'Someone else clearly thought differently, because they kindly alerted me to the fact.'

Steph's eyes widened. This was fresh information. She'd always assumed he'd been following her or paid someone to do it for him. But the idea that someone had sent him the pictures? Someone trying to stir up trouble? Unease swirled in her belly as his tirade continued. 'And that someone probably works at the wonderful place you don't want to leave.' He stood up as well then. 'But if you have to think about this, it's clear we don't want the same things. It's clear I'm not very high on your list of priorities.' He jabbed at his chest with a finger. 'You're not committed to me or our relationship. It seems your life is all about you now. So you have it, Steph. You have your life.'

She watched in horror as he left the restaurant and the murmur of conversation resumed on nearby tables now that the entertainment was over. With cheeks burning, she'd hurried outside after him, but he'd gone. The shout of a waiter made her turn. To add insult to injury, he hadn't paid, leaving her to pick up the bill.

Instead of the meal repairing their relationship, it had torn them further apart.

She thought about that now – more than three months later – as she rested back in her chair, eyes surveying her little office.

'It's not all about the job,' she muttered to herself as she tidied paperwork away into files. 'It's about trust as well. How dare he think I've been having an affair? How bloody dare he?' It was the fact that he wouldn't accept her assurances that nothing was going on with any member of staff that really rankled. It was about knowing the sort of person she was, believing that she'd never cheat on him. *Lack of trust.* That was the real problem.

It made her consider now, if the boot was on the other foot, if she'd been sent pictures of her husband kissing a work colleague on the cheek, would she have believed him that it meant nothing?

The nub of the problem then, was someone stirring up trouble for her? Why else would they send him pictures? If she wanted to change the direction of her future – if she wanted Andy to stop this ridiculous divorce – she had to find the troublemaker and make them tell Andy that it was all made up. That's the only way the future was going to change.

Who could it be?

She thought about the staff at work, to see if Andy's theory could be right. Would any of them be out to cause her trouble? She stopped when she reached Phil, the chef, who Cara was always saying had a soft spot for her. And come to think of it, he had a habit of coming to her office with bits of cake, treats to take home, especially now he knew she was on her own. He was the only person at work that it could possibly be.

Right then, she thought, jumping to her feet. *No time like the present. Let's have a little conversation with Phil, see if Andy's theory is right.*

CHAPTER SEVEN

Steph was walking through the dining room on her way to the kitchen, where Phil would be preparing for lunch, when a figure caught her eye. He was dressed in combat fatigues, wearing a baseball hat, with dirty blond hair sprouting out of the sides. His back was turned towards her, but she'd know those shoulders anywhere, the way he was standing. Her heart skipped a beat, her legs refusing to move for a moment. *He's come to find me!* After all the anguish of the last few months, this was exactly what she needed.

'Max!' she called, rushing over, putting a hand on his shoulder. 'Max, you came back.' She blinked back the tears, not wanting to overwhelm him with her emotional response, but hardly able to keep herself in check.

The man turned, puzzled blue eyes meeting hers.

She gulped and backed away a couple of steps, heat rushing to her face. 'Oh, I am so sorry. I was sure you were... But, obviously you're not.' Her hands covered her gaping mouth, appalled at her mistake. She'd been so sure.

A familiar voice, one of her regulars, piped up. 'This is Noah. Just arrived this morning.'

'Oh yes, right.' She dropped her hands and flashed him a smile, her cheeks burning as she tried to pretend everything was normal. 'Nice to meet you.'

He was grinning now, and she could see that he was younger than Max, barely out of his teens by the looks of him, his face sporting a scraggly excuse for a beard. 'Sorry, I don't know your name.' His voice had a nice tone to it, rounded with the gentle burr of a West Country accent.

'Steph,' she said, tucking her hair behind her ears as she spoke. 'I deal with housing and benefits. Any financial issues. That sort of thing.'

'Right, right.' That lazy smile, so similar to how her son once smiled. She bit her lip, having to really focus to stop the tears from coming. 'Well, I might come and talk to you later, if that's all right?'

She cleared her throat, looked at the door. 'Of course. Yes. Yes, of course you can. I'm in the first office on the right when you come in. Just knock on the door and if I'm not there, I won't be far away.' She gave him another smile, desperate to leave the room and gather her thoughts. 'Just come and find me.'

She scurried back to her office like a rabbit retreating to its burrow. Her heart was still hammering in her chest, mortified that she'd made such a fool of herself. She could have sworn it was her son. Max had been about Noah's age when he'd left. The same build. Same hair colour. An easy mistake to make when memories were all you had.

Max had been wearing a similar outfit when he'd left home for good too and because that was the last image she had of him, he always looked that way in her memories. She hated the idea of him being in the army, putting himself in danger. She had no idea what he'd trained as, but always hoped, when she lay awake at night, thinking of her only son, that he'd chosen something safe. In her fantasy world he was a chef. Or a mechanic back at base. Nowhere near the firing line.

Often, her mind took her back to the run-up to his departure, wondering if she could have done something different. If she could have stopped him from going. The parting conversation was embedded in her brain, picked apart a million times.

'Mum, I need to talk to you,' he'd said the night before he left. She was putting towels away in the airing cupboard in the bathroom. His tone was ominous, the expression on his face grim. Nervously, she followed him into his bedroom, and he closed the door behind her.

'What is it, love?' she said, not really wanting an answer. She knew he'd dropped out of college, although she hadn't told Andy. She wasn't even sure if Max knew she was aware that he spent his days at the shopping centre, pretending – as he went out of the door in the morning – that everything was normal. The truth was, things hadn't been normal for quite some time. He'd become reclusive and distant. Prickly and almost impossible to have a conversation with. Bea was positively scared of him after he'd played so many tricks on her, swearing blind that he hadn't. She often wondered how her smiley child had grown into a snarling youth.

She tried to dismiss all her preconceived ideas and gave him a broad smile.

His face didn't change, his forehead creased with troubles. 'Have a seat, Mum,' he said, indicating the chair by the desk, while he sat on the bed. She wanted to sit next to him and hold his hand. Put her arm round him and hold him to her, this man-boy of hers who'd grown up to be a mystery, tell him that she loved him, that she wanted to help him.

She did as she was told, though, her hands clasped together in her lap. It seemed so ominous, this request for a chat, but she hoped he was just going to come clean, tell her that he'd dropped out. Then, she thought, they could move forwards. Her hope was that he was about to let her into his world, just for a few moments. Let her help him with whatever was bothering him.

His eyes dropped to the floor before he spoke.

'I wanted to tell you that I'm leaving tomorrow.'

She thought her heart had stopped. Her hand went to her chest, her breath stuck in her throat. She must have heard him wrong. 'What? What do you mean "leaving"?'

'I signed up to the army. I start tomorrow.'

'The army?' Her voice was a squeak. 'No, Max. No. Don't do that. I'm sure we can sort things out. Maybe you could talk to Bea. Apologise for—'

His fists clenched by his sides, his jaw tightened. 'No. I can't live with all the bad feeling. It's doing my head in.' His eyes met hers and she could see a steely determination. 'It's all sorted. I'm not changing my mind. I just wanted you to know.'

With that, he stood and opened the door, her cue to leave.

'Everyone will be happier when I'm gone,' he said before he closed his door behind her, and the lock clicked into place.

That was the last time she'd seen him. When she'd woken in the night and crept to his room to see if she could persuade him to stay, he'd already gone. Although it was ten years ago now, the memory was as fresh as if it had happened yesterday.

There was a sadness in her soul, a feeling that she'd failed him somehow. But in all honesty, she'd done her best over the years to try and help him. She'd thought he might have ADD or be on the autistic spectrum, but tests showed not. And that could only lead to a conclusion that there was an intrinsic meanness in him, something making him want to taunt his younger sister at every opportunity and make her life a misery. He refused the offer of counselling, but Steph had jumped at the chance.

Apparently, it was not unknown for older children to rebel against the arrival of younger siblings by resorting to bad behaviour. Attention seeking, the therapist had said. Steph had done her utmost to give him more attention, but then Bea felt left out, and it was an impossible juggling act.

At the end of the day, there had to be consequences for bad behaviour. That was Andy's view of things and reluctantly, she'd had to agree.

Perhaps – as she'd told herself many times – the army was the best place for him. The discipline and sense of camaraderie. Perhaps she hadn't done anything wrong. Perhaps he just needed a different sort of family. That's the conclusion she'd come to and she could sort of live with that. But as the years went by, her longing to see him grew rather than diminished. He was her firstborn and would always have a special place in her heart.

Thinking that she'd seen Max today had really shaken her and she calmed herself with a bit of filing. Her quest to find Phil and ask him if he was responsible for sending the pictures to Andy was forgotten, until he opened the door, a plate of sandwiches in his hand.

He was pencil thin, with hollow cheeks and knobbly elbows, his face creased with wrinkles, deep grooves at the edge of his mouth. He had incredibly bushy eyebrows that shaded deep-set eyes, which gave you a sense of never knowing what he was thinking.

'I saw you rush out of the dining room, and I thought you looked a bit upset,' he said, moving towards her. He put the plate on the table. Took a step closer and reached out a hand as if he was going to touch her. She swerved away, putting the desk between them, a sheaf of papers clasped to her chest.

He pushed the plate towards her. 'Ham salad. I know you like them. On brown.' He gave her a shy smile. 'I made it specially.'

Is this a bit creepy? Or is he just being nice?

She swallowed, not sure what to do. Looked at the sandwiches, wondering if she'd eat them or not. *Have I got this wrong? Or could he be the one who started all the trouble between me and Andy?* There was no way to find out other than to ask him. She took a deep breath, plastered a smile on her face, not sure how to tackle this without causing offence if she were mistaken.

She noticed, then, the way he was looking at her; his hands fingering his food-stained apron as he waited for her approval. Her resolve to question him wavered. 'That's very kind of you, Phil.' *Just ask him!* a voice in her head shouted. She cleared her throat. 'Um... while you're here... This may seem a bit of a random question, but... do you know my husband at all?'

He looked surprised. 'Andy? Yeah, I've seen him when he's come to pick you up. Had a few chats with him while he was waiting.'

She nodded. 'Right, right. I don't suppose... did he give you his phone number?'

Phil's hands tightened round his apron, a worried look flashing across his face. 'He did. Said to call him if there was any trouble and you needed picking up.'

Her jaw hardened, Andy's theory more feasible than she'd imagined.

'Better get back,' he said, edging towards the door. 'Before they set something alight in there.' And before she could ask him outright if he'd sent the pictures to Andy, he'd gone.

She sank into her chair. *It's obviously him, isn't it?* She didn't need to ask, she could tell from his body language that he'd felt uncomfortable with her questions.

She picked up a pen, doodling on her notepad as she thought it through. Could Andy have asked Phil to spy on her for him? *Or is this Phil's own agenda?* Whichever way she looked at it, she couldn't see him as an ally.

She pushed the sandwiches away, sure that she didn't want to eat anything he'd made for her. *I can't trust him now, can I?*

CHAPTER EIGHT

Later that day, Noah knocked on her office door.

He sat in the chair on the other side of her desk like a nervous schoolboy coming to see the head teacher, bouncing his leg up and down, fussing with his hair and his hat, scratching his beard. He was a bundle of nervous energy, some part of his body constantly in motion, while she ran through the service she could offer, and they worked out where to start. She'd seen this sort of behaviour before, with clients who were waiting for their next fix, and she wondered whether this was just nerves or a lack of his drug of choice. It wasn't her place to ask him directly, but she hoped he might open up with some gentle questioning.

'So... what brought you to Leeds?' she asked with a smile. 'Your accent is Bristol, isn't it? Or down that way somewhere.'

He looked at his fingers, then started picking at his nails.

'I was a student. Came to study philosophy.' Steph was glad he wasn't looking at her because he would have seen a flash of disbelief in her face. She was curious to know more.

'Then what happened? I'm assuming you finished your degree last summer?'

He shook his head and glanced up at her, his gaze holding hers for only a second before he looked to the side, studying the pictures on the walls while his fingers fiddled with a grubby plaited bracelet on his wrist. 'Nah,' he said with a sigh. 'It didn't really work out.' He was quiet for a moment, and she could see his jaw working from side to side; could feel that it was hard for him to talk about it.

'University isn't for everyone, is it?' she said, gently. 'I know schools push kids to take that route. It was the same with my two, although I always told them to follow their hearts, not to feel that anything was expected of them except to be happy.' Still, he didn't speak, and she saw him swipe at his face, wondered if he was fighting back tears. 'You're not the only person who dropped out of uni and found themselves on the street, you know. Honestly, I've seen a number of ex-students come through here.'

He looked at her properly then. 'Really?'

She gave him a reassuring smile. 'Yep. And the good news is that all the ones I've seen have somewhere to live now and some of them have managed to land jobs. Not the jobs they'd dreamed of maybe, but it's a start. Something to give them work experience and a bit more confidence.' His eyes met hers again and she could see a spark of hope. Her heart broke for him, as it did for every young person she helped. 'Living away from home for the first time is hard, isn't it? There's a lot to organise. It's an emotional time, lots of hormonal changes going on too.' She shrugged. 'Coming to live in a different part of the country where you don't know anyone is tough as well. There's a lot of reasons why it doesn't work out.'

He sat back in his chair then, and she could see his face properly. He was so like Max she couldn't take her eyes off him, studying every contour. Even the shape of his mouth was the same – the only differences being the curve of his eyebrows and the fact that his eyes were a shade lighter than her son's. But looking at him brought a surge of emotion rushing through her, a desperate longing to see her son again, so strong that it hurt.

Noah cleared his throat, his voice soft when he spoke. 'I nearly made it. I'll admit I struggled living away from home at first, having to look after myself, get up on time and get everything sorted.' He gave a wry smile. 'I come from a village where everyone knows everyone else, and I couldn't wait to get away to a city. Honestly, it was all I could think about for years. And Mum was dead keen. But the reality... well, it was too much.' His eyes dropped from hers again and he gave a big sigh. 'I got a couple of bad marks and that's when I started suffering from anxiety. You know, full-on panic attacks about missing deadlines, not really understanding some of the logic, or the texts we had to read. I got myself so worked up I couldn't sleep and then I couldn't even get out of bed some days.' He shook his head. 'It's weird how it all got out of control so quickly. I can't really say I understand it but once I'd started with the anxiety I just couldn't seem to shake it off.'

Steph felt a strong urge to give him a hug. 'Couldn't you have gone home? You know, recharge your batteries?'

He shook his head. 'My mum was dead against my choice of course. She and her partner thought I should do something more practical. A subject that would help me get a job. But I wanted to keep my options open, and I'd always enjoyed the philosophical discussions we had in religious education at school.' His fingers were busy with the bracelet again, turning it round and round on his wrist. 'For some reason it really interested me, and my teachers stressed that if you wanted to do well at uni you had to be committed to the subject you chose.' He shrugged. 'I had my heart set on it. Then when I was struggling, I couldn't go crawling back home and admit I was wrong. Not when my mum had been working an evening job as well as her day job to help me with living costs.' He gave another big sigh. 'I felt so ashamed. Useless.' He blinked, squeezed his eyes shut like he was trying to blot out the memory. 'It's hard to explain.'

She nodded. 'It's okay. I understand, really I do, but there's nothing to be ashamed of. We're allowed to have dreams, you know, and in reality, not everything works out how we want it to. Life has a habit of throwing hard choices at us when we're least able to deal with them.' She leaned forwards, trying to catch his eye. 'The thing is, at your age, you've got your whole life ahead of you. There's plenty of time to find out what you want to do. And I'm sure your mum would understand.'

He shook his head. 'Nah.' He pressed his lips together and she thought he might be trying not to cry. 'I couldn't tell her what was happening. I'd been so full of myself before I left home, and it all came crashing down.' He was quiet for a moment. 'In the third year, I got thrown off the course for not handing work in.'

'Oh, Noah, I'm sorry to hear that.'

He gave a grunt, his eyes firmly fixed on the floor.

'Sounds like you had a rough time.'

He nodded. 'Then I got chucked out of my student house at the end of term and that's when I ended up on the streets. I've managed for just over a year now.'

'So where have you been sleeping?'

'Oh, all over the place. But I've found myself a little... well, it's a shed. It's waterproof, that's the main thing and I'm not bothering anyone, and nobody bothers me.'

Steph listened to his story with thoughts of Max in her mind. How had he managed away from home? After he left, she hadn't heard from him again. Nothing. Not even a phone call. She didn't know where he was, no idea what regiment he joined and not a clue how to get that information. She'd talked to Andy about it, increasingly worried about the well-being of their son.

'Look, love, you've got to let him come round in his own time. Let him sort out his issues, get settled into his new way of life.' He'd pulled her close and given her a kiss. 'He's a tough nut, is Max. You know he is. He's just a bit angry at the moment. Youth hormones running wild.'

Steph frowned. 'You weren't like that when you were his age. I don't understand what's happened. He used to be such a mummy's boy when he was little.'

'Oh, love, he's grown up, that's what's happened.' He pulled away and looked her in the eye, wiped a tear from her cheek. 'I know lads who I went to school with who were just the same. Nobody heard from them for a couple of years and then when they'd sorted themselves out, they turned up at home again. It's like he's got to prove something to himself. You know, feel like he's a success before he wants to come back.'

She laid her head on Andy's chest, listened to the steady rhythm of his heart, and let herself absorb his words. Men really were another species, their thought processes so different to women. But Andy didn't seem concerned. In a way he seemed quietly proud that his son had joined the army, even if he'd decided he didn't want anything to do with his family.

Did no news mean he was doing okay, or might he be like Noah, alone and on the streets? Fallen on hard times and ashamed to come home? In that moment, she decided she was going to find him.

Andy couldn't stop her now, couldn't persuade her that he just needed to come back to them in his own time. 'You can't force someone to want to be part of a family,' he'd said to her the last time she'd spoken to him about it, just after she'd started work at the homeless shelter. 'If he's not ready to come home, there's nothing we can do.' He looked into her eyes, clearly concerned that she was still fretting about his absence. Stroked her face, then pulled her into a hug. 'Just be patient.'

Ten years seemed like a very long time to be patient and she knew more now, didn't she? After dealing with homeless clients, she understood the complexity of these situations, how easily people became distanced and then estranged. He might be suffering on his own somewhere. Could he be out there, destitute, hoping that someone from his family was looking for him?

Well, she wasn't going to listen to Andy this time. She was going to follow her gut instinct and track him down. If he was well and happy living his life elsewhere, then all well and good, but she couldn't live with herself if he needed her and she hadn't stepped up and at least put some effort into making sure he was okay.

She heard Noah's feet scuffing the floor as he twisted in his chair, looking at the door. 'I'll go if you're busy,' he said, already half out of his seat.

'No, no, please stay. I'm sorry, I'm just a bit distracted today.' She gave him a reassuring smile. 'I'm sure we can help you. We have a special scheme for young people under twenty-five, so you meet that criteria. We have a new accommodation block that's just come on stream.' He blinked a few times, clearly not sure whether to believe what he was hearing. 'The idea is to give you a permanent address, you see, so you can apply for benefits and sort yourself out for work. Then when you've got a deposit saved up, you can move on to private rented accommodation. What do you think? Is that something you'd be interested in?'

His fingers stopped fidgeting, his leg stopped trying to drill a hole in the floor. He was completely still for the first time, staring at her like she'd just told him unicorns actually existed.

'For real? You can do that?'

She smiled, a glow of satisfaction warming her heart. 'I can. Your timing could not have been better, to be honest. I think there's only a couple of rooms left.' She turned to her computer screen and clicked on a spreadsheet. 'Let me check.' She carried on talking as she scrolled down, relieved to see that she was right and there was a room available. 'It's a block of twenty. Everyone has their own room and en suite. Shared cooking facilities on each floor, so five rooms share a kitchen. There's also a support worker on duty, day and night, if you need help with anything, or just need a chat.'

Noah looked dazed. 'I can't believe it. That easy?'

'Like I said. Good timing on your part. We only opened it this week. Perhaps this is the start of things getting better for you?'

He tugged at his beard and nodded, the fingers of his other hand drumming on the desk. It made her wonder again if he was on drugs of some sort and was anxious for his next fix. His eyes never stayed still, darting all over the place, like a caged animal looking for a way out.

'Wow. I just... I can't quite believe it,' he said, his voice catching in his throat.

A glow of satisfaction warmed her heart. This was why she loved her job; being able to help young people who were struggling felt like a privilege, making her feel very proud of the role she played.

'Let me run through everything.' She found the right folder and pulled out a form. 'We'll do the accommodation first, so we know that's all sorted. Then you can decide where you want to start with everything else. Or you can go to your room and get yourself comfortable and we can talk again tomorrow.'

He coughed and blinked a few times, rubbing at his eyes while she explained what information she needed, and they started filling in the boxes. Ten minutes later they were done, and Noah stood, clearly eager to go to his room. The accommodation block had been built at the back of the hostel on a bit of waste land, a fantastic initiative that was long overdue, given the scale of youth homelessness in the city. It was a pilot scheme, a new building system which was quick and cheap and if they could prove it was a success, they planned to replicate it in other parts of Leeds.

Steph went to the metal box on the wall where all the room

keys were stored and frowned when she couldn't find the one she was looking for. *That's odd. It should be here.*

She gave Noah a smile. 'I just need to go and check something, back in a minute.' *Luca must have it.* She hurried through the hostel and out to the units, finding Luca, the support worker, in his office.

'Hiya.' She gave him a quick smile. 'I'm looking for a key to room 19. Got a young man just signed up, but the key's not in the box.'

'We're full,' he said, frowning. 'Didn't Bill tell you? We had a couple of emergency admissions last night. Had to go and pick the last one up from hospital.'

Her shoulders sagged, her hand clasping her forehead. *What am I going to tell Noah now?* After she'd got him all excited about being off the streets, she wasn't going to be able to help him.

She walked back into the office. Noah's profile was so like Max's that it startled her again for a moment.

'I'm so sorry,' she said, cringing inside now that she'd raised his hopes only to dash them again. 'The system wasn't updated. I'm afraid I was wrong. All the rooms in the unit have been taken.'

Noah glanced up at her, then studied his backpack, which was resting in his lap. She could see his lips moving like he might be about to say something, but he remained silent. Without a word, he stood and when his back was to her, he mumbled a 'Thanks for trying,' and left.

She could tell he was upset by the tone of his voice, the set of his shoulders.

'Come back tomorrow and I'll have a hunt round, see if I can find you something.' He carried on walking out of the door. Would she see him again? Sometimes people just disappeared – decided they couldn't cope with all the admin, the waiting.

How hard it was sometimes to tell people there wasn't any

room. But he'd said he was staying somewhere. A shed. At least he was dry, which was more than a lot of their clients. *If Max was in the same situation, what would I want for him?* She couldn't stop asking herself that question and spent the next hour ringing round looking for somewhere for Noah to stay, but it was hopeless. And with the units full now, there really was no alternative.

It left her feeling a failure. Noah sounded like somebody she could help, with a good family in the background to support him if they could be reunited. Maybe she could talk him round, get him to call home. Then the chances were he wouldn't be homeless after all. Sometimes it only took the courage to pick up the phone, take the initiative, and decide that whatever you'd fallen out about no longer mattered.

She'd been through this a million times when she'd been thinking about Max, how she'd welcome him back in an instant if only he'd ring her. What if Noah's parents were as desperate?

That would be her plan, then, if Noah came back. She'd try and persuade him to phone home. He seemed such a nice lad, surely his parents could forgive him? She thought about his twitching, his inability to sit still and another thought crossed her mind. Maybe there was a darker story hidden in Noah's background that she knew nothing about?

CHAPTER NINE

The afternoon dragged itself to five o'clock and Steph was just packing up – ready to have a scout round the town centre and see if she could spot Noah – when her phone rang.

'Steph! I just heard about your ordeal. The intruder.' The woman tutted. 'James was talking to Andy.'

It was Lisa, the wife of Andy's best friend, James, and someone she'd thought she was close to, until Andy walked out and then it all got a bit awkward. She was suddenly unavailable for their usual Saturday morning coffee, blustering excuses that didn't always make sense.

They'd gone out as a foursome on a regular basis, even been on a couple of holidays together. Steph bristled. She didn't need fair-weather friends and she didn't need to feel embarrassed or ashamed about her current situation – the deserted wife – because she hadn't done anything wrong. Unfortunately, that's how Lisa made her feel. She'd even had the temerity to suggest that an apology might make things right. As if that was going to happen! It was Andy who needed to apologise. He was the one who refused to listen to her side of the story.

It was the strangest thing when your marriage broke down that half your friendships broke down too. People not knowing what to say, taking sides, or avoiding you because they *didn't* want to take sides. A social leper, that's what she felt like.

Bea had been very sweet about everything, always ready to jump in and keep her company, coming up with ideas of things they could do together. In fact, she'd seen more of her daughter in these last few months than she had in the last few years. But there were things you couldn't discuss with your daughter. Thank goodness for Cara, who'd really stepped up and been a great support. But apart from her, the only friends she had left were the ladies in the choir she belonged to. Although perhaps not even them anymore, after the mess she'd made of their last concert, running out of the place in tears because the song they were singing was one she and Andy had danced to at her wedding.

It was a week after Andy had left and she was still raw, her emotions refusing to stay hidden and behave themselves. She really couldn't face going back to the choir yet, although they left messages to say she'd been missed and sent her the gift and card asking her to please come back. She'd tried to make herself go to choir practice, given herself a pep talk but she'd turned back when she was halfway there, too embarrassed to meet the crowd, however sympathetic they might be.

'Hi, Lisa,' she said now, trying to hide the weary sigh in her voice. 'I'm so sorry, I'm just in the middle of something, I'll have to give you a ring back.'

'Okay.' Lisa was using her company boss voice, all clipped and efficient. 'Not a problem. I'll be quick. I have some news I think you'll find very welcome.' She sounded pleased with herself.

Steph itched to hang up, but welcome news would be good after a shitty day. 'What news would that be?'

'We're willing to buy your property. Add it to our portfolio.

We've just started investing in properties in Headingley now and thought it might help you two out. It could go through super quick, no surveys or anything like that.'

She paused for breath.

Steph said nothing.

'Andy's all for it,' Lisa continued, 'so I said I'd ring and let you know.'

She made it sound like she was doing them a favour, rather than profiting from their marital disaster. Steph could feel her blood reaching a fast simmer, on its way to boiling. The cheek of the woman. And she hated that Andy had been talking about their divorce negotiations behind her back.

A deep breath stopped her from saying something she might regret. 'That's so sweet of you to think of us,' she said, putting a sickly smile in her voice, the opposite of what she wanted to do. 'But I think James must have misunderstood. We're not selling. Andy knows that, so it was wrong of him to give James the impression the house is for sale.'

'What?' Silence for a moment. 'But surely you'll have to sell for the divorce? Split the property between you.' Lisa's voice became more gentle. 'I know it's hard to accept, but that's how it works, lovely. Fifty-fifty.'

Steph took a deep breath, hating Lisa's patronising tone. 'Yes, I know how it works, my solicitor has been through everything, so you really don't need to worry about me.' Her gritted teeth gave her voice a harsh tone and she unlocked her jaw before carrying on. *Be dignified. Don't swear.* It wasn't Lisa's fault if Andy had given her the wrong information. 'I'm sorry but selling is not the plan. I'm buying Andy out. I've got a mortgage all lined up, so we're absolutely sorted.'

It gave her a buzz of satisfaction to put her ex-friend in her place. Of course she didn't actually have a mortgage offer, but Lisa didn't need to know that.

'Oh dear, I don't think you two are singing from the same

song sheet, are you?' Lisa said with a little laugh. 'I know how these things work out, remember? Having a debt collection agency, I've seen it all. I know you want to stay there, hun.' Steph tensed. She hated being called hun and the way Lisa said it was beyond patronising. 'I know you're attached to your memories, but really it would be best for both of you to move on to something new. Have a fresh start.'

'Well, thanks for the advice, but I really do have to go. Catch you later.'

She disconnected and stuffed the phone in her bag, annoyed at the way James and Lisa had jumped in so quickly to muddy the waters. Or had Andy made the suggestion, knowing his friend was increasing his rental portfolio?

What was really annoying her was that everyone in her life had an opinion on what was best for her. Only she knew that. *Ah, but do you?* asked the little voice in her head. The voice that questioned every decision she made these days. 'Yes, I bloody do,' she said to herself as she stomped out of her office.

She decided to walk home. It was a lovely August evening and a headache had troubled her all afternoon. A bit of fresh air would clear her head and part of her hoped she might find Noah, see if she could talk him into calling his parents, or reach out to them in some way. Then at least some good would have come of her day. But after a detour round the city centre, to all the spots where homeless people tended to gather, she couldn't see him anywhere. All she could do was hope he'd come back tomorrow.

When she was halfway through the park, she saw a familiar figure sitting by the base of a tree, knees to his chest, his head bowed. It was weird seeing him out of context like this and she wondered what he was doing there. *Waiting for me?* The image spoke of despair, and she stopped, cursing her heart for wanting to reach out to him and make him feel better. She chewed her lip as she tried to decide what to do. Take a detour so he wouldn't see her? Walk past him and hope he wouldn't notice?

Don't be stupid. She walked towards him. *He's your husband. He's not going to bite.* And anyway, she had something she needed to say to him.

CHAPTER TEN

'Hiya,' Steph said, when she reached Andy, trying to keep her voice light while her thoughts wriggled in a seething mass. 'What are you doing here? This isn't your stomping ground anymore, is it?' Her husband lifted his head and blinked at her.

'Just getting some air,' he said, climbing unsteadily to his feet, brushing the dust off his jeans. 'I'm allowed, you know. It's not your park.'

Was that the smell of alcohol on his breath? He swayed, leaned against the tree to steady himself. *Yes, he's definitely been drinking.* He looked dreadful, and she wondered what had happened, concern being her first reaction. Then she caught hold of her thoughts. His health was nothing to do with her anymore. That was *his* choice. She reminded herself of her call with Lisa and why she should be angry with him.

'Stay away from me,' she hissed. 'I know what your game is. I just had Lisa on the phone trying to make me believe she and James would do us a favour by buying the house.' She jabbed a finger at him. 'It's not going to happen. I told you. I'll buy you out.' She took a breath, tried to calm herself down. 'I'm staying in the house and that's the end of it.'

She gave an emphatic nod, then stalked away, absolutely fuming, but glad she'd had a chance to make her point in person. Much more effective and satisfying than a phone call, when half the time he didn't seem to be listening to her.

Hopefully that was the end of it.

When she reached her house, it wasn't until she was putting the key in the door and glanced into the lounge that she realised something was wrong. She took a step back and her breath hitched in her throat when she saw the jagged hole in the lounge window. It looked like someone had thrown a brick through it, broken glass littering the windowsill.

Did Andy do that?

It was a strange coincidence that he'd been in the park when he lived on the other side of town now. Far too much of a coincidence, come to think of it. And he'd been drunk. He could become quite petulant when he'd had too much to drink. But would he do something so spiteful? She snatched her phone from her pocket and dialled his number.

'What are you playing at?' she snarled when he answered. 'You think I don't know it was you?'

'Steph? Hold on a minute,' he slurred. 'What you talking about?'

She opened the door as she listened and poked her head into the lounge, saw that she'd been right about the brick, which now sat in the middle of the carpet, surrounded by a glittering trail of broken glass. She took a picture and sent it to him. 'Have a look, I sent you a photo.'

It took a moment for him to respond.

'Bloody hell, that came through the window?' He blew out a breath. 'You think it was me? Why would I do that?'

'You tell me, Andy. Seems a pretty childish response for someone who keeps telling me I need to grow up.'

She disconnected, no patience for a conversation with a drunk. Where would it get her anyway? What she needed to do was sort out the problem. With a frustrated sigh, she went through to the kitchen and flicked the kettle on while she googled glaziers. After five attempts, she got through to one.

'I can come in the morning,' the man said. 'No sooner I'm afraid, I'm going to be working late as it is. Will that be okay?'

She leaned against the worktop, a cold knot of fear lying heavy in her stomach, her pulse still racing. She needed the damage repaired otherwise she wouldn't be able to sleep. 'I'd be happier if you could come today. I know it's late, but I'll pay.' It was unthinkable to have a gaping hole in her window all night. *What if somebody decides to make it a bit bigger and come inside?* She thought about her intruder from the day before. Unease crawled over her scalp and she gave an involuntary shudder, her hands closing into fists.

Is it the same person?

'Sorry, love. I'm already on an emergency call-out. Tomorrow morning is the soonest I can manage, I'm afraid.' Steph wasn't sure whether to take his offer or try someone else, but it was six in the evening, and she knew she'd be lucky to get anyone else.

'Okay.' She sighed. 'That'll have to do then.' Her voice wavered and she squeezed her eyes shut, trying to force back her tears.

'I'd patch it up for the night if I were you, love. Get a bit of hardboard nailed over it, then you'll feel more secure.'

'Thank you, yes, I'll do that.' It sounded so simple but where she'd get a bit of hardboard from, she'd no idea. Her body felt heavy, weighed down by a seemingly impossible task, but one that had to be done if she was going to have any chance of getting to sleep. She remembered that Andy kept a lot of bits and pieces in the garden shed. There was a slight chance there was something in there she could use. Other than that, she had no idea what she was going to do.

She hung up and went into the lounge to survey the damage

again, worried now that a pattern was emerging. Two incidents in two days. *I wonder what the third thing will be?*

The thought sent panic racing round her body. Her legs gave way, and she slumped on the sofa, eyes fixed on the broken glass, the sound of her pulse filling her ears.

CHAPTER ELEVEN

A ring on the doorbell made her jump and she opened the door to find a bespectacled young man smiling at her. 'Ian Johnson, Holdsworth Insurance,' he said, handing her a card. 'About the water damage to your carpet.'

She'd completely forgotten he was coming this evening, but now she managed a weak smile, relieved at least one of her problems was going to be sorted out. She was glad to have a bit of company to shake her out of her spiralling thoughts.

'Perfect timing,' she said. 'I need to add to my claim.' She held the door wide, inviting him in. 'Someone just broke my front window.' It didn't sound so scary now she'd said it out loud. It happened all the time, didn't it? *Christ, you need to stop making everything into a drama.* She wiped her sweaty palms on her jeans, hoping her heartbeat would go back to normal soon, because the speed of it was scaring her. She took a couple of deep breaths while he went through some preliminary questions with her, then she showed him the damage upstairs.

Afterwards, he put in a call to an emergency glazier. 'He can come first thing in the morning,' he said.

She shrugged. Back to square one. But at least she didn't have to pay for it now.

'You need to call the police about the window, get a report reference for the claim. You're not insured for accidental damage to windows, you see, so they'll want proof.'

She nodded, eyes fixed on the sparkling shards of glass spread over the carpet. 'Yes, I'll do that. Thank you.'

She watched him walk away, his card in her hand, feeling weary to the core. Why did one job always lead to at least one other? But she had to call the police and make her report. Do it now, she told herself, knowing that all she wanted to do was lie down and sleep. Perhaps they'd take her concerns a little more seriously now. The sporadic drive pasts clearly hadn't worked as a preventative measure, and she couldn't help thinking there was something more they could do.

Finally, someone answered and she spent another tedious ten minutes responding to their questions. No, nothing stolen. No, she had no idea who might have done it.

'Probably just youngsters causing mischief,' the officer said, after giving her a reference number. 'I doubt if it's personal but I'd get the community policing team round.'

She huffed, unimpressed. 'They came round yesterday, and it did nothing to stop this happening today. I think I need something a bit more proactive.' She sounded peeved and told herself they had real crimes to investigate. An intruder who hadn't taken anything but left the windows open was hardly a master criminal. And a brick through the window *could* very well just be bored youngsters.

So why do I feel so shaken?

Tremors were flowing through her body, the phone shaking in her hand. Whatever the officer said, it did feel personal, the two events one after the other. Somebody trying to unsettle her and make her feel uneasy in her own home. *Threatening.* That's what it felt like.

'It's on the system that they called by today, but nobody was home.'

'I was probably at work.'

'Ah, right. Can I put on the system when you're likely to be in and they'll try again?'

'Every evening,' she said, cringing because that sounded like she had no life apart from work. *Which is absolutely true at the moment.*

A swirl of sadness eddied in her heart. She'd never imagined that at the age of fifty-four she'd be having to start again. A single woman. A rejected wife. Now she was responsible for everything that had been shared before. In the past, Andy would have sorted out the insurance and the broken window. And the police for that matter. She wouldn't have had to ask or even think about these things, he would have just got on with sorting everything out. It made her realise just how much she'd relied on him.

You've got to step up. Okay, it's a nuisance and time-consuming but it's not like it's rocket science, is it? Of course she could deal with this. Didn't she spend her days helping other people to organise their lives? Now it was time to apply the same attention to her own situation.

She looked at the jagged hole in the window again, visualising the size of board she'd need to cover and secure to the window frame, then marched out to the garden shed, determined to get the job done. Andy had a stash of off-cuts in there, part of his heap of random oddments that 'would come in'. She'd teased him about them in the past but now she had to grudgingly admit they could be useful.

The shed door didn't close properly, the wood ancient and warped and she yanked it open, almost losing her balance. She was reaching for the light switch when a pair of eyes caught hers. A man sitting on the floor.

She screamed, a sound so shrill and unexpected, it chased

all thought away except the instruction to run. She turned, her heart thumping like a drummer on steroids, and was halfway to the house, when she stopped. *I know that face. I'm sure I do.* With a voice in her head yelling at her to run inside and lock the door, she wavered, glanced over her shoulder and saw him standing in the door frame. Gasping for breath, she retraced her steps.

'Noah?'

He stood still, a sheepish look on his face. 'I didn't know this was your house. Honest. I was just...'

Her mind ran back over the conversation they'd had earlier, how he'd told her he'd been sleeping in a shed. *Is it my shed?* Now that could be coincidence, or it could be... She snapped her thoughts away, not wanting to jump to conclusions. She'd wait and find out his story first.

'Flipping heck.' Steph's hands went to her chest. 'You nearly gave me a heart attack.'

She noticed a big bruise on his cheek which hadn't been there earlier. 'Are you okay?' She stepped closer. 'What's happened to you? That bruise...' Instinctively she put out a hand to turn his face so she could see better, her mothering instincts coming to the fore. Then she remembered this wasn't her son. This was a stranger. Trespassing in her shed.

He ducked his head down, picked up his bag and swung it on his shoulder. 'I'm sorry,' he mumbled, not looking at her. 'I was just...' He looked past her towards the gate and his escape. 'I'll go.'

It struck her again how much he resembled a young Max. What would she want for him if he was in Noah's position? 'I don't suppose you fancy a cup of tea, do you?' *Bloody hell*, screeched the voice in her head, *what are you doing?* 'Something to eat? I hate eating on my own and I always buy too much of everything.'

His eyebrows shot up his forehead, then he grinned at her.

And she thought, when he smiled, she could see a glimpse of something different. What he could be if he was given an opportunity. And everyone deserved that, didn't they? 'Are you sure? I don't want to be a bother or anything.'

She laughed. 'Well... I do need to ask a favour in return.' He looked worried. 'I don't suppose you could help me with a bit of DIY, could you? I need to patch up the lounge window.' She sighed. 'Someone put a brick through it.'

His eyes widened, an expression on his face that she couldn't quite decipher. 'No way.' She gazed at him for a moment, wondered again about the coincidence of him being in her shed just after a brick had been put through her window. *But then why would he?* Because she'd promised accommodation and then had to go back on her word? No, that didn't really make sense because how would he know where she lived? They'd only met today. Unless... it was her shed he'd been living in and he'd been watching her. Maybe followed her to work?

She cast aside her suspicions, fumbled for the light switch and snapped it on, Noah blinking in the glare. 'Let's see if we can find something to tack over it for tonight.'

Together they sorted through Andy's pile of off-cuts until they found a piece of plywood that looked like it might be big enough. Noah found a hammer and saw, and Steph took Andy's toolbox.

Thankfully, Noah turned out to be quite handy and insisted he could sort out the window. He obviously felt bad about sneaking into her shed, and she was happy to leave him to get on with the job, feeling like he was making amends, while she made mugs of tea. When she went back into the lounge, she was pleased to see that he was already sawing the wood to size and together, they soon had it nailed in place.

Steph stood back to admire their handiwork, pleased with herself that she'd actually managed to get the job completed, even if Noah had done most of it. 'Not bad,' she said, grinning at Noah, hoping it would give him a confidence boost to have done a good turn.

His eyes slid away from hers as he bent to pick up the tools and the remaining bits of wood. 'I'll put this back in the shed, then I'll be off,' he said. 'And... you know... I'm sorry.'

Before she could say anything, he'd headed off to the kitchen and she hurried after him, watched him disappear out of the back door, not sure she was ready to be on her own just yet.

She waited until he came back from the shed, gave him a smile. 'You'll stay and have something to eat, won't you?'

He shook his head. 'Nah, it's okay. I'll just get off.'

'Please stay.' She recognised how needy she sounded, gave a laugh. 'I've only got dinners for two in the freezer. I just seem to shop on auto-pilot and then I remember there's only me now.'

He looked towards the back gate again, obviously how he'd got in. It was five feet high and permanently locked but she supposed it would be easy enough for someone agile to climb over. It must be how the intruder got in too. She looked at Noah again. *Could he be my intruder?* The police had thought it might be a homeless person sheltering from the weather. Hmm. Now she was even more keen that he should stay so she could question him. Just gently, see if he might give something away.

Somehow, the thought of it being Noah made her feel better. From what she'd seen of him he seemed like a nice lad and from their conversation earlier it sounded like he came from a good, hard-working family. If it had been him in her house, then she was sure the damage was probably a mistake, not shutting the loft window properly.

But why had he been up there?

She thought back to all the times she'd thought someone was in the house, when the rooms had been empty. Could he have been sneaking in and hiding from her? The thought made her stop and assess the wisdom of inviting him inside. *But he's just a young lad, away from his mum. Struggling.* The idea that he represented any threat to her safety melted away. He needed a bit of mothering, that was all, and she'd let him down today, promising a place to stay then having to turn him away.

'Come on,' she said, her hand reaching for his arm. He winced and she snatched her hand back. 'I'm so sorry, I didn't mean to hurt you.' She'd only touched him lightly, and was a bit perplexed by his reaction.

He grimaced, shook his head. 'It's okay. You weren't to know.'

So his injuries weren't just to his face – she couldn't think about letting him go off into the streets without knowing what had happened. 'Look, Noah, please stay. You'll be doing me a favour and we can get you cleaned up. I've got some ibuprofen gel in the house, that might take the pain away.'

Their eyes met. For a moment she was sure he was going to leave, but then he nodded, and she grinned, surprised at how relieved she felt. The events of the last couple of days had spooked her more than she'd been prepared to admit and if the police didn't have the resources to investigate in a timely manner, then there was nothing stopping her asking a few questions. Perhaps Noah had seen something if this was his stomping ground? Or perhaps he was her intruder and the brick through the window was someone completely different. No connection at all.

As her brain whirred on, taking her theories apart, separating things out, she didn't feel quite so worried. There could be a perfectly rational explanation. As the police officer had said, perhaps this wasn't personal at all.

But maybe it is, said the voice of reason, making her heart skip. *You should be careful.*

CHAPTER TWELVE

'Have a seat.' She pointed to a chair at the kitchen table, watching as Noah sat, his knee jiggling up and down again. He looked nervous, teeth gnawing at his lip, so she chattered on, thinking that might help him relax. 'It won't take long to get supper on. Like I said, I've just filled the freezer with dinners for two.' She grinned at him, raised an eyebrow. 'Supermarket's finest, don't you know.' She opened the freezer, rummaged around. 'Ah yes, how about chili con carne?'

'I love a chili,' Noah said.

Inside, under the bright lights, he looked younger. Vulnerable. Her heart went out to him, as it did to every young person she met in a similar situation. But she'd learned that nothing was ever what it seemed, and it often took a little while to get to something near the truth of each individual's situation.

Wait until we've eaten. Then he might feel more relaxed, more inclined to tell her the truth.

She found herself singing as she put the food in the microwave, got plates from the cupboard, cutlery from the drawer. To her surprise, Noah joined in, harmonising with a lovely falsetto. That was not what she'd been expecting, and she turned to him open-mouthed.

'How on earth do you know all the words to that song? It's way before your time.'

His face cracked into a wide smile that lit up his eyes. *Is he blushing?* It was hard to tell with his scraggly beard. 'It's one of my mum's favourites. She loves Take That. Robbie Williams. Spice Girls.' He shrugged. 'I was brought up with it. Mum singing along while she did the housework. I didn't get pocket money unless I helped with the cleaning, and it became our thing on a Saturday morning. The singing made it a bit of fun. Then she bought a karaoke machine one Christmas and it snowballed from there.'

He swallowed, looked down at his hands. The microwave pinged and she took the food out, gave it a stir and put it back in for a little longer. 'It sounds like you're close to your mum,' she said, gently. 'And what about your dad? Where's he?'

Noah didn't reply for a moment. 'He passed away when I was a toddler. I don't even remember him.'

'Oh, I'm sorry. That's tough.'

She pulled a bottle of sparkling water from the fridge, poured them drinks and put them on the table, not sure how much she could ask about his background before he clammed up. He didn't seem inclined to volunteer anything else, so she decided to let it be for now. *Change the subject.*

'What's your favourite song, then? We've got time for another before the food's ready.'

Noah gave her a sheepish grin, then started to sing 'Angels' by Robbie Williams. It was one of her favourites, too, one that the choir often sang, and she found herself getting lost in the melody, their voices soaring together.

When they finished, they looked at each other and laughed.

The microwave pinged and Steph busied herself with dishing up the food, a warmth flowing through her that she recognised. This is what singing did for her. It took her away from her worries, it brought her joy and my goodness how she'd missed it. She resolved to go back to choir practice the following week. Maybe she could persuade Noah to come with her? What a confidence boost that would be for him and the girls would love him. Her mind sauntered off into a little fantasy world for a moment until she realised she'd finished putting the food on the plates and was staring out of the window.

She jolted to her senses, turned and set the plates on the table.

'Have you ever belonged to a choir?' she asked as they started to eat.

'Nope,' he said, with a shake of the head, before he started shovelling food into his mouth as if he hadn't eaten for days. Perhaps he hadn't and she wondered if she'd given him enough. Decided they could have pudding.

'Let me tell you about the choir I belong to. Well, it's an a capella group. Just the six of us. Or it used to be anyway. I haven't been for a while.'

The conversation flowed and they talked about their favourite songs, how singing made them feel and she noticed that his leg had stopped bouncing, his eyes were shining, the creases gone from his forehead.

'Do you fancy some ice cream?' she asked when they'd finished. 'I've got loads in the freezer that needs eating up.' Andy loved his ice cream, but now it would just go to waste. It felt like a little victory, a positive step forward offering it to somebody else. Letting go of a bit of her past, even if it was just her husband's penchant for Ben and Jerry's salted caramel brownie.

He grinned at her. 'Lovely.'

She plonked a little tub in front of him, then sat back down. 'Now... tell me to butt out if I'm being nosy, but... what happened to your face? How did you hurt yourself?'

He looked startled for a moment, and she wondered if she'd misjudged the mood, ruined her chance. He took the top off the ice-cream tub and looked at it before dipping his spoon in, a little flash of ecstasy on his face when he popped the ice cream into his mouth.

'This is between you and me,' she said, wondering if he'd been doing something illegal and he was worried she'd go to the authorities. She gave a wry smile, said in stage whisper, 'What's said in this kitchen stays in this kitchen.'

He nodded, took another spoon of ice cream.

She thought he wasn't going to answer, but he began to talk, his voice a low murmur. 'For someone who's supposed to be intelligent, I have done some really stupid things.'

Steph laughed. 'Join the club. I think that's all part of being human.'

He caught her eye. 'But this was ridiculously stupid.' He shovelled a couple more spoons of ice cream into his mouth. 'I trusted someone.'

Steph watched him eat, wondering if that was all she was going to get. 'It's not stupid to trust people,' she said, hoping that he'd come to trust her.

'It is when they've done nothing to earn that trust. When you don't actually know them.' His jaw hardened. 'Then it's worse than stupid.'

'And they hurt you?'

Noah gave a derisive snort and touched his face, wincing as his fingers located the darkening bruise. 'Oh, this is nothing. He has this baseball bat. I've had broken ribs before now.'

Steph frowned. 'He's done it before?'

'I owe him money.' He sighed and put his spoon into the empty ice-cream tub, and sat back in his chair. 'When I was first evicted from my house share, I used to go down to the railway station and busk for money. Then somebody stole my guitar, so I just used to beg. Anyway, one day he comes up to me and asks if I'd like something to eat, told me I could have anything I wanted.' He gave a derisive snort. 'I didn't think he was for real. You get all sorts of jokers leading you on when you're begging. And when he disappeared off down the street, I thought that was the last I'd see of him. But he comes back with a cheeseburger and fries and a big drink of Pepsi.' His eyes met Steph's. 'It was the first proper meal I'd had for a few days. Honestly, I couldn't believe my luck. He sat down with me while I ate and told me how he'd been homeless when he'd come out of the army. Told me not to give up.'

He fiddled with the spoon, a frown wrinkling his brow. 'Anyway, I saw him a couple more times after that and each time he brought me a meal and we'd chat. I told him how I'd come to be on the streets, and he told me about his experience.' He shrugged. 'I honestly thought he was a nice guy. Easy to get on with. Then he lent me some money to buy new shoes because mine had holes in. And then...'

Noah's mouth moved from side to side, and he blinked a few times, then reached down and picked up his bag. He stood, eyes searching for the door.

'Look, I've taken up way too much of your time.' He wouldn't look at her. 'Thank you for the food and everything, but I'm going to head off now.'

And with that he was gone, before Steph could ask him to stay a little longer and finish his story. *But I can guess, can't I?* It was a familiar tale; one she'd heard a few times from the young people who came through the doors of the homeless shelter. Youngsters who were vulnerable and alone and desperate to find someone to help them out of trouble. Once they took the loan, the amount they owed escalated until it was impossible to find the money to pay it back. Then they were coerced into all sorts of activities in lieu of repayments. And if they refused, they were beaten up. Just like that, they were caught up in a situation that seemed to give them no way out.

Poor Noah. He seemed like such a nice young man, polite and thoughtful, but it looked like he was in a whole lot of trouble. *I can help him.* She was sure she could, just like she and Bill had helped the many before him. The trick was to keep him engaged, keep him coming back to the shelter until they could get him some accommodation. In the meantime, maybe Bill could chat to him, see if they could get a description of the guy who he was in debt to and work with the police to get him caught; they'd had a few successes recently. She decided she'd talk to her boss in the morning, make sure he kept an eye out for Noah.

She hummed as she cleared up the dishes and wiped down the table and worktops. It had been nice having company, lovely not having to eat alone. But now Noah had gone she was aware of the empty space, a house too big for her alone. She shivered, although the night was warm, an image of the broken window filling her mind.

Cara's suggestion popped into her head – the idea of a lodger – and she let herself think about that, how she might feel with somebody else in the house. It would be nice to have a student, someone like the nurses next door, help a young person who was away from home and might struggle a bit to find their feet. She could be there as a mentor for them. Now that felt like a positive thing to do, a chance to help someone rather than think of it as a strategy to earn some cash.

The more she thought about it, the more she warmed to the idea. Except her timing was all wrong. It was the end of term and students wouldn't be back until October. She needed somebody now if she was going to get a mortgage and buy Andy out.

She poured herself a glass of wine and walked through to the lounge. The boarded-up window shrank the room, disfigured it, making the space ugly and inhospitable. It was in her eyeline as she sat to watch TV, reminding her that someone had dealt her a malicious act which had no rational explanation.

It was impossible for her to ignore it now she was on her own, with no distractions to make the implications fade to a point where it was somehow acceptable.

She couldn't avoid the question now. *Could it have been Noah?* He had a motive, but then so did Andy and despite his protests that he was innocent, that didn't mean she had to believe him. Or it could be someone else entirely? Someone she'd upset unintentionally?

What about Lisa? She had a reason to make her too frightened to live in her own home.

Her head ached, the idea that she had an enemy out there such an alien concept that she was struggling to believe it was true. She pulled the fleece blanket from the back of the sofa and wrapped it round her shoulders, cradled a cushion in her lap, desperately seeking a bit of comfort, reassurance that she was okay. Safe. But was she?

CHAPTER THIRTEEN

The next day dragged by as she waited for Noah to turn up at the shelter. She'd briefed Bill and he'd promised to keep a look-out, put the word out among the regulars to try and get him to come in, but there was no sign. Nothing the next day either. Or the day after that. After two weeks, she had to accept that Noah might have moved on to a new place, to get away from his troubles, and who could blame him? She hoped he'd had the courage to go home.

Life seemed to have settled down for her. The police had been again and taken a statement, the insurance claim was going through, the contractor had been to measure up for the carpets, and the window had been repaired.

Cara popped her head round the door at lunchtime. 'Fancy going out for something to eat? My treat.'

Steph smiled. Lunch out was exactly what she needed to distract herself. She'd got herself a bit obsessed with the idea of helping Noah and she couldn't quite understand why. Was it because he reminded her so much of Max? By helping Noah it was sort of making up for not being there for her own son? Anyway, lunch with Cara would be fun. She jumped to her feet, grabbed her bag. They hadn't had a chance for a proper chat in days.

'Let's try the new vegan place,' Cara said. 'I've heard good things.'

Cara's new boyfriend, Dev, was a vegan, along with being a fitness fanatic, and it was funny seeing how she'd changed from a full-on carnivore to devout vegan in the space of weeks. She'd even started going to the gym after work. But that was probably more to do with the fact that her boyfriend worked there than a desire to exercise.

'Okay, let's give it a try,' Steph said as they exited the shelter and Cara linked arms with her. She enjoyed vegetarian food herself and was sure she'd find something on the menu to her liking. The main thing was having a catch-up with her friend.

'How are things with your neighbours?' Steph asked.

'Oh God, don't start me on that. I think we've reached the point of no return. In fact, I wanted to talk to you about that very thing.'

'Okay, fire away.'

'Let's wait till we're sat down. I can't hear myself think with all this traffic. It's just down here.' Cara steered them down towards the canal, the vegan restaurant being on the bottom floor of one of the new apartment blocks there. They'd been developed from the old red-brick industrial buildings and the setting by the canal was peaceful and quiet.

They found a table by the window, then Cara went and placed their orders, coming back with glasses of iced water and lemon.

'There you go. That'll clear out your system,' she said, handing Steph a glass and sinking onto the seat opposite.

Steph laughed. 'I'm not sure my system needs clearing out.' She took a sip. 'But it's lovely and refreshing.'

'Anyway... I was wanting to ask you a favour.'

Steph tensed, sensing this might be a big favour rather than something trivial. Cara was treating her to lunch. That had never happened before. It was usually the other way round, Steph moving into her default mothering role and taking Cara out when she was feeling down.

'I was thinking about you needing a lodger. And I was also thinking about my horrible neighbours and then I thought... why don't I come and rent a room from you? Well... actually, not just me. It would be me and Dev.' Cara picked up her napkin, carefully unfolded it and put it on her lap. 'He's about to be thrown out of his place. The landlord is selling up and wants them all out so he can do the place up before he puts it on the market. He doesn't want to move in with me because of my neighbour situation.' She rolled her eyes. 'Needs his beauty sleep, does Dev.'

Steph could feel a bead of panic tightening in her chest. Much as she liked Cara as a friend, that didn't mean she wanted to live with her. They were very different people. And if Cara's boyfriend was living there as well, Steph would be in the minority. Two of them, one of her. That had the potential to get really awkward. But saying no was going to be tricky too.

She ran her tongue over her lips, looked up to see a waiter heading in their direction, carrying two plates of food.

'Poor Dev. That must be stressful for him, being thrown out. He's been there a while, hasn't he?'

Cara nodded. 'He's so disorganised, he's left it until the last minute to start looking. Hasn't got it into his head that these things take time. But he could come and stay with you, couldn't he? Just to tide us over till we find something long-term?'

Steph smiled at the waiter as he put her food in front of her, a glorious multicoloured salad, with ingredients she'd never heard of before, let alone tasted. The basket of garlic bread smelled delicious, so she reached for a piece, took a big bite to give herself a bit of time before she replied.

'I told Dev you wouldn't mind. He's quite excited.' Cara

laughed. 'He's always wanted to live by the park. Perfect place for a fitness nut to live, isn't it? Honestly, I tell you, he'll be doing laps of the park at sunrise. Then yoga on the grass. And that's before he's had breakfast.'

Cara was positively glowing, wrapped up in an imaginary future living at Steph's house. Steph ripped off another chunk of garlic bread, chewing furiously. *It's my house. Not their house.* It was so presumptuous of her friend, assuming that she'd say yes, making plans before she'd even asked. It seemed like a big thing. Like a line had been crossed in their friendship.

'I'd be there most of the time too. I could sell my place. Dev won't stay there anymore after he had that bust-up with next door. He says they're toxic. Anyway, your place would be perfect. But we might have to separate out different spaces in the fridge so our food isn't contaminated with meat or dairy. And the same in the freezer. He's funny about things like that.' She laughed, leaned forwards. 'I hope your house is well sound-proofed. He's a bit noisy when he's... you know.'

Before Steph could check herself the words were out of her mouth. 'I'm so sorry, Cara, but you're too late. I've already agreed to take on a tenant.' She blushed at her lie, tucked her hair behind her ears and dabbed at her mouth with her napkin.

Cara stopped chewing. Stared at Steph.

'What? You never said.'

'That's because I haven't really seen you these last few days. And it's only just been agreed.'

'But I... we'd got our hearts set on it.' Cara swallowed, a tell-tale sheen in her eyes. She put her knife and fork down, still staring at Steph. 'I can't believe you'd do that without giving me first refusal.'

'What do you mean "first refusal"?' Steph's voice squeaked with indignation. 'You didn't say you wanted to be my lodger. You literally *just* suggested it as an option, remember?'

'Yes, but I thought you'd take the hint. What with all my

problems with the neighbours. I was sure...' She blinked. 'Can't you say you've changed your mind? It's not too late. Just tell them you made a mistake or something.'

Steph shook her head. If Cara came to live with her, it would be just like this. Barging Steph out of the way of any decision she didn't like. Imposing her will. It was a side to Cara that was great at work, but at home, well it could be really difficult.

'I'm really sorry. But it's all sorted.' Steph started on her salad, not wanting to catch her friend's eye. She felt awful for not helping her, but she had to stop herself from agreeing to something that would make her marginalised. That wasn't what her new life was about. She was aiming for empowerment, independence, a life where she was in control for once.

'Okay,' Cara said, with a sniff as she picked up her bag. 'Well, I'm sorry, but I'll have to go and tell Dev. He's got to move out at the weekend.' Her chin wobbled. 'I don't know what we're going to do now. We were so sure you'd say yes. Especially when you've had all the troubles recently and didn't want to be on your own.'

She walked out, leaving Steph to finish her meal on her own, and pay for it after all, wondering if she'd done the right thing, or if she'd just lost a friend.

CHAPTER FOURTEEN

Steph felt at a bit of a loss that afternoon. Cara didn't come back to work and wasn't answering her phone. Bill had meetings with the council, and she had a daunting pile of paperwork to wade through.

A tap on her door made her look up and there was Noah, standing in the doorway, his bruised face now tinged with yellow, making him look jaundiced. Had he lost weight? He'd been lean when she last saw him but now his cheeks seemed to have new hollows, his eyes larger in his face. Her mind swapped his face with that of her son, and she had to blink, recalibrate and push all thoughts of Max away. Surely Max was doing better than this. Surely her son wouldn't have fallen foul of the same sort of people who had Noah in their grasp?

'I can come back if you're busy,' he said, already inching out of the door.

'No. No, please come in,' she said, jumping to her feet, ready to dash after him and drag him back if he tried to disappear. She'd been waiting days for him to turn up and helping him would make her feel better about herself after the incident with Cara. He edged inside the office, stood against the wall. 'I was hoping you'd come back.' She indicated the empty chair in front of her desk. 'Have a seat.'

He pulled his hand from behind his back, presenting her with a bunch of flowers. She recognised them as wildflowers which grew by the canal, sprouting out of the walls. Valerian, she thought they were called, with long tips covered in dense clusters of dusky red blooms. Their stems were wrapped in a plastic bag to stop them from drying out.

'I wanted to say thank you for the meal the other night. And for not being mad at me for being in your shed.'

Her hand went to her chest, her throat too choked to speak for a moment. She took the flowers from him, blinking back the sting of tears, feeling stupid for getting emotional over something so trivial. But it reminded her so much of Max. He'd loved flowers when he was little and when they went to the park or the playground, he'd always find something for her, even if it was just a handful of daisies, or dandelions. Such a thoughtful child and it had always touched her heart.

She stared at the flowers, gathering herself before she dared glance at Noah. 'Oh, they're lovely. Thank you. And like I said, you did me a favour keeping me company.' Her smile broadened. 'It was fun.' And that was the truth. It had been fun, especially once they'd found the common bond of singing. The last few days had felt empty with Andy gone and Bea over in Europe with Mark for a short break. Now she'd upset Cara she had more lonely evenings ahead of her. *Perhaps he'd like to come for another meal?*

He blushed and tugged at the knotted bracelet on his wrist, then slid into the chair, giving her a shy smile.

She went round her desk and sat opposite him, putting her flowers down while she sorted through a pile of paperwork. 'I've got some forms here which we need to complete to get you on the waiting list for the youth accommodation. You'd be first in line, and it might only be a couple of months' wait.'

'Okay, it's worth a try. I can't stay where I was at the allotments, so I need to find somewhere else.'

Well, that clears up a puzzle. It wasn't her shed he'd been living in; he'd obviously just been hiding in there. 'Oh, that's a shame. What happened?'

Noah grimaced. 'He found me. You know, the guy I told you about.' He sighed. 'I manage to avoid him for ages and then... well, someone probably snitched on me.'

'I'm sorry to hear that.'

He shrugged. 'It's okay. It's all sorted now.'

'Does this man have a name?' Steph was thinking about putting a report in to the police.

'Not that I know of.'

'Well, what does he look like? Just so we know to keep him away from the shelter.'

Noah thought for a moment. 'He looks nice. Big smile. Short dirty-blond hair. You know, like a buzz cut. He usually wears a black baseball hat. Aviator shades. Stocky, like he works out. Tatts up both arms.' She jotted down notes as he spoke, thought there were a few things that would make the man distinctive, easy for the police to track down. 'He told me he used to be in the army, but I don't even know if that's true. He's got a bit of a gang, you know, lads who he sends out to do discipline if people don't pay or do the jobs they've been asked to do.'

She stopped writing and looked up, feeling increasingly uneasy. 'What sort of jobs?'

Noah didn't answer for a moment, his teeth chewing at his lip. 'All sorts of things.'

She knew not to push it, didn't want to scare him away with too many questions. In time, she hoped he'd confide in her, but she knew it had to be at his speed, when he trusted her enough.

'Okay,' she said, brightly, pulling the forms in front of her. 'Let's get these filled in, shall we?'

He nodded and she saw the hope in his eyes, understood the circle of despair he'd got himself into because she'd seen it so many times before.

She rang through to the hostel kitchen and asked Phil if he'd bring Noah something to eat and a couple of mugs of tea – it was going to take a good half hour to get all the information she needed if she was going to be able to look at all the options for accommodation. Five minutes later, the chef's assistant appeared in the doorway, a volunteer who was staying at the shelter and was keen to learn new skills as a route to getting a job.

Noah snatched up the sandwich as soon as he was handed the plate, and started eating, clearly ravenous.

'How would you like to come round for tea again?' she asked before she'd thought about it. 'Pepperoni pizza tonight.' It had been Andy's favourite, but not something she enjoyed. It could be part of her mission of clearing up her life. Emptying the freezer of stuff she wouldn't eat and feeding Noah at the same time. 'Please? My daughter's away at the moment and I could do with a bit of company.'

He stuffed the rest of his sandwich in his mouth and grinned at her. 'For real?'

'Absolutely. But only if we can do a bit of singing practice.'

His grin widened. 'You're on.'

She checked her watch. 'Okay, well we can get this form done, then if you want to wait in reception while I tidy up, I'll be ready to go.'

They got the bus home and she couldn't help noticing a strong aroma of stale sweat as he sat next to her. His clothes were filthy, his fingernails black with dirt. 'You know, you could have a shower if you wanted, while I get the food ready,' she said as they walked up to the house. 'And I could probably find you some clean clothes. My son... he was same size as you when he left home.'

She startled herself with that suggestion, but it made sense. Andy had been on at her for ages about clearing out Max's stuff, but she'd resisted, wanting everything to be as he'd left it when he came home.

'There's a chest of drawers you can have a root through. Find a few things you like to keep you going. He was eighteen when he left and still growing, so I doubt any of it would fit him now and he's not likely...' She tailed off, not wanting to admit that her son was estranged. Just like Noah was from his parents. She understood how it could happen, she really did.

She opened the door, letting it swing wide so Noah could go in ahead of her. But he seemed to be stuck to the gravel, and she wondered if she'd gone too far. Her heart skipped a beat. She really didn't want to be on her own.

She glanced at Noah, desperate for him to stay. 'It's just a suggestion. No pressure. Only if you want to.'

Noah wiped his hands on his grubby trousers, the knees caked with mud, his trainers so worn his toes poked through at the ends, then nodded. 'That would be great, thanks.'

She led him upstairs and into Max's room. He stopped in the doorway, looking at the posters on the walls, images from the Xbox games Max had been so keen on. War games. It should have been obvious where his obsession would lead him. He'd spent years holed up in his bedroom, shooting things on video games, so why not go for it in real life? Just coming in here opened a room full of regrets. Could she have talked him out of it, encouraged him down a different path? Could the circular arguments have been avoided, could she have stopped him from...? She mentally shut the door, not wanting to see or hear any more. *No point mulling over what's been.* She had to think about now. About the future.

Noah gave a low whistle as he scanned the walls. 'Wow. I

loved all that stuff when I was a kid. Didn't have an Xbox myself but my mates did. We played all these games.' He laughed. 'I can't say I was any good at it. I know this might sound weird, but it was a bit full-on for me. So noisy. The novelty wore off pretty quickly, to be honest.' He sighed, a pensive expression on his face. 'I saw friends who were addicted to this stuff, though. Stayed up half the night playing and looked like they were doing drugs or something.' He shrugged. 'I suppose they were, in a way, the amount of energy drinks they were getting through to keep themselves awake.'

It sounded very familiar, Max fitting the description perfectly. These games had become his world and there had been nothing she could do to encourage him to open his mind to anything else. He'd shrunk away from his family, a ghostly presence in the house, hardly emerging when the rest of them were home.

She couldn't help thinking she'd failed him. It had been too easy to leave him to it and spend time with Bea, who actually wanted her company, rather than hustle a surly youth into doing things he clearly had no interest in. But then... it had been more peaceful that way. Better for Bea who had fallen victim to Max's vindictive moods. How many times had she comforted her daughter when her things had been ruined by her brother?

When they were little it had been petty things like making her drop her ice cream on the floor. Or hiding her favourite teddy. Or a pivotal memory of her daughter running downstairs one the morning, tears streaming down her face, her long braid in her hand. Max had cut it off when she'd been asleep. He'd been eleven at the time, just about to go up to secondary school. Steph had spent a long time talking to him about boundaries and the difference between practical jokes and bullying. He'd stared at her, anger in his eyes, not prepared to admit his guilt.

He was older, and Steph put it down to jealousy. He'd been an only child for almost three years, but when Bea came along, he'd had to learn to share. It had been pretty much okay until Bea was five or six and developing into a little person with an opinion of her own. That's what Max didn't seem to like. That's when he started the mischief and it escalated into a full-scale war between them as they got older. Always accusing each other, lots of shouting, banging doors. Until Max retreated into his bedroom with his video games for company and finally left.

Whatever your children did, you never stopped loving them. That was Steph's experience. More than ever, she just wanted a chance to talk to Max, see if they could patch things up, now he was an adult with some life experience under his belt. She thought about Noah's story, how he felt ashamed to go home. Maybe Max felt something similar? Felt he couldn't come back because of the bad feeling when he left?

Andy still maintained that they should let him come back when he was ready. But how could he come back if they'd moved house? He could be in trouble, just like Noah, and the thought of that made her heart clench. Even if he wasn't in trouble, she wanted him to know that she was always there for him, that she loved him as much as ever. Over the years, she'd let herself be distracted by Bea, trying to make amends for the trauma she'd suffered at her brother's hands. Allowed Andy to persuade her not to start searching. *You can do what you want now.* It was time, she decided, to focus her energy on finding him.

She turned her mind back to the job in hand, glanced at Noah as she opened drawers. 'Here. Have a look through these, see if anything will fit. I'm sure you'll find something.' She gave him an encouraging smile, held up a couple of faded black T-shirts. The next drawer was stuffed with jeans and joggers, and she pulled out a few pairs. The next drawer was full of sweat-shirts and hoodies.

Ten minutes later, she'd found him a pair of trainers that fit and left Noah sifting through a heap of clothes on the bed.

'Bathroom's on your left down the landing when you're ready. I'll put the towel on the wall heater in there.'

'Are you sure this is okay?' Noah asked, holding up an Adidas sweatshirt. 'You don't want to keep anything?'

Steph thought for a moment. 'They're only clothes and they won't fit Max anymore. No use sitting in a drawer, are they? Honestly, take what you need.'

She walked down the landing, nerves twisting her stomach. Her head telling her that it was fine, but her heart telling her that those things belonged to Max. They weren't hers to give away as they were all she had left of him.

CHAPTER FIFTEEN

'Food's ready,' she called up the stairs a little while later. She'd caught herself humming to the songs on the radio as she got plates and cutlery out, making an effort to set the table for their meal.

There was no reply and after a while she went upstairs, surprised to find Noah asleep on Max's bed. She leaned against the doorway, her heart melting as she watched. He looked even younger. A handsome lad now he'd shaved off the wispy facial hair that couldn't really have been classed as a beard. She'd put out a pack of disposable razors and shaving foam that Andy had left, hoping that he'd take the hint. How exhausting it must be to sleep outside, always a bit cold, a bit hungry. You probably never really got a proper night's sleep. But he needed food, he could sleep later, and she moved towards him.

'Noah,' she said, gently, bending over him and rubbing his shoulder.

He jumped, his arm swiping the air as his eyes blinked open and she had to duck to avoid being hit. He stared at her, fear in his eyes as he scanned the room. Then his face fell.

'Oh my God, I'm so sorry. I'm so sorry. I didn't mean to...'

He jumped off the bed, picking up his bag, which was now full to overflowing with clothes. 'I'll go. Please don't call the police.'

Had he intended to hit her? *He didn't know where he was.* That was the truth of it, and she knew rough sleepers were regularly attacked. She'd know in future to find another way to wake him, should the need arise. She studied his face, his eyes darting to the door, looking for a way to escape.

She held up a hand as if that would stop his fear in its tracks. 'It's okay. My fault for startling you.' She gave him a reassuring smile. 'Honestly. I know it was just an instinctive reaction. No harm done.'

He nodded, lips pressed together like he was trying not to cry. Poor lad was in a bit of a state. *But I can help, can't I?* And she really didn't want to be on her own just yet, still a bit jumpy after the intruder and the broken window.

'Come on, supper's ready,' she said, leaving the room and walking downstairs, hoping that he'd follow.

After a moment he did. But he stopped by the front door. 'I really think it's better if I just go.' He hefted his bag onto his shoulder.

'No,' she said, diving between him and his escape route. 'Please, Noah. Just stay for something to eat. You might as well. It's all ready now.'

His stomach grumbled. He looked unsure. She laughed. 'Come on. Lighten up. Like I said, no harm done.' Then she remembered his story, how the man had showed him kindness, then wanted something in return. 'You'll be doing me a favour if you stay.'

He smiled at her then, such a lovely warm smile it was like a forbidden treat. Something just for her.

She walked down the hallway into the kitchen, Noah following behind. 'Have a seat, I'll just dish up. Won't be a minute, then you can be on your way.'

'Are you sure? I don't want to be any trouble.'

'Oh, stop it. I wouldn't have invited you if it caused trouble.'

She brought the plates over to the table. 'I've not been on my own for very long, you see, and I'm finding it quite weird having the house to myself.' She sighed. 'I used to love cooking for my family, but now it's just me I find it hard to bother.'

'What happened to your family?' Noah asked as he took the plate from her. 'No, no, sorry, that was way too nosy. You don't have to answer that. Honestly... I'm sorry.' He picked up a slice of pizza, took a big bite.

She laughed. 'It's okay. It's not like it's any big secret. My husband left me a few months ago. My two kids, Bea and Max, have grown up and left home.'

She sighed, nibbling at the crust of her pizza. 'It's weird how you think you know someone and then you realise you don't know them at all. I would never have imagined Andy would walk out on me. Never.'

'My mum said the same about her dad. My grandad left my nan when she was going through cancer treatment. How bad is that?'

'That's really, really bad.'

'Luckily Nan pulled through, but Mum never spoke to Grandad again. Says she won't ever speak to him after that. Seems some things can't be forgiven.' He chewed his pizza, thoughtful. 'But some things can. Mum's partner went on a stag do with his mates, and there were pictures of him kissing this woman all over social media.' Noah shrugged. 'They had a hell of a row and then it was okay.' He shrugged. 'People are weird. That's all there is to it.'

She smiled and chewed and thought he was probably right.

'I think it's all down to what you want and what you need being different things,' he said. 'I thought I wanted a degree, but then I found that wasn't what I wanted at all. What I wanted was a home that was mine, where I felt I belonged. You see, when Mum's partner... well, he's actually my stepdad now.

When he moved in, I felt like I was in the way. Going off to do a degree was probably just me finding an excuse to get out of there.' He took another piece of pizza, his eyes staring into the distance. 'Really, being on the streets has been much more of a learning experience than university.' He laughed. 'It certainly made me grow up, that's for sure. And I've learned some hard lessons.'

'You must have got something from your degree, though. It can't have been a complete waste of time.'

He stopped chewing, considered for a moment. 'I've got a head full of useless quotes and a debt of around twenty-five grand. So what I discovered was... well, my mum was right.'

He went quiet then, while he finished off the rest of the pizza and she picked at hers.

'So what are your hopes for the future?' she said when he'd finished. 'What would you like to happen?'

'It's like you said, I need a permanent address. And a job. Then everything else should start to fall into place.'

'Don't worry, I'm sure we'll find you something soon.' The words felt hollow in her mouth, and she changed the subject, started talking about the courses available at college and how she was hoping to do a counselling course, trying to tease out of him what career direction he might choose.

The conversation flowed and she studied his face as he spoke, watching the way his mouth moved, the way his eyebrows shot up and down when he became animated, the warmth of his smile. She remembered watching Max growing up, noting every little change in him, wishing he would talk to her, instead of shutting her out. This felt like a second chance.

However much she told herself – and everyone else who would listen – that she was happy to live on her own, in her heart she yearned for company. Someone to have proper conversations with, have a laugh, share meals. Companionship and, if she was being honest with herself, an element of security.

Of course, Bea had suggested she go and stay with her, but her recent convalescence after the broken ankle was still fresh in her thoughts; she really didn't want a repeat of that.

Bea had picked her up from the hospital and instead of taking her home had taken her to their house outside Harrogate, which was like something from *Hello!*. In fact, it had been featured in that very magazine when Mark first had it built, four years ago. She still had the article at home, Bea dressed to the nines, looking like a model. She was supremely proud of her daughter but it was hard, sometimes, to believe they shared the same gene pool.

'No, Bea, I want to go home,' she'd said as she watched the car take the wrong turning on their way back from the hospital. She was feeling jittery and shocked after her tumble down the escalator, reliving it over and over. Now she wanted the comfort of her own bed.

'Don't be daft, Mum, you're not safe to be home. Not until you can put some weight on that ankle. It's going to be a little while before that happens, isn't it?'

'Will Mark be there?' she asked, nervously twisting her hands together, thinking she could always call a cab and come home. There was nothing overtly wrong with Mark. To be fair, he was amazingly generous, but he was always on the go, talking so fast she could hardly keep up. She found his company exhausting and he had a habit of asking question after question. In his mind he was showing a polite curiosity about Steph's life, but she always left his company feeling like she been through an intensive interrogation.

'Mark's in Italy doing some business with Inter Milan. Then he's off to Portugal, so he won't be home for a week or so.'

Bea gave her a beaming smile. 'Just you and me, Mum. It'll be fun.' She stretched a hand and patted her Mum's knee. 'Loads of treats. Anyway, think of it as a little holiday and all you have to do is relax.'

Steph had stayed for a couple of weeks until she was able to put weight on her ankle. Bea had protested, didn't think she was ready to go home, but Steph was adamant she was going back to work.

Now, her thoughts came full circle, back to loneliness. And here was Noah, sitting in her kitchen, his company so easy she couldn't remember the last time she'd felt this relaxed.

Then a question popped into her head and flew out of her mouth. It had been sitting there, niggling at the back of her mind, waiting to ambush her enjoyment.

'You know the other night? What were you doing in my shed?'

CHAPTER SIXTEEN

Noah's eyes dropped to his plate, empty apart from a couple of burned crusts. She watched his Adam's apple move up and down, the atmosphere in the room feeling charged. It had all been going so well. Too well probably. His leg started to bounce up and down under the table, a sure sign he was nervous. *What's he hiding?*

He heaved a big sigh, tugged at the bracelet on his wrist. 'I was looking for somewhere to sleep. I walked down the back alley and when I popped my head over the gate, I saw your shed door wasn't shut properly.' He held his hands up. 'I had no idea you lived here. Honest to God, you've got to believe me. I wasn't doing any harm.' He picked up a bit of pizza crust and crumbled it into dust.

Steph's voice hardened. 'I want you to be honest with me, Noah.'

He swallowed again but didn't speak.

'That's a new bump of your forehead, isn't it?'

'I had a bit of a tumble, that's all. Fell over in the park when I wasn't looking where I was going. Tripped over a tree root.' He rubbed his nose, head dipped so she couldn't see his face.

'Oh, Noah. You must think I was born yesterday. Somebody did that to you, didn't they? Was it the same man? Because if it was, you've got to talk to the police, see if we can get him locked up.'

He looked at her properly then, blew out his cheeks. 'It's what happens when you're sleeping rough. It's like a game to some people. They don't seem to see us as human, just something to kick for a bit of a laugh, or to impress their mates, or take out their anger on.'

A flash of rage sparked through her. 'I'll never understand people.' How could someone just kick out at another person, a stranger, for no reason. *Perhaps that's not what happened.* She stopped and was just about to go back to her original question when he spoke.

'You must feel a bit nervous here on your own.' He caught her eye. 'I feel nervous every night, wondering if someone's going to come and nick my stuff, or have a go at me. You never really sleep properly.' He ran his tongue round his lips. 'If you want the truth, I was in your shed because I was hiding. I don't want to be a lackey anymore, but I owe that guy I told you about some money. So I'm just ducking and diving trying to keep out of his way.' He sighed. 'Anyway, one of his lads followed me across the park. I've been living in a shed on the allotments not far from here, but they found me there, so I was looking for somewhere new. I manage to slip away from them, climbed over the gate and ducked into the shed until they'd gone. Then you found me.'

She gazed at him for a moment, considering. 'It just seems a bit of a coincidence that it was my shed.'

He shrugged. 'That's the God's honest truth. Coincidences happen, don't they? Your house just happens to be between the park and where I've been living.' She studied his face but could see no evidence of a lie. *Maybe it was just a coincidence.*

She hated the way she'd become suspicious of everything,

looking for ulterior motives. But with the recent incidences, her trust had been shaken. She crossed her arms over her chest. 'Well, that's okay. I don't mind, as long as they didn't see you go in there.'

'I'm sure they didn't.' He looked her straight in the eye. 'If they had, I'd be in hospital now.'

She gave an involuntary shiver. Noah's situation was so desperate. Imagine living your life wondering if people are going to come and beat you up? She frowned. 'You don't think it could be them who put the brick through the window?'

Noah's eyes widened. 'I hadn't thought of that. But that's really not their style at all. They don't bother with property. It's people they damage.'

A silence fell between them.

'I do feel nervous, though. You're right about that.'

He considered her for a moment. Opening his mouth and then closing it again before finally speaking. 'Steph, I hope you don't mind me asking... but, you know, the brick through the window thing. Has somebody got it in for *you*?'

She sighed and dabbed her mouth with a napkin, not sure how to answer that. *Perhaps if I talk it through it'll make some sense?* 'There *is* something odd going on. The police seem to think it's separate things, but I've been thinking about it, and, well, I have to admit I'm feeling... unsettled. I mean, what if these things are connected? That means you're right. Somebody has got it in for me.'

He frowned. 'Sorry, I'm not sure what you mean. What things?'

She adjusted her position, realising that Noah didn't know the whole story. 'Three things that have happened recently.' She took a deep breath. 'I'm pretty sure someone pushed me down the escalator at the shopping centre. That was the first thing.'

'Nasty,' he said, grimacing.

'I ended up with a broken ankle, which was bad enough, but it could have been a lot worse. I told myself it was an accident at the time, but now, after these other things, I'm not so sure.' She picked up her knife, scraped at some melted cheese on the side of her plate. 'Then I had an intruder. The weird thing about that was nothing was taken, just windows left open in the pouring rain. That caused a bit of damage, but I think it was more to do with somebody wanting me to feel... vulnerable.' She huffed. 'The police thought my intruder was a homeless person just getting a bit of shelter from the weather.' She caught Noah's eye and had to ask, 'It wasn't you, was it? I won't be cross, honestly, but in a way, I'd feel a whole lot better if it was.'

He shook his head, his mouth a thin line. 'Honestly, nothing to do with me. Sheds, that's my thing. I'd never dare break into someone's house.'

She watched his expression, satisfied that he was telling the truth. 'The last thing was the brick through the window.'

Now that she'd laid it all out, she could think of only one person to blame, one person who would benefit from her feeling so insecure she'd want to leave her home. Her eyes met his. 'I think my husband's been doing it.'

'Wow. That's quite some accusation.'

'Yeah, well, he's the one who wants me out of the house. We're going through divorce proceedings, you see. He wants to sell, and I don't. I refuse to be forced out just because he chose to leave me.' She frowned. 'Does that seem fair to you?'

'Nope. That sucks, to be honest.'

'It does, doesn't it? Anyway, I won't be intimidated.'

'But don't you think... he might try something else?'

'I've told the police about everything, so they've got him in their sights if anything else happens. And my friend came up with a great idea. She suggested I could get a lodger. Then I'd have enough income to get the mortgage I need to buy him out and there'd be someone else here for a bit of security. So that's my plan.'

They sat in silence for a little while.

'You know, I think you should chase up the police about the brick through the window. Tell them exactly what you've told me. Now you've gone through the whole story, there's definitely a pattern.' His brow crumpled, concern in his eyes. 'Three times now. What if it escalates?'

What if it does? It was something she hadn't thought about. But now Noah had mentioned it, she felt a little shiver run through her, fear settling like a lead weight in her stomach.

She gave Noah a weak smile. 'I don't know. I might be making a mountain out of a molehill. As threats go, it's pretty lame, isn't it? That's why I think it was my husband. I'm not sure we can add up everything that's happened and think there's one person behind it. Now that I've said it all out loud, it sounds like paranoia to me. I think the shopping centre accident was just that. The intruder didn't actually take anything, and the broken window has been fixed.'

Noah looked at her askance, clearly unconvinced.

She felt her resolve wavering. If Noah was concerned, should she be too? After all, he was the streetwise one. She'd led a pretty sheltered life, really. Very cautious. What did she know about threats and the dark underbelly of life? She'd wised up a bit since she'd been working at the homeless shelter, but that was all second-hand information and in terms of personal experience, she had little to draw on.

'I can keep an eye out for you,' Noah said. 'Loiter around outside, like a lookout.'

Steph laughed. 'That sounds very melodramatic but thanks for the offer.'

She watched the hope fade from his eyes and understood then that he needed something from her. That's what this was about. It was about a connection. Him not feeling that he was completely alone – being able to do something positive – and she felt bad for refusing his offer so quickly.

'I've got a better idea,' she said. 'It'll help me and solve a problem for you at the same time. Why don't you stay with me for a little while?'

CHAPTER SEVENTEEN

What are you doing? yelled a voice in her head, one that sounded a lot like Andy. Her behaviour was impulsive to say the least, she knew that, but her brain was refusing to be objective, her heart having taken control. *Bill took homeless people in when there was nowhere else for them.* She repeated it a few times in her head, convincing herself that she was doing the right thing. The compassionate thing. *It's just for a few days*, she reassured herself as she carried on with her justification out loud, as much for her benefit as Noah's.

'Perhaps this person will stop their little power play if they know I'm not alone. It would make me feel safer to have you here. And I'd be happier if I knew you weren't out there being kicked about by random idiots. What do you say?'

Noah stared at her like she'd sprouted wings and started breathing fire.

'For real?'

She smiled and caught his eye. 'Definitely for real. I'll be honest. I'm not that keen on living on my own. I've never done it, you see. I moved straight out of the home I grew up in into this house with my husband. We'd been together nearly thirty years.' She had to stop for a moment, a rush of regret filling her throat so she couldn't speak.

She gave herself a mental shake. There was no road back to the past. No choice but to face a different future and why couldn't she help this young man? Surely that was a good thing to do – and wasn't it was close to what she'd planned anyway, renting out a room to a young person who she could mentor? Why shouldn't that person be Noah?

She relaxed a little, happy with her reasoning. 'You can have the attic room. There's more space up there. And you can help me pull up the ruined carpet ready for the insurance people.' She grinned at him, relieved at the thought she'd have company. 'What do you think?'

He frowned, looked wary. 'Are you sure?'

'Definitely. Let's give it a go for a couple of weeks. If it doesn't work, we can part company, no hard feelings. If it does work, we can think about formalising it and apply for housing benefit. Then I can charge you as a lodger and it sorts out my financial problems.' She held out her hands. 'It's a win-win, isn't it?'

'Bloody hell,' he said, still staring at her.

She laughed. 'Was that a yes?'

He nodded and his face broke into a grin. 'It was.' His eyes shone. 'I'm so grateful, I really am. And like you say, if it doesn't work out, I'll be happy to go. Just say the word.'

She stretched her hand over the table. 'Let's shake on it.' Noah hesitated, then his hand clasped hers, dry and rough but his handshake was firm. They had a deal.

Her heart skipped, exhilaration making her feel a little giddy. How good did it feel to be doing someone a favour? A little act of kindness. It really was food for the soul, and she was feeling thoroughly nourished by the thought of helping Noah through the sticky patch he'd found himself in. She was already compiling a tick list of things she could do to help, conversations they needed to have, people she could speak to. He could be her project.

'Come on, let's get your room sorted out,' she said, bouncing to her feet, ready for action, casting off all thoughts of the unsettling events of the last few weeks.

She bustled round, gathering bedding as she led Noah up to the loft.

'Sorry, it's not really a man's room.' She cringed as she saw the room with fresh eyes. It was a bit Laura Ashley – all flowers and bows and very pink. 'It was my daughter's, you see.'

'Won't she mind me staying here?' Noah's eyes flicked down the stairs and she knew he'd rather have *Call of Duty* posters on his wall than the décor her daughter favoured. It wasn't to her own taste either, but Bea had paid for it to be redecorated so she hadn't had much choice. It was Bea's little bolthole, and she was happy for her to make it her own in whatever way she wanted.

'Let's just think of the décor as a temporary thing for now,' she said.

Noah nodded, looking a bit distracted, like he might be regretting his decision. But why wouldn't he want to stay? Surely it was better than being on the streets? Then she remembered her boss's pep talk on the first day.

'You are not here to make their decisions for them. You are here purely in an advisory capacity. Some people are ready to hear what you have to say, and some people aren't quite there yet. But we don't give up. We let them decide when the time is right.' He made eye contact, making sure she was listening. 'We don't know what's gone on in their lives, do we? Who are we to say what's right for them?'

Of course she'd nodded and agreed with him. But she'd often found herself putting a little pressure on her clients to take the help she was offering. It was hard to understand why they wouldn't want to. Now she looked at Noah, took in the defensive hunch of his body and wondered if she'd pushed him into a decision he was regretting.

'Look, I want you to know that you're very welcome here.' Noah chewed at his lip, staring at the stairs as if he wanted to run down them. 'You obviously don't have to stay if you don't want to.' She shrugged. 'Completely up to you.'

He allowed his backpack to slip down his arm onto the floor. 'It just feels a bit weird being in a house again, that's all.'

Steph turned towards the stairs, thinking it would be better to give him some space to settle in. 'Make yourself at home. Help yourself to anything in the kitchen. I'm going to read for a bit, so I'll see you in the morning.'

She looked over her shoulder at him before she went downstairs, catching a fleeting expression on his face. A secret smile, like he'd won something.

CHAPTER EIGHTEEN

The following day on her way home from work, Steph listened to the phone ringing while she waited for Bea to pick up.

'Hello, love,' Steph said when Bea finally answered. 'Good trip?'

'It was lovely. I've never been to Belgium, but I think it might be my new favourite place. Lovely architecture, fabulous coffee and chocolates to die for. Talking of which, I brought some back for you.'

'That's so sweet of you.' Bea always brought her a little gift from her travels and Steph really appreciated the thought. Not to mention the fact she was a bit of a chocolate addict. 'Thanks, love.'

'Do you want me to come over? I've just this minute got back, but I really don't mind if you're a bit lonely.'

'No, it's okay. I need to give you a bit of an update, actually. There's a few things happened since you've been away.'

'What things?' Bea sounded panicky. 'Why didn't you ring me? You're okay, aren't you?'

'Don't worry, I'm fine. You're not going to believe this, but somebody put a brick through the front window.'

Bea gasped. 'Oh my God, Mum. You should have rung! Have you called the police? What about—'

'I didn't want to bother you when you were on holiday. Anyway, I have called the police and they're investigating. They don't think it's anything to be too worried about. Probably just youths.' She sighed. 'Actually, I suspect it was your dad. I bumped into him in the park on my way home, just before I found out what had happened. He was drunk, can you believe? God knows what's going on with him.'

'What? You're joking? What was he doing in the park?'

'Loitering, that's what. Anyway, I can't think who else would have a motive and it's all mended now, so nothing to worry about.'

'I don't know, it doesn't feel right to me.' She sounded indignant. 'Dad wouldn't do that!'

Steph could feel her teeth grinding and loosened her jaw. 'Let me tell you what that scheming weasel of a father has been up to. His best friend has offered to buy our property and he's agreed to it!'

There was a clatter, then silence. 'Bea, are you still there?'

'Sorry, I dropped my phone. But... Mum, are you sure?'

'Absolutely sure. Lisa rang me, made it sound like they were doing us a favour. It seems obvious to me that this is your dad trying to scare me out of the house. Get his own way, as usual.'

'You really think so?' Bea still didn't sound convinced and Steph knew it would be hard to persuade her that the father she had once doted on would do such a thing. She moved the conversation on, not wanting to get into an argument.

'You'll be pleased to know that I'm not on my own in the house anymore. I've just got a lodger.'

Bea started to cough, like she was choking on something, then there was another silence.

'You okay, Bea? Are you still there...? Bea?'

'Sorry, Mum,' she said after a minute or two. 'Biscuit went down the wrong way. I'm not sure I heard you right.' She gave a laugh. 'I thought you said you'd got a lodger.'

'That's right. Tall, blondish and handsome.'

Bea giggled. 'For God's sake, Mum. You had me going then, I thought you were being serious.'

'I am being serious. Honestly, he's so like Max, it's uncanny. Anyway, he came to the shelter a while ago and there was nowhere for him to stay. I've got to know him a bit and he's a lovely lad, just fallen on hard times.' She smiled as she spoke. 'We get on ever so well. Would you believe he likes singing? Knows all the old hits we did at the a capella group.' She laughed at that because she still couldn't believe it. 'Anyway, it solves a financial problem for me, gives him a place to stay and I have to admit I do feel happier with someone else in the house at the moment. I know you'd been worried about me being on my own.'

'Wait, wait... A homeless person?' Bea's voice rose to a squeak. 'You've picked up a homeless person? Someone you know nothing about and invited them to stay in your house?' There were tears in her voice. 'A stranger staying in our family home!'

'Oh, Bea, he's not really a stranger and you'll just have to trust my judgement on this one. It's only for a few weeks until he gets back on his feet. He's a philosophy student, no less. Does that make you feel better? He had a bit of a falling-out with his parents, but he's staying here while I help him sort out something permanent.'

'What can I say?' Bea seemed to soften, and added, 'You're full of surprises these days, Mum. I can't keep up.'

'It's the new me, love. Mrs Independent.'

They both laughed then, and the conversation moved on to Belgium and what Bea had been doing on her holiday. Steph felt her neck muscles relax as the conversation reached safer ground. To be perfectly honest, she'd been a bit worried about telling Bea about her lodger because Noah was going to be using her old bedroom, but she didn't need to know that just yet.

Later that evening, she and Noah had just finished their meal – cooked from fresh ingredients for once – when the doorbell rang. Steph opened the door to find Andy and Bea standing there, grim expressions on their faces.

'What's the matter with you two?' she asked, her heart sinking, aware that there was going to be a row now about Noah staying. Why her family thought they could interfere in her life she didn't know. But then having a life of her own was a novelty to them and she supposed it would take them a while to get used to the idea she was actually an individual, not just a wife and mother. Two roles which had made her invisible in the past.

Andy barged past while Bea pulled an apologetic face and gave her a hug.

'Sorry, Mum, he insisted on coming, so I thought I better come with him. But I've been thinking about the brick through the window and I can't see why youths would do that? It feels more like intimidation to me. Dad and I were wondering whether your homeless youth had something to do with it.'

Steph glanced at Andy's back as he walked into the kitchen. 'You'd have to ask your father about that brick, I think.'

Bea sighed and pulled away. She looked quite weary, her usually perfect make-up smudged under her eyes. 'I did and he says it's nothing to do with him. Pure coincidence that he was in the park.'

'Really.' Steph couldn't help the tinge of sarcasm.

Raised voices floated down the hallway from the kitchen.

'Oh God. He's at it already.'

'Well, I hate to say it, but he's got a point, Mum. It is half his house, so you can't really have a lodger without asking his permission, can you?'

Steph hadn't thought about that. In fact, she hadn't really thought it through much at all. It had been her heart speaking when she'd asked Noah if he wanted to stay. It had seemed like a good idea at the time, but she would admit, she hadn't been thinking about Bea and Andy. For a change she'd been thinking about herself. *Why does that always seem to end in trouble?*

When she got to the kitchen, Bea on her heels, the men were squaring up to each other, circling slowly like they were going to start fighting. Noah looked quite different now. Gone was the innocent young man and in his place was a feral youth, eyes sparking, teeth bared as he took the blast of Andy's angry words. Steph did a double take, a shimmer of unease running through her, but who wouldn't go on the offensive if somebody came and started shouting at them? Noah had been living on his wits, facing trouble just about every day of his life for the last year. Of course he'd learned to stand up for himself. *Nothing to worry about.*

'Bloody hell, Andy. Just stop it,' Steph snapped, standing between them and pushing the two men further away from each other. Beyond hitting distance. 'You can't just come barging in here, you know. This isn't your house anymore.' She jabbed a finger at her husband's chest. 'You chose to leave.'

Andy turned to her then, his face thunderous, spittle flying as he spoke. ''Course it's my house. We're not divorced yet, are we?'

'Come on, let's just sit down like civilised people and talk about this,' Bea said in a voice you'd use to soothe children's tantrums, shooting a curious glance at Noah. She pulled out a chair and sat at the table. Steph sank into a chair opposite, her body shaking. It was scary when men looked like they were going to start fighting because how on earth would you stop them? It could all get out of hand in an instant.

Noah backed away from Andy and leaned against the worktop, arms crossed, leaving Andy alone in the middle of the kitchen looking like someone who'd just been too slow in a game of musical chairs.

He glared at Steph. 'You can't have him staying here. Look at him? Who knows what trouble he'll bring here?'

'It's a temporary arrangement. He's my friend and I'll be honest, having him here makes me feel more secure after the recent trouble,' Steph said, evenly.

'How do you know he's not the one who broke in the other day?' Andy sneered at her. 'Or broke the window. Looks very convenient to me that he's wheedled his way inside. You don't know what his agenda is, do you?'

Noah narrowed his eyes as Andy spoke about him like he wasn't in the room, his hands bunched into fists.

'When did you get so obnoxious?' Steph snapped, her eyes scanning the dishevelled appearance of her husband. 'You don't get to tell me what to do anymore.'

'Like I said, it's not your choice to make,' Andy snarled.

Steph folded her arms across her chest, thinking that it was her husband who looked more like a vagrant. She was determined now that Noah was staying. 'I don't think you can stop me.'

Andy's jaw tightened. 'I'm pretty sure my solicitor will have something to say.'

Anger flared in her chest and Steph pushed her chair back from the table and went over to Noah. She'd never wanted to slap her husband more in her life. 'I think you should both go.'

Bea's jaw dropped. 'Come on, Mum, don't be hasty. Why can't we just talk about this?'

'Because it's my decision. There's nothing to talk about.'

She pointed to the door. 'I'm sorry, love, but could I ask you to take your father back to where he's staying?'

Bea's chin started to wobble, her emotions bubbling perilously close to the surface and Steph relented. None of this was Bea's fault, she'd just been caught in the crossfire. Not a great place to be. 'Oh, Bea, I know you mean well but I don't think your father's in a fit state to have a sensible conversation. He's just going to shout and you know what? That's not going to change anything.'

She glowered at Andy who gave a weird, frustrated growl before he turned and left.

'I'll call you later,' Bea said, eyes flitting between Steph and Andy as he stormed down the hallway.

When the front door closed, she blew out a long breath.

'Bloody hell,' Noah said, looking quite pale. 'That was intense. I thought he was going to hit me.'

She laughed. 'It's all show with him. Honestly, you were never in any danger.'

'You were well scary.' He put his hand up for a high five and she slapped his palm, pleased that for once in her life she'd stood her ground.

She clung on to the worktop, feeling a bit light-headed, eyes gazing out of the kitchen window as she tried to calm down. The events ran through her mind like a movie reel, stopping on Noah's snarling face, that glint in his eye. It reminded her there was a feral side to this young man, a past she knew nothing about. And it did still feel like a big coincidence that he'd been hiding in her shed right after the brick went through the window.

She turned and looked at him. Understood that she didn't really know him at all.

Have I invited trouble into my home?

Noah disappeared to his room, saying he was going to have an early night. Exhausted after all the confrontation, Steph finished tidying up then headed upstairs too. She ran a bath, throwing in one of her favourite bath bombs, a present from Bea, full of essential oils that helped you to relax. *My goodness, do I need that.* She locked the door and slid into the water, relishing the delicious aromas. It did the job and feeling pampered and relaxed, she snuggled into her bed, deciding that she had to trust her instincts where Noah was concerned.

CHAPTER NINETEEN

The next couple of weeks gave Steph the reassurance she needed that her judgement had been right. Noah was a well brought up young man who'd just lost his way. Slowly but surely, she felt they were beginning to trust each other. They settled into an easy routine. Steph started cooking again, and Noah tidied up afterwards without even having to be asked. He also hoovered while she was at work and cleaned the bathroom. The house felt like a proper home again and even Bea was impressed when she came round to take Steph out for an evening meal. It was a spur-of-the-moment thing and Steph felt ridiculously excited about an evening out.

'I think it's because he's been homeless for a while, he really appreciates it,' Steph said as Bea led her to a new upmarket Italian that she'd been dying to try. 'He doesn't take a home for granted and wants to keep it nice.' She laughed. 'He even tidies up after me – puts my things in a little pile on the hall table.'

'Well, I'm glad for you, Mum.' Bea flung her arm round Steph's shoulders and gave her a hug. 'If it's what you want, then that's fine. I'm sure Dad'll calm down eventually.'

'I haven't heard a peep out of him, so I'm hoping he's accepted that I'm not selling.'

'I did try and have a quiet word with him, you know. Reminded him that although half the house is his, the other half is yours.'

Steph smiled at her daughter. 'Thanks, Bea. Maybe that's given him something to think about.'

The aroma of garlic and tomatoes made Steph's stomach gurgle and the maître d' showed them to a window seat, handing them bound menus. 'Order whatever you want, Mum.' Bea leaned over the table towards her, eyes sparkling. 'Mark just rang to say he's on the verge of signing a mega deal, so let's treat this as a celebration, shall we?' She giggled. 'Tell you what, shall we order champagne?'

It was a lovely evening and Steph arrived home feeling more relaxed than she had in weeks. Noah was still up, watching TV, when she got home.

'You look happy,' he said. 'Nice night?'

Steph grinned at him, her speech slightly slurred from the champagne, her body buzzing with an afterglow that made her feel all was well with the world. 'Lovely night, thank you, but I'm going to head up to bed, if you'll turn everything off.'

'No problem,' he said. 'I'll do a last check round, then I think I'll be going to bed too. Honestly, I've never slept so much in my life.'

'Catching up for lost time,' she joked and staggered up the stairs, thinking how much she enjoyed having someone to come home to.

She woke at 2 a.m. to a cacophony of sound. It was so loud, her bed felt like it was vibrating, making her leap up, heart racing as she tried to work out what was going on. It sounded like voices, coming from downstairs. *Intruders?* She stood still, holding her breath while she listened. A blast of music made her gasp with relief. It was the theme tune of a TV programme. *What the heck is Noah doing having it on so loud?*

She threw her robe on over her pyjamas, wincing at the volume of the noise as she dashed downstairs, ready to give him a telling off. But the lounge was empty. She grabbed the remote and turned the TV off, wilting with relief from the absence of sound. 'Noah?' she called, as she stalked into the kitchen, ready for a row. But he wasn't there either.

The sound of footsteps on the stairs made her return to the hallway to see a sleepy-eyed Noah sitting on the top step.

'Something woke me up. Did you call?'

'Did you leave the TV on? Because it was ridiculously loud.'

Noah shook his head. 'I haven't been down. I came up to bed right after you. I've just woken up now.'

She studied his face and was pretty sure he was telling the truth.

'What the hell is going on?' she muttered to herself, looking round the lounge, but there was no clue. The window was intact, the side windows locked. She checked the front door, but that was locked too, the chain in place. She wandered back into the kitchen where a chill blast of air led her through the utility room to the back door. It swung to and fro in the breeze.

She turned, startled to find Noah right behind her. 'Did you go outside and forget to close the door? I thought you said you were going to check everything?'

A look flitted across his face, gone before she could decipher its meaning. *Guilt? Fear? Annoyance at being questioned?* She really didn't know but her instincts told her there was something he wasn't telling her. She shivered and closed the door, making sure it was properly locked. It was obvious Noah had forgotten to secure the back door and wasn't owning up to it. Mystery solved.

But who came in and turned on the TV?

More to the point, why would somebody do that? *To scare me?*

'I think you really need to talk to the police,' Noah said, making her jump. 'I remember locking this door. Honest to God, I know it was locked.'

A weight dropped to the pit of her stomach. 'So how did someone get in and turn the TV on?'

He shrugged. 'They must have a key.'

The only person with a back door key was Andy. Was this him getting his own back for Steph taking in a lodger?

She clenched her jaw. *This has got to stop.* In the morning she would call the police again and tell them everything. She had to convince them there was a connected series of events going on which could be traced back to her husband. Then they could go and talk to him, make sure he stopped this nonsense.

But what if it isn't him? asked the voice in her head, curdling the contents of her stomach.

She knew her husband, knew that this really wasn't his style. Was it just convenient to pin it on him, when it was the work of someone else?

Her mind lined up everyone she needed to consider, like an identity parade in a police investigation. Phil was there. And for a fleeting moment, Noah's face appeared. But the biggest surprise was Cara. Steph considered that for a moment. She liked her acts of revenge and Steph had let her down. *Could this be her doing?*

CHAPTER TWENTY

After a restless night, she arrived at work feeling like she was sleepwalking rather than being fully present.

'You look rough,' Cara said, when she walked into the staff kitchen. 'Heavy night?'

'Something like that.' Steph felt uncomfortable in Cara's presence. She watched her carefully as she made her a coffee and brought it over to the table. Was she acting like someone with a guilty conscience?

Things had been awkward between them since she'd refused to take her and Dev in as lodgers, Cara taking every opportunity to make it known how difficult things were at home. They were both living at Cara's house now, an arrangement that was far from perfect, especially now Dev had lost his job. But Steph kept having to tell herself that Cara's personal situation was not her responsibility. Still, she felt pangs of guilt whenever Cara's neighbours started misbehaving.

She decided to hide her suspicions, tell her tale, and see how Cara reacted. 'You won't believe what's happened now.'

Cara sat opposite, tutting and nodding as Steph ran through the events of the night before.

'Wow,' she said, when Steph had finished. 'It's got to be Andy, hasn't it? Who else would have a key?'

'Well, I've been thinking about that. Do you remember I lost my keys a few weeks ago? We had to search everywhere for them, didn't we? And then they turned up on my desk.'

'Oh yeah. That was weird, wasn't it?' Cara's eyes narrowed, as if she were trying to remember what had happened. 'You thought you might have left them in the dining room. Put them down while you were talking to one of the service users, I seem to remember.'

'That's what I thought I'd done. That's how I rationalised it when they turned up again. I thought someone had realised I'd lost them and brought them into my office. But what if that's not what happened? What if someone took them deliberately to get a key cut?'

She studied Cara's face. *She could have done that.*

Cara's eyes widened. 'Bloody hell, that's a horrible thought. I hope you've got a locksmith lined up to come and change the locks.'

Steph nodded. 'I have. Noah said he'd wait in, then he's bringing the new keys down later for me.'

Cara took a sip of her coffee. 'It still seems like a weird coincidence that the person you had lined up as a lodger dropped out just when Noah needed somewhere to stay.' Steph avoided eye contact, a blush colouring her cheeks. She was sure Cara must have guessed that she'd made up the original lodger because she didn't want her and Dev as lodgers, but she'd never admitted it. 'I still can't believe you invited him into your home.' She looked quite stern now, her voice snippy, and Steph knew what was coming. 'That's usually a real no-no in this line of work. Obviously, we're sympathetic to the plight of homeless people, but that doesn't mean you need to open up your house to strangers. We're not like an animal shelter, and these are people we are dealing with, not pets. They have complex problems and what you see is usually not what you get.'

Steph had heard all this before. Several times. In fact, Cara took every opportunity to lecture her on how she'd broken a golden rule. Bill had been more relaxed about it, suggesting that it probably wasn't a good idea, but that he'd experienced similar situations himself, and as it was her house, she was free to make her own choices. She remembered her introductory training. The warnings. But she'd studied Noah these last two weeks, looked for signs of errant behaviour, but he'd really been the prefect housemate. So much so that she'd agreed to make the arrangement permanent.

She looked Cara in the eye, saw a glint of something she didn't like. There was definitely bitterness where there used to be friendship. She sipped her coffee, overwhelmed by a need to justify her actions. 'He reminds me so much of Max, that's the thing, I suppose. I can't seem to disconnect from feeling if Max was in the same situation as Noah, I'd want someone to take him in and look after him. Give him a break, you know? And he'd been beaten up, poor lad.' She shrugged. 'My conscience wouldn't let me turn him away.'

Cara rolled her eyes. 'Beaten up? You didn't mention that before. Can't you see that spells trouble? Are you sure you want that coming to your door?'

'I think he was just unlucky and got picked on by some random stranger.'

Cara tutted, unconvinced.

'Anyway, after the brick through the window incident, I didn't want to be in the house on my own.'

'Yeah, like having him in the house prevented an intruder getting in again!' Cara was sounding increasingly frustrated. 'What are the police doing about it?'

'They're sending someone round.'

Another eye-roll from Cara. 'That's not good enough, is it?'

She tapped at the table with a finger. 'Have you told them about last night?'

'I have.' Steph stared into her mug, unable to meet Cara's fierce glare. To be honest, she wasn't sure what the police could do. She looked at her watch, keen to end the conversation. Giving Cara a quick smile, she finished her coffee and stood up. 'Sorry, I better get started, lots to do today.'

Cara caught her arm as she was on her way out of the room. 'I just had a thought about the keys. You don't keep your office locked, do you?' Steph shook her head. 'Which means anyone could have walked in off the street and taken them.'

Steph swallowed that unpalatable thought and left the room, speed walking to her office and closing the door behind her. She sat at her desk, head in her hands. Cara was right. Anyone could have walked in and taken her keys. *Would Cara point that out if it was she who'd taken them?* Probably not.

Security of her personal belongings was a bit of a weak point for her, coming from a bank environment, where everyone just left their bags by their desks. Working in a homeless shelter was completely different, with the doors always open to anyone who wanted to wander in during the day. She had to wise up. And fast.

She opened the bottom drawer of the filing cabinet, stuffed her bag in and locked it. There. That would be her safe place from now on. The start of a new regime.

Her phone rang. Bea. She let it ring while she debated whether to answer, knowing what her daughter's reaction would be to the events of the night before, with the back door left open and TV set to blaring. She didn't feel up to another lecture, so she let it ring, thinking she'd call her back later when she'd had a chance to talk to the police again.

Bea's mothering instinct towards Steph could be a little overwhelming at times and she often thought what Bea needed was a child of her own, then all her attention wouldn't be focused on Steph when Mark was away. She let her mind wander over what that would be like – to be a grandma – knowing that she'd enjoy it immensely. Then she remembered Bea being upset at the spa because she wanted to start a family but Mark was away so much she obviously thought it might never happen.

It struck her then that there was a lot she didn't know about her daughter and her marriage. A pang of guilt made her ring back.

'Mum, how are you after last night?' Bea giggled. 'That pasta was lovely, but I have one hell of a hangover. Honestly, I'm all over the place today.'

'I've got a bit of a headache, but other than that I'm not too bad. It was a lovely evening, though. Thanks again for treating me.'

'We'll have to do it again, won't we? There's a new Indian opened in Harrogate. Gets rave reviews, perhaps you could come over the for the weekend and we could try it out?'

'You're spoiling me, Bea. Honestly, you don't have to keep taking me out.'

'But you deserve it, Mum. I know it's been a hard time for you on your own.'

Steph smiled. Bea was so generous with both her time and money, she couldn't believe her luck sometimes. 'Anyway, I feel more relaxed now that Noah's staying. And I've rediscovered cooking, so my diet is much better than it was. In fact, why don't you come to us for a meal soon? I'd like to cook you something special and it'll be nice for you to get to know Noah. He's like part of the family now.'

Bea was quiet for a moment.

'I suppose having Noah there is a way of you getting over Max at last. I hope you cleared his room out properly before you let your lodger in there.'

'Oh, I've put him in the loft. I didn't have time to—'

'What? You did what?' Bea snapped, clearly horrified.

Steph cringed, could feel her daughter's anger sparking down the phone.

'That's my room. How could you put him in there?' Her voice was plaintive now, upset rather than annoyed. 'Why not in the spare room?'

'We don't have a spare room,' Steph said, evenly. 'The attic is bigger and gives us more separate spaces. I didn't think it would be a problem.'

'I don't want some random nomad in my bed, Mum.' Bea sounded distressed. 'That's... horrible.'

She was crying now, and Steph felt her heart clench. *Oh dear*, she hadn't expected such an extreme reaction and had no idea how to make things right.

'You sound a bit... I don't know. Is everything okay with you? Is Mark all right?'

Bea's tears hiccupped to a halt. 'Nothing's okay. He's going to be away for another fortnight at least, he says.' Her voice was thick and stuttering. 'Honestly, he's never home these days. I don't know what he expects me to do, just hanging around waiting for him to come back.'

Steph gave a silent sigh of relief. This wasn't about her or Bea's room at all, it was more to do with Bea's husband.

'I'm sorry you're having a tough time, love. Why don't we organise a meet-up this weekend? A drive out to the Dales maybe?' Bea hadn't responded to Steph's invitation to dinner at home with Noah, so it was probably better to go somewhere neutral for the time being.

Bea's tears snuffled to a stop. 'I'd like that, Mum,' she said. 'We used to do that quite a lot, didn't we? As a family.' A quiet sniff. 'I miss those trips out.'

Steph felt a flush of heat run through her. She hadn't been thinking about Bea's situation at all. How she missed her husband and needed a bit of attention to help her through a bit of a rough patch. And now she'd given her room to a stranger. She could see why Bea might be upset.

'We can go shopping after, pick out some new stuff for your bedroom as well, so you can have it just how you want it again.'

'Can we? I thought you were short of money?'

Steph closed her eyes. It was true; what on earth was she doing making these promises? She was going back to people-pleaser mode – her default setting – especially when anyone was upset.

'I'm just trying to sort that out, love. I'm sure I'll be okay. Anyway, let's go out at the weekend, shall we?'

'I'll treat you, Mum. But that would be lovely.'

Steph saw the shadow of someone waiting outside her door. She'd done very little work today and it was time to do what she was actually being paid for. 'I'm sorry, love. But someone's waiting to see me. I'd better go.'

'I'll pick you up Saturday morning,' Bea said, sounding much more cheerful as she rang off.

Steph went to open the door, shocked to see Phil standing there.

He whipped out a plate from behind his back, a misshapen scone sitting in the centre, filled with jam and cream. 'I thought you might like this,' he said with a shy smile. 'I had it left over. It's a bit of a reject, but I didn't think you'd mind.'

He held it towards her, and she took it from him, stepping back to put it on her desk and create a little distance between them.

He stepped closer. 'I heard there'd been a bit of trouble over at your house.'

Steph nodded, wondering why Cara would mention it to him. Nobody else knew about her troubles. 'That's right. Nothing much, just a bit of mischief.'

'I can keep an eye out if you like.' His caterpillar eyebrows moved up his forehead. 'I only live up the road.'

This was news to Steph. She frowned, confused. 'I thought you lived over in Armley? That's not up the road.'

His smile broadened. 'I just moved over your way. About five or six weeks ago now. It's handier for work, you see.'

Quite a coincidence, Steph thought. That was when the trouble had started. *Could it be connected?* He shuffled another step closer, and Steph could smell the faint whiff of cigarettes.

She turned and moved round the desk, putting it between them, then looked at her watch. 'Oh dear, I'm so sorry, Phil, I've got to get some work finished and I'm way behind. Thank you so much for the scone. I'll catch you later if that's okay. I just need a bit of quiet to get this thing done.'

She forced a smile, her gaze flicking to the open door as if that alone would move this creepy man out of her office.

Her skin crawled. *Could it be him causing more trouble?*

CHAPTER TWENTY-ONE

Noah arrived at lunchtime with her new set of keys and an invoice for an amount that made her gulp. Amazing how expensive it was to have a couple of locks changed, but then she had asked for top spec, and peace of mind was worth it, wasn't it?

'Thanks for supervising him,' she said tucking a set of keys into her pocket.

Noah shrugged. 'I left him to it, to be honest. I had to go out for a bit, but he just got on with everything. Looks like he's done a tidy job. I'm sure you'll feel better now.'

Steph's breath caught in her throat, not sure if she'd heard him right. 'What? You left him on his own?' Surely he wouldn't do that after everything that had happened.

Noah blushed, scuffed the carpet with the toe of his shoe. 'It wasn't for long. Half an hour maybe. Anyway, his job is security so I thought it would be fine.'

Steph sighed and closed her eyes, pinching the bridge of her nose, while she tried to contain her frustration. 'I can't... I don't...' It was hard to know what to say without causing offence or an argument. It was done now, wasn't it? She took a deep breath, told herself it didn't matter. 'It's always better to be there if anyone's doing work at the house.' She smiled as he looked up. 'Just good practice.'

'Okay.' His jaw tightened, his voice no more than a mumble. 'Point taken.'

Steph held up the keys. 'Thanks for bringing these, though.'

Noah was right. She did feel better now the locks had been changed. Whoever had let themselves in last night wouldn't be doing that again, so at least that was something she didn't have to worry about now.

Cara's words of warning seemed fresh, though, and she wondered if she really *could* trust Noah. He was giving her a funny look and she realised that her internal debate had probably played out on her face. Something that Andy had always teased her about, telling her she'd be a rubbish poker player. A blush crept up her neck, but before she could say anything, he was halfway out of the door.

'I'll see you later,' he called and then he was gone, leaving her staring at the space where he'd been, half of her desperate for his company, the other half thinking that life would be easier if he moved out, then there'd be no argument with her family or her work colleagues.

At least security was all up to scratch again in her home, she thought, feeling the keys in her pocket. The last thing to sort out was the water damage in Bea's bedroom. The insurance company's contractor was coming in the morning to take up the old carpet and fit the new one, so she'd have to make sure she was home for that.

Feeling satisfied that she was getting on top of things, she was about to go and make a cup of tea when a new email pinged into her inbox. It was from Andy. Recently, his messages had never heralded good news and she hesitated before opening it.

I do not agree to anyone staying in our house. I am talking to my solicitor about this and unless you want to defend costly legal action, you have to get rid of him. I'll be round later to check he has left.

Steph bit her lip. Bossy, arrogant man. When had he started to tell her what she could and couldn't do? He was the one who'd left her to run a house on her own with all the bills to pay, not to mention solicitor's fees now there were divorce proceedings to deal with. Could he actually do anything? She really wasn't sure, but her boss, Bill, would know. He seemed up to date on housing law, having been a solicitor in the past, before he succumbed to mental health problems and his life fell apart.

He'd alluded to it in passing and she hadn't liked to pry, but Cara had no such compunction and she'd filled her in one lunchtime.

'Looks like our boss is a bit of a colourful character,' she'd said with a wink.

'What do you mean?' Steph was all ears and would admit she was intrigued. She'd had a few conversations with him where he'd mentioned his dark days and the events leading up to his homelessness, but his comments were cryptic at times and she couldn't be sure if she'd understood his meaning.

'He was on the streets for five years.'

She took her sandwich out of its wrapper. 'Oh yes, I know that.'

'He's an alcoholic.'

'I know that too. But he's not drinking anymore.'

'Says you.' Cara leaned across the table. 'I've smelled booze on him on more than one occasion.'

Steph's eyes widened. She hadn't noticed herself, but then Cara worked very closely with him as his assistant, whereas since Andy's allegations, she'd been keeping her distance, so she might not have detected it. She frowned, putting her sandwich back down again. 'Really? You think he's fallen off the wagon?'

'I asked him.'

Steph's hand flew to her mouth. 'You didn't! Oh my God, that's so cheeky. You're going to get yourself fired if you're not careful.'

'He said he'd had a bit of a relapse, but he'd sorted it out now. Some woman trouble, apparently.'

Steph blushed. *Was I the woman trouble?* He had been very attentive when she'd first started, always checking that she was okay, never too busy to explain things to her and talk through the projects she was working on. She picked up her sandwich again, took a big bite, and chewed while her embarrassment subsided.

Cara took a sip of her coffee, cradling the mug in her hands.

'But the most interesting thing is why he lost his job as a solicitor.'

'I thought he just left. His marriage broke up, he went into a depression, and everything fell apart for him.'

Cara gave her a knowing look. 'That's the edited version. I did a bit of research, and it turns out he was accused of fraud. They said he was falsifying documents on his clients' behalf.'

Steph stopped eating mid-chew, struggling to swallow her mouthful of food before she could speak. 'No! I don't believe you.'

Cara sat back in her chair, her voice full of confidence. 'I'll send you the links. Anyway, it came to nothing, he was exonerated. But by that time, his wife had left him, he'd lost his job and whisky was his best friend.'

Steph blew out a long breath. 'Just shows how easily things can all fall apart. Poor Bill. I really don't think we should be gossiping about this though. It doesn't feel right.'

Cara leaned forwards, lowering her voice. 'I was a bit

shocked, to be honest. Just wanted to run it past you to see if it was common knowledge.'

'Well, it's not. Everyone knows about the drink, depression and being homeless. They know his marriage broke down. But the rest of it, well, I think you should keep that to yourself.'

'Don't worry, I will. But since we're both dealing with financial issues, and regulations – not to mention vulnerable people – I thought we should just keep an eye.' She met Steph's gaze. 'I'm a great believer in there's no smoke without fire. So it's up to us to make sure this place is running by the rules otherwise we could all be out of work. Or worse if the police get involved.'

Steph wrapped her sandwich back up and stood, throwing it in the bin, wanting to put an end to the conversation. It had stuck in her mind, though, that there was a lot of potential for fraud with the client group they looked after, even though she was convinced that Bill was genuine.

Now, she popped her head round his office door, but he wasn't there. Cara was sitting at her desk, which was squeezed into the corner of the room, frowning as she typed.

'Boss not here?' Steph asked.

'He's got a lunch meeting in town, so who knows when he'll be back.'

Steph tutted.

Cara stopped what she was doing. 'Have you got a problem? Anything I can do?'

Steph sat on the edge of Bill's desk and explained Andy's message. 'I just wanted to ask Bill's advice. I need to know what I can do to stop Andy selling the house from under me.'

'Oh, I think there's plenty.' Cara swung round in her chair to face her. 'And surely you'd have to agree the sale given that half the house is yours?' She held up a finger. 'Plus... you're living there and possession is nine-tenths of the law, as they say.' She cocked her head to one side, her brow creased into a frown. 'That husband of yours. What's got into him?'

Steph leaned against the wall, weary with the constant conflict. 'God knows. He never used to be like this.'

Cara opened her mouth to speak then closed it again, silent for a moment. Her voice was gentle when she finally spoke. 'Look, I don't want to pry and I'm sure you've already thought about this, but do you think there's somebody else in the background?'

Steph tensed. 'What do you mean?'

'Like a girlfriend?'

She blinked. Of course she'd thought about it. Their break-up had been all about his misperceptions about *her* behaviour, but as Bea had suggested, he could be putting the blame on her so he could leave and start up with somebody else. After that conversation, she'd watched for signs – new clothes, a bounce in his step, a secret smile on his face, but there'd been none of that and she'd discounted it as a possibility.

She rubbed her hands over her face as if washing the thought away.

Perhaps if she went to talk to him – stopped being so stubborn with him – then they could have a proper conversation about everything. That hadn't really happened yet, both of them so keen to be in the right that they couldn't work through their problems in anything resembling a calm manner.

'Earth to Steph, are you receiving me?' Cara looked concerned. 'You went all blank on me then. Are you okay?'

She ran a hand through her hair. 'Oh, I'm just tired after the disturbance last night. Worrying about things.'

'So... do you think he's got somebody else?'

Steph felt her eyes sting. She swallowed and looked at the floor. 'I don't think so.'

'But you don't know for definite?'

She pushed herself off the wall, stood up straight, fired up now. 'You know what? I have his address and I'm going to go round there after work and ask him that very question. Along

with a whole list of other questions.' Her voice rang with determination. 'Honestly, it's ridiculous that we can't talk without an
instant argument. I'm going to really try this time not to get
annoyed with him. Maybe it'll be easier if we're on neutral
ground.'

'Atta girl,' Cara said, giving her the thumbs-up. 'And can I
suggest if that doesn't work, you really should ring that marriage
guidance counsellor I told you about. Obviously it didn't save
my marriage, but it helped to identify what the problems were,
and we both came to accept that our relationship didn't have a
future.' She shrugged. 'After that, we stopped blaming each
other and got things settled pretty amicably.'

Straight after work, Steph hurried up the road towards Brewery
Wharf, next to the river. It had been completely redeveloped
from its industrial days and was now the location of upmarket
apartments with restaurants underneath. It was a very convenient location in the heart of the city, close to the station, and
she could see the appeal of living here if you were young and
wanted a social life. But for Andy? She hadn't thought it would
suit him at all. She considered his recent sullen demeanour, his
drunken state in the early evening. That wasn't like her
husband either. It was clear he wasn't happy, of that she was
certain.

The lobby was tastefully decorated. Very grown-up and
sophisticated. There was a board next to the lifts giving details
of apartments for sale and to rent and she couldn't help
checking them out, doing a double take when she saw the
prices. Then her eye settled on the details for apartment 406.
That's where she was headed. *Interesting.* Maybe Andy wasn't
feeling secure in his new digs. *Is this the reason for all the hurry?*

She stepped into the lift and sent it up to the fourth floor,
the view from the window at the end of the hallway making her

stop and look for a moment, the river taking centre stage as it snaked between the wharf-side buildings. She wandered down the hallway, looking for number 406, a dark brown door, like all the others. She rang the bell and stood back, waiting.

The door swung open to reveal a young woman with a bouncy blonde ponytail, dressed in exercise gear, a sheen of sweat on her face.

'Sorry, I was on the bike. Spin class on Zoom.'

'Oh,' Steph took a step back, 'I'm so sorry, I must have got the wrong apartment.'

The girl smiled at her. 'Happens all the time. Who are you looking for?'

'Andy Baker, do you know him?'

The woman laughed. 'I do indeed. You've got the right place, though. He lives here.' Then her smile dropped, as her hands flew to her mouth. 'Oh God, you're the wife, aren't you?'

The door slammed shut.

Steph took another step back, leaning against the wall as her thoughts slotted together, revealing a truth which genuinely shocked her. Charlie – Andy's workmate, and now the person he shared a very small apartment with – was a woman.

She hurried back down the corridor, taking the stairs instead of waiting for the lift, not wanting anyone to see her angry tears.

Evidently, Cara's hunch had been right, while she'd been in denial. He did have someone else.

She felt a bit stupid that she'd dismissed the idea so readily and her jaw clenched tight as she marched out of the apartment building and headed up the main road towards the bus stop. *Right, no need for niceties now. No need to consider his feelings.* Her marriage was dead, and she was decided. She was staying in the house whether he liked it or not and she would invite who the bloody hell she liked to come and live with her.

Despite any concerns she may have had, Noah was staying.

CHAPTER TWENTY-TWO

The parcel lying on the mat caught Steph's eye as soon as she opened the door. It was the size of a book, wrapped in brown paper. Noah's name was in thick black marker pen on the front. It hadn't been posted, she noticed, but hand-delivered. Curious. It wasn't in her nature to be nosy, but she couldn't help wondering who might be delivering parcels to him. She put it on the hall table ready to pass it on to him later.

That's when she noticed a skateboard propped against the wall. *It must be Noah's.* Strange that she hadn't seen it before, but it seemed a popular mode of transport amongst the students, she'd noticed.

She was just starting to chop up some carrots to go with the roast chicken she had in the oven when she heard the door bang shut and she hurried into the hallway.

'Hi, Noah, I thought I heard you come in. There's a—' Her eyes flicked to the empty hall table. 'Oh, you've seen it.'

Noah was pushing the parcel into his backpack, a blush creeping into his cheeks. He seemed a little flustered, glancing up the stairs. 'Yeah, I've got it, thanks. Just a book I left at someone's house. When I was sofa surfing. I was chatting to them last night and they said they'd drop it off.'

He stood, one hand on the bannister, a foot on the bottom step, then turned and gave her a smile. 'Sorry, that's rude if I just go rushing upstairs, isn't it?' He pulled an apologetic face. 'I just have this running-away-from-people thing going on at the moment.' He shrugged. 'I suppose it's just become second nature.'

Steph's expression softened and she put a hand on his shoulder. 'Well, that's very understandable given what you've been through.' She let her hand drop. 'Come and have a cup of tea. I've got a chicken in the oven for tea if you fancy some. Roast potatoes as well. There's plenty for both of us and there will be leftovers for tomorrow. I'll leave it in the fridge, and you can just help yourself.'

Noah put his bag down and followed her into the kitchen.

'I wanted to have a chat with you,' Steph said as she poured boiling water into a teapot and picked two mugs out of the cupboard.

'I need to have a chat with you as well,' Noah said before she could continue. 'I went to the Jobcentre, as you suggested, and the housing department. I need to show them my tenancy agreement before I can sign up for benefits.' He caught her eye. 'I hope you don't mind, but I said I did have one, because you did say about making everything permanent, didn't you? So we did all the paperwork and I just have to drop off a copy, then I'm all signed up.' He beamed at her. 'At last I'll have a little bit of money. And you'll get a rental.'

Steph poured the tea into the mugs. 'Well, it just so happens that was exactly what I wanted to talk to you about.' She handed him his drink. 'Seems great minds think alike. It doesn't matter what my husband says, as far as I'm concerned, this arrangement seems to be working fine.' She thought back to the fear she'd felt when she'd had an intruder and then the brick through the window. The strange incident with the TV being turned up high and the back door left wide open. Whatever anyone else might think, she felt safer with Noah here than she did on her own and hopefully all that nonsense was behind them now she'd had the locks changed.

Noah let out a relieved breath.

'You've got to promise me that you'll be extra careful about locking up, though. I can't cope with any more of that weirdness.'

'I honestly *did* lock up.' His face said he was telling the truth and she thought again about the mystery intruder and who it might have been. 'Cross my heart, I really did.'

'Well, at least with the locks changed we can't have strangers wandering into the house in the middle of the night. I didn't sleep a wink. Honestly, I was convinced that every little creak was somebody creeping up the stairs.'

'I can sleep downstairs if that would make you feel safer.' He clearly meant it. 'I can sleep anywhere. The sofa would be fine.'

She smiled at him, touched by his thoughtfulness. 'Oh, Noah, that's a lovely suggestion, but we should be okay now. Mind you, I do think it might be an idea to see about CCTV outside. Or one of those doorbells that films people.' She tucked her hair behind her ears. 'The trouble is, I have no idea about any of that stuff. But Bea's husband is a bit of a techno geek, so I might ask him when he's back from abroad.'

They sipped their tea in silence for a moment.

'I have to say your daughter looks like a film star.'

Steph laughed, and noticed his cheeks redden. 'I know. I can't quite believe I made her, to be honest. But her husband is a football agent. Loads of money. And everything is shared in their marriage.' She smiled to herself. 'I'm so proud of her.'

Noah sighed. 'I wish my mum was proud of me like that.'

Steph reached across the table and squeezed his arm. 'I bet

she is proud. But how can she tell you when you don't speak to her? She must be worried sick if she hasn't heard from you.'

His eyes dipped to the table, his hands wrapping round his mug of tea as if he needed its warmth. 'I can't tell her all that money has been wasted. Tens of thousands of pounds. All her hard work for nothing.' She watched his Adam's apple bob up and down, saw a tremor in his chin and knew he was fighting back tears.

'But no experience is a waste,' she said, gently. 'You learn something from everything that happens to you, even if it does feel like failure at the time.'

'"Thinking is difficult, that's why most people judge."' Noah looked up. 'That's one of the best quotes I learned from my degree.'

Steph nodded. 'It's a good one.'

'But that's what my mum and her partner will do. They'll judge me, find me a failure, without thinking about why it happened.'

'Well, they'll never understand if you don't speak to them, will they? I can help you make contact if you like? Maybe I could ring them first, just to let them know you're okay.'

'No!' Noah's eyes sparked with panic.

Steph sat back in her seat, pushed away by the force of his words. Clearly there was more to this that she didn't understand. She held up her hands. 'It's okay. I just want to help. But I won't do anything you're not comfortable with.'

She stood and finished preparing the vegetables, checked the chicken, turned the roast potatoes, while Noah sat and drank his tea in silence.

The next morning, Noah came down to the kitchen and she did a double take, imagining for a moment it was her son standing in front of her. It was the clothes, she realised. They kept catching her out when she was least expecting it, making her gasp every time, a hand clutched to her chest as her heart skipped. She heaved in a breath to steady herself, told herself to stop being so stupid. She forced a smile.

'Good morning. That hoodie and those jeans – they're a great fit.'

He nodded, clearly distracted, his face crumpled with worry lines. 'I've got to go back to the benefits office with the tenancy agreement, to prove I've got a permanent address. They said I had to do it today. Then I can get going with applying for jobs.' His eyes met hers. 'I don't want to be a pain, but do you think you could sort one out for me, please?'

The ring of the doorbell made her remember the carpet contractors. They were due any time.

'I'm so sorry, I'll have to deal with the carpet guy now. Can I do it later? I'll be in work this afternoon, once they've gone, then I can print you one off. We've got pro formas on file, so it won't take me long and I can give it to you tonight but... well, there's probably a few house rules we need to go through first.'

Noah frowned at her, a hard edge to his voice. 'It's got to be today. That's what they said. Otherwise there will be a delay with my benefits and it'll be longer before I get any money.'

Steph felt a pang of guilt and reached into her bag, pulling out her purse. She held out a twenty-pound note. 'Here you are. Will this do for today?'

Why are you giving him money? She had no answer, flustered by the question. The doorbell rang again. Noah snatched the note from her hand, grabbed his skateboard and made a swift exit, pushing past the surprised man standing on the doorstep, leaving nothing behind but the faint whiff of smoke.

'Someone's in a hurry,' he said, watching Noah's back as he sped down the road.

'Youngsters,' Steph said, opening the door for the contractor to come in, wondering what had got into Noah. He was usually so polite, but he'd turned a little sharp there; the way he'd dashed off was not like him at all. 'I'm afraid the carpet's in the attic.' She waved a hand at the stairs. 'Will you manage on your own?'

'I'm not on my own. My workmate's just finishing his breakfast.' He rolled his eyes. 'Anyway, he'll only be a minute. Okay if I go and get started?'

Steph showed him up to the attic, leaving the door open for his workmate while she went to tidy up the kitchen. What a strange start to the day. Unnerving. Because it reminded her that Noah had another side to him. One that she'd glimpsed before when he'd been cornered by Andy, and she wasn't sure she liked it.

CHAPTER TWENTY-THREE

Steph had put aside the morning for cleaning while the carpet fitters were working upstairs. The kitchen needed a proper wipe down and she was going to go through the cupboards in the utility room and start clearing out Andy's stuff.

Over the sound of the radio, she could hear the men's footsteps, heavy on the stairs. Up and down, up and down. *How fit must they be, doing a job like that!* It went quiet for a bit, methodical banging from the loft, then the sound of feet running up and down again. She envied them their energy because hers was waning fast after scrubbing floors and walls. She was finished now, though, so unlocked the back door to empty the dirty water in the drain outside. Then she sat on the doorstep to catch her breath.

She thought about the door being left open and the TV on full blast. Could that have been Noah and he just wasn't owning up to it? Had she misjudged him? And then there was the parcel arriving yesterday; he seemed a bit furtive about that. It felt like a book, but lighter and had a weird smell to it. Sort of sweet and musty. *Like weed?* She'd smelled it on many of the people at the homeless shelter, but not on Noah. She was sure of that but she had a nasty feeling that's exactly what was in the parcel. And she was sure he'd said he'd been sleeping in a shed, not sofa surfing at a friend's house. *Which is the truth?* On top of that, he'd acted a bit weird this morning, almost insisting that she give him a tenancy agreement. That look in his eye which she couldn't quite place. Annoyance? Determination? Or had it been something else?

She made herself a cup of tea and sat at the table, pondering everything that had happened. It was weird, wasn't it, how he'd been hiding in her shed on the very night the brick had been put through the window. *Was that really a coincidence?* And this morning, the smell of him as she'd stood close, reminded her of the smoky smell in the house when the intruder had been in. Had he been smoking?

Oh my God, was Andy right? Was Noah her intruder and now he'd wangled his way into her home?

She shivered, suddenly chilly.

He'd been beaten up, she reminded herself. He was scared, hadn't expected to be found. Then he'd helped her, and he'd been good company, or she wouldn't have invited him to stay, would she? But then there was the Max connection, that overwhelming feeling that if Max had been in the same situation as Noah, she would have wanted someone to be kind and compassionate. *Have I made a terrible mistake?*

The ringing of her phone made her jump. It was Bea doing her daily check on her.

'Hello, love,' she said, trying to inject a smile into her voice.

'Mum, how are you today? I'm coming to Leeds later this morning and thought we could meet up for lunch. I'll be close to your office, so we might as well.'

'I'm not at work. The carpet is being fitted in your old room, so I had to stay home this morning. I said I'd go in after lunch, but you can come here if you like, and I'll rustle something up.'

'I'll bring something. You deserve a treat after everything that's happened. Be there in an hour.'

Then she was gone before Steph could say anything. Lunch with Bea might be a nice distraction, she thought as she started clearing out one of the cupboards in the utility room.

The sound of footsteps coming down the stairs made her turn, and the older man came into the kitchen. 'All done if you want to come and have a look.'

She followed him upstairs into the loft bedroom, pleased with the job they'd done. The men left and she stayed in the loft, thinking she should try and put everything back in its right place, because Bea was bound to want to come and have a look. She opened the skylight to let some fresh air in, the room having a chemical smell of new carpet. She leaned on the window frame, looking out over the park while her mind wandered.

At least she could show Bea now and try and calm her down about her lodger. Well, he wasn't officially a lodger yet, was he? She checked her thinking, unsure now whether she wanted Noah to stay. But she didn't want to be on her own either. And would it be fair to throw him out when he had nowhere else to go? Look what a state he'd been in when he first arrived. He was like a different lad now, no longer the beaten-up vulnerable youth she had first met. It was a tricky one.

Just talk to him. Tell him what you're thinking and see what he has to say for himself. If you don't like it, you can tell him to go.

Her thoughts flicked through the list of things that had happened, trying to find a culprit that wasn't Noah. There was still Andy, of course. And his lover, Charlie. Hmm. Her flat was for sale so did that mean they were going to pool their money and buy something better together? Was that the root of Andy's urgency? The hairs stood up on the back of her neck. It made so much sense when she thought about it. Charlie had to be added to the list. She definitely hadn't been happy to see Steph on her doorstep, that was for sure.

It was still a puzzle what the person was trying to achieve, though. They'd made her uncomfortable in her own home. Scared even, and that's why she'd asked Noah to stay. So it could be Noah after all. Because he was the one who stood to gain the most, wasn't he?

She shook her head, befuddled with the circle her thoughts were taking her round. She'd have a nice lunch with Bea, give her brain a rest and it might sort out the answer on its own.

Her gaze wandered over the park, to groups of students sitting on the grass. Mothers with toddlers and babies sitting on rugs. Children playing with balls, wrestling, screaming as they chased each other. Dog walkers. A skateboarder, travelling at quite a speed, weaving around the people in his path.

Somewhere out there somebody was watching her. *Are they watching me now?* Her breath caught in her throat and she ducked her head back inside, glad that Bea would be here soon to distract her from this overwhelming feeling of dread. Wondering what was going to happen next, always on edge when she came home, not knowing what damage she might find. It was a terrible feeling, making her stomach churn, her legs shaky.

She focused her energy on tidying up the bedroom as best she could without wanting Noah to think she'd been meddling with his things. But the carpet fitters had piled everything on the bed, and she didn't want Bea seeing it in this state or she really would go mad. It needed to look just like it always had, all traces of Noah hidden away for now. Then she could avoid an inevitable telling-off for letting him stay in the first place.

She knew it had been an impulsive decision on her part, taking pity on him. But then, what mother wouldn't have done the same? It's not just me; Bill did the same. She comforted herself with that thought as she made the bed and put Noah's clothes in a pile underneath. As she was folding a shirt, something fell out of his pocket. She bent to pick it up. A lighter and a hand-rolled cigarette.

Lots of homeless people smoked. She supposed it was something to help with their anxiety, but this didn't look like a normal cigarette. Or smell like one either. The tobacco was a greenish grey, that same sweet musty smell she'd detected on the parcel that had been delivered. Her brain fitted the puzzle together and there was only one answer. *He's dealing drugs!*

With a groan, she sank onto the bed. It hadn't even occurred to her that he might be involved in shady business. Although, now she thought about it, the beating should have been a clue. She cursed the way she always thought the best of people, assuming they held her own values without considering how they might be different.

Andy would have a field day if he found out and Bea would blow a gasket. *How on earth could I have been so stupid?* What if the police came round again and found out? Her heart hammered in her chest. This was the last thing she needed.

Her brain started putting the puzzle together, the image of the skateboarder flashing in front of her eyes. The fact that Noah had a skateboard. A terrible thought brought a chill to her body. *Was it Noah who pushed me down the escalator?*

A ring on the doorbell heralded Bea's arrival and she stuffed the lighter and cigarette back in Noah's pocket, rammed his shirt under the bed and hurried downstairs. *I'll have to ask him to leave.* It really was the only answer. How could she trust him now?

CHAPTER TWENTY-FOUR

'Hey, Mum,' Bea said with a wide smile. She held up a bag from her favourite deli in town. 'I got us smoked salmon bagels with cream cheese and watercress salad. And for dessert, we have salted caramel cheesecake.' She winked. 'Naughty but nice.' She studied her mum's face, the smile fading from her lips. 'You look a bit frazzled. Is everything okay?'

Steph held the door open wide and gave Bea a quick hug as she passed. 'Everything's fine. I just had the carpet fitters here and then I had to sort out the bedroom after they'd finished.' She blew out her cheeks. 'Bit of a rush.'

'Oh, let's have a look.' Bea was already halfway up the stairs before Steph could reply and she tramped up after her, legs heavy and tired after her morning cleaning and putting the bedroom back together. 'But first, I'm desperate for the loo,' Bea said, disappearing into the bathroom.

She staggered back out, just as Steph got to the landing. 'Bea, what's wrong?'

Her daughter pointed at the open bathroom door, eyes wide, her mouth opening but no words coming out. She'd gone a deathly pale and looked like she might faint, her hands clutching the bannister as if to stop herself from falling.

Steph frowned. *What on earth has got into her?*

She poked her head round the bathroom door. 'Oh my God!' she gasped, hands covering her mouth as her eyes travelled round the room, the walls splattered with what looked like... 'Is that—' She gulped, her voice a whisper, 'Is that blood?'

It was dripping down the walls, trickling onto the floor, covering the toilet and the basin, pooling in the bottom of the bath. She backed out, just as Bea had done. Her legs threatened to give way and she sank onto the windowsill, her chin trembling as she tried to hold back her tears. Then the smell hit her and she understood.

'It's paint. I can smell it. Gloss paint.' She buried her hands in her hair, her heart beating so fast she was feeling light-headed.

If she could dismiss everything else that had happened as explainable, this act of vandalism was something else. This was definitely somebody trying to scare her, wasn't it?

Bea peered round the door again. 'What a mess!' She came and sat on the windowsill, her arm reaching round Steph's shoulders, giving her a reassuring rub as her body shook. 'I don't understand. You changed the locks, didn't you?'

Steph nodded. 'And I was here all morning.'

'So whoever did this... how did they get in?'

'I don't know. Oh, wait a minute...' She closed her eyes, gave a low groan. 'The carpet fitters had the front door open so they could come in and out with everything.' She rubbed at her forehead as she thought it through. 'I was in the kitchen doing a bit of cleaning. I had the radio on. You know me, singing along. So I wouldn't have...' She gasped, turned to Bea. 'Oh my God, I think I heard them.'

Bea frowned. 'What do you mean you heard them?'

'Well, I could hear the carpet fitters tramping up and down

the stairs, slow and steady because they were carrying stuff. Then I heard someone running up and down.' The more she thought about it the more certain she was. 'That must have been them.'

'Wow, they were taking a big risk, weren't they? You could have easily seen them.' Bea didn't sound convinced. 'Are you sure this wasn't your lodger?'

Steph shook her head. 'No. I came up after he'd gone out. I showed the carpet fitters where the bathroom was if they needed it and it was fine then.' She scrunched up her nose. 'Anyway, it doesn't make sense for it to be Noah. Why would he vandalise a house he was wanting to call home?'

Bea's mouth twitched from side to side. 'Look, Mum, I don't want to be alarmist or anything, but the situation seems to be getting out of hand.' She pulled out her phone. 'I'll ring the police.' She stopped what she was doing, fingers hovering over the screen. 'Come to think of it, do you have a contact name and crime number? That'll speed things up.'

Steph grimaced. 'I suppose I'll have it somewhere. But they haven't been round since I reported the TV incident. I don't suppose they think it's urgent. Not when you compare it to kids being stabbed or domestic violence or armed robberies. You know, serious crimes. This is probably just some petty vendetta.'

Bea had an impatient edge to her voice. 'It might be petty, but it's pretty horrible, isn't it? Someone's determined to make your life a misery and we can't let it carry on.' She squeezed Steph's shoulder. 'Come on, Mum. There's no point being in denial. We've got to do something if we want this to stop.'

Steph puffed out her cheeks. 'I'm not sure there's much the police can do. Or will do, to be honest. You know how short of staff they are. Wasn't the Chief Constable on the news just the other day complaining about lack of manpower?'

Bea pursed her lips as she scrolled through her phone. 'Let's see if I can get something to happen.' She dialled and spoke to the call handler, quietly but firmly pointing out all the incidents that had been reported and the lack of any recent follow-up. She was so clear and concise, very definite about what she wanted to happen and the consequences of nothing being done. Steph was proud of her daughter and alarmed by what she was saying in equal measure. Was she really in danger?

Bea disconnected and smiled at her mum. 'There you go. Sorted. Someone is on their way. They should be here in the next hour anyway.'

Steph checked her watch and jumped to her feet, panicking. 'I've got to go to work. I said I'd be in after lunch and it's one o'clock already. I've got so much to do.'

Bea put a hand on her shoulder, pulled her to a halt. 'No, Mum. You do not have to go to work.' That authoritarian voice again. 'What you have to do is come downstairs, have a cup of tea and calm down. You need to have something to eat and be here when the police arrive. And then tell them everything. Once all that's done, we can clean up the bathroom together, okay?' She gave an emphatic nod. 'Sorting this out has got to be a priority.'

Steph sighed. Opened her mouth to argue then shut it again. Bea was right. This *was* getting out of hand. She nodded. 'Okay, I'll just ring my boss and let him know what's happening or he'll wonder where I am. We're supposed to be going through plans for a grant application to extend my post this afternoon.' She sighed. 'Such bad timing. We've got a deadline to hit and if we miss it then my post will come to an end, and I'll be out of work again.'

Bea gave her a hug. 'Oh, Mum. So many worries all at once. I wish I could take them away from you. Are you sure you wouldn't like to come and stay for a few days, just like a little break?'

Steph gave her a weak smile. 'That's a lovely offer, but it doesn't solve my problems, does it? Your father is trying to sell my home from under me and somebody is making my life a misery. I can't just run away from everything. I've got to stand my ground. You know I do.'

She made her way downstairs, Bea right behind her, picking the deli bag off the hall table as they passed.

'I'll sort out lunch while you make your call, Mum,' she said as she filled the kettle.

Steph went into the lounge to retrieve her phone from her handbag and after an apologetic conversation with Bill – who was concerned about her welfare rather than upset that she was missing their meeting – she headed back into the kitchen. She noticed another parcel on the hall floor and picked it up, put it on the hall table. It had been hand-delivered again. She sighed, dreading her conversation with Noah.

In the kitchen, the table was set, the food laid out, drinks made, and Bea was waiting patiently.

Steph realised she was starving and for a few minutes they ate in silence. 'Did you know that the Charlie your dad is living with is a woman?' Steph said, not sure why that particular thought had pushed itself to the front of the queue.

Bea started to splutter and it was a moment before she got her breath. 'Don't be daft. No, you've got that wrong.'

Steph shook her head. 'I've got it absolutely right. I went round there yesterday to speak to him, to tell him to stop his nonsense, and she opened the door. Then slammed it in my face.'

Bea's eyes grew round. 'Wait a minute... Could this be her doing? The paint, I mean. And maybe the other things too.'

'It did cross my mind.'

Bea looked puzzled. 'But why would she want to be bothered? She's got her man, why be nasty like this?'

'Well, I've been wondering that myself. But I noticed her flat is for sale and my theory is they want to buy a bigger place and need the proceeds from the sale of this house. They want me out of here as fast as possible.' She nodded to herself, her theory sounding very plausible now she'd said it out loud. 'That's why your dad agreed to sell it to his mate. But I've been digging my heels in, so maybe she thinks it's the only way to make me change my mind.'

'Wait? What? Mum, you're going to have to slow down. I'm way behind here. He's selling it to who?'

'James and Lisa are buying rental properties in this area apparently. Remember, I told you about this? They've offered to buy and your dad said yes. Without even consulting me.' She took a bite of her bagel, licked cream cheese from her lips.

'You can be quite stubborn, Mum.' Bea took a sip of tea. 'But I can see why you'd be annoyed if he did that without even asking.'

Steph concentrated on eating, not willing to discuss the sale of the property. It wasn't happening. Full stop. An awkward silence settled over them and Bea finished her bagel first. 'I'll just go and have a look at the new carpet while you're finishing, then we can move on to dessert.'

Steph could hear her running up the stairs, one flight, then two. Thank goodness she'd had time to clear up.

Bea reappeared just as Steph popped the last bit of bagel into her mouth. 'That was delicious. Thank you. And that cheesecake looks even better.' She took a sip of her tea and pulled the plate towards her, saliva already filling her mouth.

'It looks as good as new up there,' Bea said as she scraped a spoonful of caramel off the top of her cheesecake. 'I'm glad to see you decided against the lodger. At least you don't have that worry anymore.'

Steph stopped eating. 'Ah, well... Technically, I do still have a lodger.'

Bea put her spoon down, a warning glint in her eye. 'You mean he's still in my bedroom?'

'It's only temporary. No need to worry. I'm going to tell him later that he has to move on.'

'Oh, Mum, do you want me to wait and tell him. You know, for moral support. Two against one. Just to make sure he does actually know he'll have to go? He might not listen if it's just you.'

Steph licked a blob of cream cheese from her upper lip, annoyed that Bea didn't think her capable or sorting out her own problems. *Am I such a pushover?* She forced a smile, determined to put this right herself. 'No, it's fine. He's already said he'll go if the arrangement isn't working out. I'll just wait until we've managed to find a permanent placement for him.' She took another spoonful of cheesecake. 'It shouldn't take long.'

What about the parcels? That's got to stop if he's going to stay for even another day.

Her mind gathered up all the bad things that had been happening, along with her concerns about Noah and laid them all out in front of her. A coldness filled her chest. Was Bea right? Did these things always develop into something far more sinister?

CHAPTER TWENTY-FIVE

Steph finished her cheesecake, the sickly sweetness making the contents of her stomach curdle. The silence had allowed her to sort through everything in her head and although she was happy to fix her own problems, she wanted to make sure she wasn't going to embarrass herself when the police came. Bea's thinking had always been incisive. She had that sort of analytical brain – took after her father in that department, always two steps ahead, able to work out the plots of convoluted dramas on TV when Steph hadn't a clue what was going on.

'Can I just talk this through with you, love? I don't think I've told you everything and I want to be sure I've got it all straight in my head.'

Bea nodded and stacked the plates, moving them out of the way, so there was nothing to distract them. She gave her a quick smile. 'Okay. That's a good idea.'

'I don't want to get your dad in trouble. That's the thing. Because he's the obvious person behind all this trouble. Him and that Charlie woman he's shacked up with.'

Bea's eyes narrowed. 'I honestly can't see it being Dad. I mean, when has he ever done anything nasty in his entire life?'

Steph huffed, her voice sharpened by bitterness when she spoke. 'Apart from leaving me and having an affair, you mean?'

Bea swiped crumbs off the table and into her palm, sprinkling them onto the top plate. 'You might have got it wrong, Mum. Jumping to conclusions. But I say you tell the police everything, let them sort it out. And if it is Dad or that woman, then having the police go round and interview them should stop all this trouble.'

'Hmm. Yes, you're right. They won't be arrested or anything, will they?'

'I suppose splattering paint all over someone's bathroom is criminal damage. Breaking and entering, even if nothing is taken is still criminal, isn't it?' She shrugged. 'I honestly don't know. Maybe a caution?'

'There's your father's friend, James, as well.' She glanced up at Bea. 'He's got a motive to scare me out of here, hasn't he?'

Bea looked thoughtful. 'I suppose he has.' She leaned towards her mum. 'I never liked him, you know. A bit too smarmy and full of himself, isn't he?'

That brought a flicker of a smile to Steph's lips, her daughter's opinion of Andy's friend very much like her own.

'And then there's a creepy guy at work, who's recently moved around the corner from here. Phil. I think he's got a thing about me, keeps bringing me cakes and stuff, and he could have had access to my keys. He might be setting himself up as a knight in shining armour to save me from harm, making me scared so I'll ask him to come round.' As Steph said it, she thought it sounded a bit fanciful, a blush warming her cheeks.

Bea pulled a face. 'I don't like the sound of that. He's definitely got to go on the list. Is there anyone else?'

Steph thought for a moment then shook her head. 'Not that I can think of.'

Bea pursed her lips. 'I'm going to say it again, Mum: I'd be much happier if you'd come and stay for a few days. Just until the police have had a chance to investigate.'

Steph could feel her pulse racing, her shoulders so tense they ached. She'd been like this ever since the trouble had started and that couldn't be healthy, could it? All that adrenaline – hadn't she read somewhere that adrenal glands could get exhausted and then you became ill with all sorts of ailments. Maybe she should take up Bea's offer. A couple of days might be nice, and she knew she'd get pampered.

'Is Mark still away?' she asked, her gaze on the table, her fingers fiddling with a teaspoon.

'Another week or so, he said. He's got negotiations with Real Madrid. He said there's big money at stake, so he's going to stay over there until it's all tied down.' Steph watched Bea's hand reach over the table and squeeze her own. 'I'm not sure why he makes you feel uncomfortable. He thinks you're great, you know that. But when he's home, he spends most of his time in his office so you don't really have to see him if you don't want to.' She grinned. 'We can spend our time in your suite.'

Steph thought about the luxurious set of rooms her daughter had decorated for her, with a bathroom, living room and bedroom. Bifold doors opened out onto the patio with views out to the landscaped gardens beyond. It really was quite lovely and if Mark wasn't around...

She smiled at her daughter. 'That's a lovely offer. And maybe I will take you up on it.' Bea's face lit up with delight. 'But I've got some really important things to sort out at work first. Including that grant application I told you about. That's got to be in by the end of the week and it's already Wednesday. It'll take me two days to get it finished and that'll be a push.' She sighed, frustrated. 'I should be doing it now, instead of having to sort out this... situation.'

Bea's mouth turned down at the corners, and she was clearly disappointed.

Steph squeezed her daughter's hand, a stab of guilt making her wonder if she was doing the right thing. 'We were going to go out to the Dales this weekend, weren't we? Let's still do that. I will have finished this application by then and I'll be able to relax a bit.' She caught Bea's eye. 'I know you're trying to help, but I feel if I leave here, then whoever is doing this has won. And I might even lose the house.' She sighed. 'I don't know, but it doesn't feel right to run away. I'm staying here until I'm ready to go. Nobody is going to scare me away.' She gave an emphatic nod. 'For once I'm going to stand my ground.'

Bea got up and put the plates and cutlery in the dishwasher, clearly unhappy with her mum's decision.

After a few minutes of clattering, she stood up and slammed the dishwasher door shut. 'I want you to be safe, Mum.' Her voice was clipped, impatient. 'That's what you're not getting. People who do this stuff, well it gets worse if they don't get what they want. I've watched all the police programmes. And their advice is always to be careful. Things escalate. Think about all those women murdered by their partners. There's usually a warning, you know, a series of events leading up to the final terrible conclusion.'

Steph's heart skipped in her chest and she tried to make light of things. 'You're not suggesting your dad's going to come and try and do me in, are you?'

'No, but...' Bea frowned, arms crossed over her chest as she leaned against the worktop. 'I'm worried about you.' Her eyes sparked then. 'Tell you what... I understand you've got work to do but... why don't I come and stay here for a few days instead?'

Steph grimaced, caught between a rock and a hard place. She started to bluster. 'I've got to sort things out with Noah first. I mean, I can't just throw him out until he has somewhere else to stay. Honestly, I couldn't do that.'

Bea's mouth pressed into a thin line, her eyes boring into Steph's.

She swallowed. 'It's imminent, but with the best will in the world, it's going to take a few days to find him somewhere to stay.'

Perhaps she should have put Noah in Max's room, and left Bea's room alone. But that had felt wrong, like she was closing the door on her son. After waiting so long for him to return, that was the last thing she was willing to do.

Maybe the answer *was* to go and stay with Bea over the weekend.

The doorbell rang and Steph shot out of her chair to answer the door, glad she didn't have to answer any more of Bea's questions.

CHAPTER TWENTY-SIX

The two community policewomen, who looked like a mother and daughter – a similar size, both blonde with their hair tied back – were very sympathetic as they sat in the lounge and listened as Steph went through everything. When she'd finished, Steph leaned forwards, clasping her knees, her eyes on the carpet so the women wouldn't see the sheen of tears. Just recounting her story had brought all the incidents into focus. Including the accident with the skateboarder and the broken ankle. When you added that in, everything felt that bit more menacing. 'I honestly don't know what to make of it all.'

'It's very scary for Mum,' Bea said, putting an arm round her shoulders. 'She has to stay here because of work commitments, but I'm worried for her.'

'Of course you are,' the older woman said, compassion in her eyes. 'I'm sure it's shaken you both up, but we'll definitely go and speak to the three people you've identified, and I promise I'll call you back once we've completed our initial investigations.' She held out a card to Steph. 'Here's my number. If anything else happens, please don't hesitate to give me a ring. And can I suggest that you keep everything locked;

doors and windows? I know it's a bit humid with this weather, but maybe you could get a fan to cool you down rather than keeping windows open. Especially given it looks like that's how the intruder might have come in before.'

Steph nodded, although she wasn't sure if she knew where the keys for the window locks were, not having used them for years. She'd never felt vulnerable in this house before now.

She looked at the two policewomen and hoped they were the solution to her troubles.

They stood and said their goodbyes, leaving Steph and Bea shoulder to shoulder in the doorway, watching them walk down the path to their car.

'Well, at least they sound like they're going to do something,' Steph said, arms folded tightly across her chest. Talking everything through had unnerved her, making her more jittery than she'd been before, panic fluttering beneath her ribs. Bea's offer seemed ever more tempting and she was about to say something when a sharp voice in her head made her close her mouth again.

Nobody is scaring me away. Her jaw hardened. If this was Andy's doing, then she'd fight him all the way. *Lying, cheating, good for nothing—*

'Is that Dad?' Bea's voice made her eyes focus on where she was pointing and sure enough, she could see Andy striding purposefully across the park towards them.

'Oh God. I'm not sure I can face him.' Anger burned in her chest. She hadn't spoken him since she'd found out about Charlie and could feel a shouting match coming on, even from this distance.

Bea glanced at her, gave her arm a squeeze. 'I'll head him off,' she said, obviously sensing trouble. She gave her mum a kiss on the cheek. 'I'll call you later.' Steph watched as she ran across to meet her dad, then gratefully closed the door.

The parcel on the hall table caught her eye. She picked it up and studied the writing. It was the same as the first parcel. Again, it was the size of a book, but much lighter. She sniffed it, relieved to find nothing unusual this time. But when she gave it a shake, she heard a faint rattle. *Pills?* Quickly, she put it back on the table. It was Noah's. What was in there was none of her business. It could be perfectly legitimate and she told herself off for being so suspicious. So he had a spliff in his pocket. Wasn't that the norm amongst kids these days? Nothing to worry about. Nothing at all. Except that other parcel definitely smelled of weed. There was no getting away from it. And that would be a lot of weed for one person to get through, which meant...

The ring of the doorbell made her turn. She opened the door without thinking and did a double take when she saw a tattooed young man outside. He was chewing gum at an alarming speed, hopping from foot to foot like he was standing on burning coals.

'Is Noah in?' He looked behind him, first over one shoulder, then over the other.

She frowned. 'No, he's not.'

He tried to push past her, but she slammed the door shut and put the chain on, opening it slightly so she could peer at him through the crack.

He took a step forward, his face practically wedged in the gap, so close to hers she could smell the mint of his chewing gum. 'I just want to come in and wait. He said to meet him here.'

'Well, I know nothing about that. I don't know who you are. So... why don't you wait outside for him?'

The young man glared at her and stopped chewing for a second. 'Tell him Jez called, will you?' He straightened up, put his hand to the side of his face, signalling a phone call 'Tell him to give me a bell.'

'I'm not his secretary,' Steph snapped.

The young man narrowed his eyes, and pointed at her.

'You'll tell him, though,' he said, giving her the thumbs-up before he turned on his heels and jogged off down the road.

She unchained the door so she could look out and check he'd really gone, then closed it firmly, leaning on it while her hands rubbed her face, as if she was trying to wash away what she now knew. Noah was dealing drugs from her house.

How dare he?

And how had her judgement been so far wrong? She kicked the door, furious, not only with Noah for being so stupid, but with herself for seeing only the good in him and not considering the bad. As Cara had warned, he'd brought trouble to her door. She cursed herself for thinking she could change things round for him. Only Noah could do that and dealing drugs was never a way out, even though kids were dragged into the game with promises of easy money.

She remembered what Noah had told her about the man who'd shown him kindness but led him into debt, demanding favours in payment. Was he the one Noah was selling the drugs for? It seemed likely. She resolved to have that conversation with him. Get the police involved. They'd be coming back to her house, for God's sake. What if they found the drugs? She groaned. What a mess she'd made for herself.

And it's not like you weren't warned. Everyone close to her had told her she was making a mistake, but would she listen? She was so stubborn at times she annoyed herself, unable to understand what logic she'd applied, what had made it seem like a good idea.

I wanted to help a young person who was struggling. That had been her goal. Thoughts of Max and the lovely relationship she had with the student nurses next door clouding her judgement. Perhaps she could still help him, but now it would have to be tough love.

She made her way to the kitchen and put the kettle on, remembering there was still the bathroom to clean up. *How on earth am I going to deal with that?* It was gloss paint, so she'd need white spirit to get it off. There was probably some in the shed, maybe not enough but she could make a start.

She heard the front door bang, footsteps on the stairs. Then footsteps coming back down the stairs.

Noah came into the kitchen looking puzzled. 'Hey, Steph. What happened in the bathroom?'

She sighed. 'More of the same, I'm afraid. I think it's very clear now that somebody is trying to scare me out of the house. Anyway, the police have been round again. I have a few suspects and they're going to check them out so hopefully that'll be the end of it.'

Noah paled. 'The police? They've been here?' He swallowed, tried to look casual, but failed miserably. His hands flapped at his sides as if he didn't know what to do with them, a note of panic in his voice. 'Did they... um, have a look around?'

She leaned against the worktop, arms crossed, steeling herself for the difficult conversation, because there was no time like the present. She watched him for a moment, his hands having found his pockets now, but his weight was shifting from foot to foot and he was chewing nervously on his bottom lip.

'Yes, Noah, they did. They had a very good look round.'

He couldn't look her in the eye, a sheen of sweat breaking out on his brow. She relented, could see how uncomfortable he was. He reminded her so much of Max she couldn't be cross with him, wanting to undo all those arguments with her son. There were two sides to every story, as Max had often told her, and this time she'd make sure she listened.

'Fortunately, I tidied up in the bedroom before they came, and I stuffed your shirt and your spliff under the bed. So they didn't find anything, if that's what you're worried about.'

Noah's eyebrows shot up his forehead and he ran his tongue round his lips, obviously not sure what to say.

'Sit down.' Steph pointed to a chair at the kitchen table, her voice firm. 'We need to have a proper chat.'

He slid into the seat, head bowed, hands fiddling with his bracelet.

'What's going on, Noah? There've been two suspect parcels arrive for you in the last couple of days. Hand-delivered. Then a strange guy turned up at the door and—' The doorbell rang, loud and insistent, somebody leaning on it.

Steph looked down the hallway.

Noah jumped up. 'I'll get it.'

And before she could say anything, he'd gone, the front door banging behind him. She wondered if it was Jez. She sighed with frustration as she cradled her mug against her chest, the warmth of it giving her some comfort, while her worries crammed themselves into her head. She felt so conflicted about Noah, she wasn't sure what she was going to do.

Five minutes later, the doorbell rang again. She stomped down the hall and opened the door to find a young woman with blue dreadlocks, a pink summer dress and sparkly Doc Martens. She wore heavy make-up, and had bright red lips.

'I'm looking for Noah,' she said, peering past Steph's shoulder as if she'd see him there.

'He's out,' Steph said, trying to close the door, but finding the woman's Doc Marten wedged in the way.

'Can I come in and wait? He said he'd be here.' She looked around as if he might materialise out of the garden wall, or the hedgerow. Her eyes met Steph's and the young woman grinned. Her pupils were dilated, her gaze drifting like she was watching an invisible movie. *Is she high on something?*

'You can wait in the front garden,' Steph said, giving her a gentle push backwards to make her move her foot, before closing the door.

She crept into the lounge and peered outside from behind the curtain. Another woman arrived and sat next to dreadlocks girl on the garden wall. *What on earth is going on? Are they all coming to buy drugs?* She checked in the hall, saw that Noah had taken the parcel with him. The one that rattled. She went up to the bedroom where she'd have a better view without being seen and settled by the window, in the shadow of the curtain. A young man arrived next, thin as a twig in skinny jeans, a grey hoodie and enormous trainers, twitching and nervy. He had a quick conversation with the two women, then checked his phone before heading off into the park. He sat on the grass, eyes on the house. Clearly, he was waiting for Noah too.

Steph's anger pulsed in her ears, tension pulling at her neck muscles. She knew beyond doubt now that Noah was dealing drugs from the house. Furious, she ran downstairs and put the chain on the door. Now she wouldn't let him back in until she had a sensible explanation. And if he couldn't give her one then he was back out on the streets. *He's not my problem.* Then she remembered that he still had a set of keys, having only given her one when he'd come to see her yesterday lunchtime. She gritted her teeth, telling herself she'd get those back off him as soon as he turned up.

Over the next hour, another six people rang the bell looking for Noah. At the seventh ring she was at boiling point and yelled through the letter box. 'He's not here,' at whoever was at the door.

'Mrs Baker?' A woman's voice, one that sounded familiar.

The policewoman? She couldn't even remember her name. It was Polish, she thought. Impossible to pronounce without a bit of practice.

She unlocked the door, opened it a crack.

'Everything okay?' There was concern in the eyes of the older policewoman who'd visited earlier.

She blushed, flustered now and took the chain off, opened the door.

'I'm fine. Come in.' She locked the door behind her, led the woman through into the lounge. Steph flopped onto the sofa, the woman perching on the armchair by the window. 'I've just had all these random people coming round, looking for my lodger. It's driving me mad.'

The woman's eyebrows rose an inch. 'Lodger? I don't think you mentioned a lodger.'

'Oh, it's not official.' Steph sighed. 'I work at the homeless shelter and this young man came in who reminded me of my son and anyway... to cut a long story short, he'd been beaten up and I got to know him a bit, so I invited him to stay. Just until we can get him something permanent.'

The policewoman couldn't hide the flash of disbelief which crossed her face. 'I'm not sure that was the wisest move, given everything that's been going on.'

'You sound like my daughter.'

'She seems very sensible.' The implication being that Steph wasn't.

Her gaze dropped to her hands, her fingers turning her wedding ring round and round. 'The thing is... I like him. Honestly, I thought—' She stopped herself from blurting out the whole story, and sagged back against the cushions.

The policewoman took her notebook out of her pocket and flicked through the pages. 'I thought I'd pop round to give you an update on what we've done so far.' She gave a reassuring smiled. 'I've spoken to all three of the people you gave me contact details for. Nobody has admitted anything, but I have given them all the same warning that any further incidents will be taken extremely seriously by the police.'

'Good to know,' Steph said, unconvinced. 'My husband was heading over here after you left. My daughter went to talk to him.'

The policewoman nodded. 'Yes, she was there when I caught up with him at the address you gave me.'

'What about this Charlie woman?'

'She was there too. And after assessing their responses, I really don't think they are behind your troubles. I know they might seem the obvious culprits, but often, in these cases, it's not the obvious people who are to blame.'

Steph thought about that for a moment.

'What about my husband's friend, then? James. The one who wants to buy the house.'

'I've checked him too and he's been out of the area for the last week, working in London.'

'Oh right.' Steph's shoulders drooped, the enquiry having reached a dead-end.

'So I just need to ask if there's anyone else we need to consider?'

The policewoman looked at her, pen cocked, ready to write. Steph shook her head, despondent. 'I don't think so.'

The policewoman flipped her notebook shut and tucked it back in her pocket before standing. 'We'll carry on checking in with you and doing drive pasts, but make sure you keep your windows and doors locked.' Steph hauled herself to her feet and walked with her to the door. 'Give me a call if there's any more trouble,' she said as she left, Steph locking the door behind her and putting the chain back on.

The house felt different when she'd gone. It was no longer her peaceful sanctuary, her space having been violated once again. She went up to inspect the bathroom again, her heart skipping a beat as she took in the paint splatters across the walls, running down in rivulets to pool on the tiled floor, in the bottom of the bath, the sink. The colour of blood.

CHAPTER TWENTY-SEVEN

She found a big bottle of white spirit in the shed, and when she'd started cleaning, she realised that there wasn't as much paint as she'd thought – it had just been splattered to good effect. It had stained the grout, but on the whole, she managed to get most of it off. At least the bathroom was in a usable state again and really that was all that mattered.

By the time she'd finished, her arms were shaking with the effort of scrubbing, her mind full of everything she needed to say to Noah. *If he comes back.*

'He might have done a runner,' Cara said when she'd rung her up, needing someone to talk to who'd understand. 'Especially if he knows the police have been round. I wouldn't be surprised if that's the last you see of him.' She sounded a little smug, in a told-you-so sort of way.

Steph took a big breath, ready to apologise. It had been a long time coming. Too long probably, but she wanted their friendship to go back to how it was. 'I'm sorry, Cara. I don't know what's got into me at the moment. I should have listened to you. And I'm sorry I knocked you back when you asked if Dev could come and stay. I'm all over the place at the moment with this divorce and Andy wanting to sell the house and not knowing what's going to happen.' A sudden flush of emotion caught her unawares and her voice cracked. 'Can we still be friends?'

She could hear Cara's breath, white noise in her ear.

'Of course we're still friends,' she said at last and Steph had a struggle to keep her tears at bay. 'But I can't pretend it didn't hurt.'

'I'm sorry. I didn't mean to upset you, honestly I just...'

'It's okay. The neighbours have been behaving themselves, so it's all good at the moment.' She cleared her throat. 'You just keep those doors locked so he can't get back in if he tries.'

Steph was grateful for the change of subject, relieved that she'd been forgiven and hopeful that the awkwardness would now melt away. 'I have a bit of a problem because he's still got a set of keys, but I can double-lock the doors while I'm in the house. It's just if he comes back when I'm out that I could have a problem. Honestly, I'm so angry with him. Imagine dealing drugs from the house.'

'Look, love, I hate to say this, but maybe you've been a little gullible. I mean, I'm sure he's a nice enough lad, but that doesn't mean he isn't trouble. Or in trouble. And I know you mean well, but you really don't need that on your doorstep. These people can sniff out the vulnerable.'

Steph had gasped at that. Gullible? Vulnerable? *Am I?* Naïve, Bea had called her.

'I don't think I'm—'

'Sorry, sorry, that came out wrong.' Cara's voice softened. 'What I mean is you're too nice for your own good sometimes. You give everyone the benefit of the doubt, don't you? And just because someone looks harmless and friendly it doesn't mean that they are. Young lads are the worst, to be honest. They're used to tying their mothers in knots and think they can do it to everyone.'

She frowned, a little wounded by her friend's words. 'You think I'm being played for a fool, don't you?'

'No, love. Not necessarily, but you do need to take a step back. Take the emotion out of the situation.'

'Hmm. Maybe. You know he reminds me so much of Max, that's the thing.'

'Exactly. That's the problem. In your mind, you're thinking he *is* Max, making him into the same person and he really isn't. He can't be, can he? The reality is you don't know this lad from Adam. He's a stranger. You have no idea of his history, what he's capable of.'

Steph's mind ran over Noah's story. She remembered how he'd changed when Andy had started to have a go at him. *Has he been telling me the truth, or wheedling his way into my house?* She gave a nervous laugh. 'You're freaking me out now.'

'Good. Just double-lock the doors. Put an end to it and whatever operation he's got going on from your house.'

'I couldn't believe all those people. They just kept turning up.'

'You've heard of cuckooing, haven't you?'

Steph hesitated. 'No, I don't think I have.'

'It's when drug dealers or criminals take over a vulnerable person's house and use it for their own purposes. There might be an element of that going on here.'

'What? You think so?' Steph bristled. 'I wouldn't class myself as vulnerable... No, I don't think that fits at all.' Just because her husband had left her and she lived on her own, it didn't mean she'd lost her judgement. But then... she stopped her defensive babbling and made herself listen. Perhaps she had been taken in. Perhaps Noah *had* been playing her. Look at his insistence that he should have a tenancy agreement. Determined to get it in writing and official. The mysterious parcels and then all those people.

'Anyway,' she said, thankful that nothing had been signed.

'He's gone out now and I won't be letting him back in. Hopefully that's the end of it.'

She thought of the clothes in the attic bedroom that she'd given to him, his little pile of possessions, hidden under the bed. *What if he does come back?* Would he knock on the door when he found himself locked out? Demand to come in? She could always call the policewoman, she reminded herself, feeling for her card in her pocket. There was backup if she needed it.

That night, she'd lain awake, listening for a ring on the doorbell, but after a while, her exhaustion won, and she fell into a deep sleep.

Her alarm startled her awake the next morning and she reached for her phone, turned it off, not sure she was ready for a day at work. But it was imperative that she get there. The deadline for the grant application was due in tomorrow and she had a lot of number crunching to do if she was going to make a convincing case.

She hopped out of bed and went for a shower, frowning when she saw a damp towel on the floor. That wasn't there last night, was it? She stopped and listened, the house quiet.

After a quick shower, she hurried downstairs to make breakfast, stopping when she saw the crumbs on the worktop, the open margarine tub. She definitely hadn't left it there. Her skin prickled, heart racing. *Noah?* It was the only answer. But she'd double-checked all the locks before she went to bed.

She ran upstairs, then slowed and crept up to the attic bedroom, pushing the door open as quietly as she could. He was fast asleep, sprawled in the bed like he had every right to be there.

How the hell did he get in?

She knew she'd double-locked the doors because she'd checked three times before going to bed. It didn't make sense, but there was no time to do anything about it now. She had to get to work.

Tonight I'll sort it out, she told herself, not wanting to think about it when she had more important things to focus on.

She was just about to leave for work when she heard the thunk of the letter box. A parcel lay on the doormat. The same as the previous days. She picked it up, smelled it, gave it a shake, and heard that telltale rattle. *More pills? Is that what the people were queuing up for yesterday?* Anger burned through her. She slapped it down on the hall table, took a photo for evidence, intending to tackle Noah about the drug dealing when she got home. There would be no denying it then.

It was almost lunchtime when she got a phone call. The policewoman.

'Sorry to disturb you, Mrs Baker, but we've had a complaint from a neighbour. Several complaints, actually. He's got himself quite worked up.'

She frowned, confused. 'Which neighbour?'

'Elderly chap. Next door. He says there's a gang of young people outside your house. Said it was the same last night and they're worrying him. They've been sitting on his wall. Throwing rubbish in his garden.'

Steph's heart sank. 'Oh God, I'm so sorry. I think it's to do with my lodger.'

'Yes, well we've been round and a young man was just leaving the property when we arrived. I'm afraid to say we seized some suspicious packets. He's in custody now.'

A weight settled on Steph's shoulders, pressing her into her seat. A dull ache pounding at the base of her skull.

'But he says you gave them to him.'

CHAPTER TWENTY-EIGHT

Steph rang the only person she knew who could really help her. Bea answered on the second ring. 'Oh, thank goodness.' She was so anxious she could hardly breathe let alone speak. 'I'm in a right mess, love.' She gulped back a sob.

'Mum, what's wrong?'

'I'm at the police station. There's been a bit of trouble with Noah. You know, my lodger.' Tears were streaming down her face now, the enormity of her situation hitting home.

'What the hell has he done now?' Bea gave an annoyed grunt. 'Look, you can tell me when I get there. I'm on my way.'

'Oh, thank God. I didn't know what to do, who to call now your dad's not...' She was sobbing, fumbling in her pockets for a tissue.

'Oh, Mum. Don't go getting yourself all upset. I'm sure we can sort it out. Which station?'

'Leeds Central. Thank you,' she gulped. 'Thank you so much.'

The line went dead, and she visualised her daughter running to her car, thankful that at least one member of her family was always there when she needed them.

. . .

Forty minutes later, Bea was shown into the meeting room where Steph was being kept, following an initial grilling. She wiped her tear-stained face, and sprang to her feet, rushing to her for a hug. Never had she been so glad to see anyone.

'Oh, Mum. What on earth is going on?'

Steph sniffed, clinging tighter and Bea buried her face in her mum's hair, something she'd always done since she was a child.

Eventually Steph pulled away. 'God, you must think I'm an idiot.'

'No, not an idiot. Just too nice for your own good.' Bea pointed to the chairs. 'Let's just sit down and you can tell me all about it.'

Steph explained – in stumbling sentences – about the drugs and how the police thought Noah had been dealing from her house and how he'd told them she'd given the drugs to him to sell. 'I'm apparently a person of interest in their enquiries now. They've taken my fingerprints.' She sniffed, her panic starting to rise again as she spoke to Bea about her predicament. 'The thing is... another parcel arrived this morning and my fingerprints will be all over it because I picked it up and put it on the side.' She caught Bea's look of horror. 'How can I prove it's nothing to do with me when Noah says it is? It's his word against mine.'

Bea looked thoughtful, got out her phone, scrolled for a moment. 'Here we go,' she said, dialling a number.

'Who are you calling?'

'Our solicitor. It's an excellent practice. I'm sure they'll have someone who can come and sort this out for you.'

'You think so?' Steph slumped back in her chair, her relief palpable. Maybe with the right legal support, she'd have a chance of getting out of this mess.

. . .

Two further hours passed, until – after another lengthy interview with the police with the solicitor present – Steph was allowed to go home.

Bea linked arms with her and steered her out of the station. 'I'm parked over here. Now I'm going to take you back to my place, away from all this trouble.'

Steph pulled away. 'Oh, love, I told you. I can't just yet. I still haven't finished that grant application. I got interrupted today when the police got involved in all this mess. I just want to go home.' She looked at Bea, eyes sore from crying. 'Please?'

'Really?' A flash of disbelief crossed Bea's face, the colour rising in her cheeks. 'You're joking. After all this trouble, you still want to go back there?'

'Even if I was going to stay with you, I'd still have to go back to get my clothes and everything. But honestly, love, I feel so dirty I just want a shower and a proper cup of tea and something to eat.'

Bea gave a frustrated sigh. 'Okay. If that's what you want. But the offer is there. And you promise you'll ring me if you change your mind. Honestly, it's no trouble coming to get you.' Her eyes met Steph's and she could see the concern; she felt bad for dragging her daughter into a predicament that was completely of her own making.

She pulled Bea into a hug. 'I'm so lucky to have you. And I promise, if I feel at all spooked, I'll give you a ring. But after the police have been crawling over the house, I can't help feeling the problem is solved now.' She pulled away. 'I don't understand the logic, but I think now that it must have been Noah who was my intruder. He's found a way to get into the house. I know I locked everything, but my bedroom window doesn't shut properly, so I think he must have climbed onto the kitchen roof and got in that way. It's the only possibility.'

It was an unsettling thought to say the least because she'd heard nothing. *How many times has he done that before?* It didn't bear thinking about.

Bea stopped and stared at her. 'Bloody hell, Mum. Well, we'll have to get that fixed somehow before I'm leaving you on your own.'

'I think we could nail it shut for now.'

Bea nodded. 'Right, that's what we'll do, and I'll get a glazier organised to come and sort it out properly.'

Steph clung on to Bea's arm, her body feeling weak now the adrenaline rush was starting to fade. 'If I ever mention anything about lodgers to you again, please stop me.'

Bea laughed and steered her to the car. 'As if I could ever stop you from doing anything.'

'Thank goodness for your solicitor friend. He knew exactly what to say. Had it all sorted out without me having to say much at all.'

Bea grinned. 'He's one of Mark's mates. He's always there when we need him. Not cheap but worth every penny.'

Steph tensed. She hadn't thought about the cost. Another unforeseen expense that she'd struggle to pay. It was bad enough with the excess from the insurance to find this month. 'You'll have to let me pay his bill.'

Bea opened the car door. 'Don't be daft. I'm sure he owed us a favour.'

'I swear you have superpowers, love. Flying in to the rescue. Again.'

Bea considered that as she put her seat belt on. 'I suppose having the right contacts and knowing when to use them might be a superpower.' She grinned. 'I like the sound of that.'

They travelled in silence, the thought of Noah creeping in and out of the house through her bedroom while she was asleep, filling her head, bringing her out in a cold sweat.

Other people could have got in that way too.

And that was an even scarier thought.

CHAPTER TWENTY-NINE

Bea insisted on doing a search of the house before Steph was allowed inside, which Steph was grateful for. She sat on the garden wall, chewing what was left of a fingernail while she waited.

'The police clearly made a bit of a mess when they did their search,' Bea said, when she reappeared in the doorway. 'Did Noah honestly invite them in? I can't believe he would have done, but I suppose it's his word against theirs.' She gave an impatient huff. 'You'd think they might have put things back.'

Steph stood, disheartened that she'd have another mess to clear up. That's all she seemed to be doing these last few days. Bea ushered her inside, put a reassuring hand on her shoulder. 'Don't you worry, Mum, I'll help you tidy up. In fact...' She guided her through the hallway. 'You've had a nasty shock. Why don't you sit in the kitchen? I'll make you a proper cup of tea, while I scoot round and clear up in the lounge.'

Steph blinked, feeling totally helpless. She had no energy, her body all shaky after the trauma of being questioned. She nodded at her daughter, tried a smile, which felt like it would

crack her face. Bea guided her to a chair at the kitchen table
while she put the kettle on. Drawers and cupboards had been
opened and emptied, not everything put back in the right place.
She sighed, her elbows leaning on the table, head in her hands
wondering how she'd let her life get so out of control.

It was hard to come to terms with the ordeal she'd just been
through. The eyes of those police officers boring into her, asking
the same questions over and over, trying to catch her out. Did
she look like a drug dealer, for God's sake? How could she have
been so stupid, though? A woman of her age manipulated by a
young lad like that, especially given where she worked and the
people she dealt with on a daily basis. And then he had the
cheek to point the finger at *her*. Ironically, she'd always thought
she was a good judge of character, but she'd got it totally wrong
this time.

It was the Max connection. That was the thing that had
thrown her judgement out. Somehow, they'd merged together
in her head, and she'd bestowed Noah with qualities he clearly
didn't have in reality. It was a hard lesson. *My God, I'm going to
feel stupid when I go back into work. Having to explain
everything.*

Maybe Bea was right. Maybe she was in the wrong job,
always thinking the best of people who had complex histories
and personalities, troubled track records. *Perhaps finishing that
grant application doesn't matter after all.*

But then... she needed that job to keep the house.

Bea pushed a mug of tea into her hands and she sipped at it,
lost in her thoughts, while Bea moved into the lounge to carry
on with her tidying, humming to herself as she worked.

Thinking about judging character, she'd got Andy wrong as
well, hadn't she? Married to the man for nearly thirty years and
he now felt like a stranger. How could that happen? After
blaming her for flirting with her boss, he was having an affair

himself. What a load of misplaced suspicion that was and yet it had led to them separating.

Her phone rang. She pulled it from her pocket and looked at the screen, frowned. *Talk of the devil.* She hesitated, then answered, deciding that her day couldn't get any worse and a shouting match with Andy might just make her feel better.

'What?' she said, all snappy.

'Are you okay? Bea said you'd been arrested.' He sounded properly concerned, which threw her for a moment.

'I'm... fine and I was just helping the police with their enquiries, isn't that the phrasing they use?'

'That lodger. I told you it was a bad idea.' He sighed. 'When are you going to start listening to me?'

'When you stop lying maybe? Accusing me of having an affair when you're the one who's shacked up with someone else.'

'Don't be ridiculous. I told you, she's a work colleague.'

'Oh yeah.' Steph sneered, her voice getting louder as her anger came to boiling point. 'I can't remember you telling me that Charlie was actually a woman.'

Andy stayed calm, his voice very even considering she was yelling at him. 'What difference does it make? Bill, who is a man, is your work colleague.'

She bit back what she was about to say, thought about it. Then quietly said, 'I didn't move in with him, though, did I?'

He gave a frustrated sigh. 'Look, Steph, I didn't ring up for a fight. I was just wondering... could we meet up? I need to see you. Have a proper conversation.' He sighed again. 'I'm sorry. That's what I really want to say.' Steph held her breath. *An apology.* Wasn't that all she'd wanted when this bad feeling between them had started? 'I'm so sorry, love. I've been an idiot and...' His voice thickened, like he was close to tears. 'I don't want to lose you.'

Steph couldn't speak. Couldn't think. Did she believe him?

Or was this a ploy, was he playing her in some way she couldn't quite grasp?

'I want us to start again. Put everything behind us. We've got a buyer for the house, so let's move somewhere new, have an adventure? See if we can get back to how we used to be.'

It's all about the house, making me move.

Did she believe that he wasn't in a relationship with Charlie? She remembered the look of horror on the woman's face when she'd seen her at her door. *No, there's something going on.* That wasn't a rational response, she was definitely emotionally invested. If Steph allowed herself to be taken in by his pleas, she could end up homeless and she wasn't going to let that happen.

I'm not going to be gullible again. She gritted her teeth. *I'm not.*

'I've got to go,' she said and disconnected, tears filling her throat.

She went to find Bea – not wanting to be sitting on her own – and found her plumping cushions, the lounge as tidy as it had been for some time. Bea smiled at her, dropped the cushion into place and stood back to admire her handiwork. 'There, all done.'

'Wow, thanks, love. You've done an amazing job.' Her chin quivered. 'It's very kind of you to help like this.'

'Don't be daft. I want to help. I've always wanted to help, but you keep...' She closed her mouth, lips working from side to side as if the unspoken words were trying to wriggle out.

Steph frowned. 'What do I keep doing?'

'Pushing me away.' Bea's voice was small, like she was a little girl again and her words hit Steph hard.

Is that what I've been doing? For a moment she was lost for words, casting her mind back to see what Bea might be referring to. 'I'm sorry if you feel like that. I'm... just trying to be independent for once in my life.' She sank onto the sofa, clasped a cushion on her lap, hands kneading the fleece fabric of the cover. 'I've never lived on my own. I've always had your dad and I realised I've never had a chance to just be me. Nobody else to look after or wind my life around.' She shrugged. 'I need to prove to myself that I can do it.'

'Oh, Mum.' Bea sank down beside her and took her hand, weaving their fingers together. 'You can be independent and still let people help you sometimes, you know.' She leaned against Steph, their heads touching.

'I know. It's just... It's something I've really got to do. Prove to myself that I don't need your father. That I can run a house, my life, on my own.'

'Thing is, Mum, honestly... I don't think you're the sort of person who thrives on their own.' Bea's hand squeezed hers. 'I think you're a nurturer. You need people to look after. That's why you asked that homeless punk to come and stay.'

Steph thought about her daughter's words and had to admit she'd hit the nail squarely on the head. But looking after other people didn't mean she couldn't be independent. She could do both, couldn't she?

'I think I've inherited that from you,' Bea continued. 'That's why I like to be able to help you. Especially when Mark's away. So... I want you to let me in a little. For my sake as well as yours.'

Steph turned and looked at her daughter, could see the gleam of tears in her eyes and felt a pang of guilt.

'Anyway, please just come back with me. Let's have a lovely weekend together. I'll book Veronique to come and give us a pamper. What do you say?'

Steph thought about the paperwork on her desk. The grant application she needed to complete. 'I'm sorry, love, but I can't. I've missed so much work and I've got a really important application to catch up on.' She looked at her watch. 'In fact, I'm going to go to the office now and get some more done on it. It's got to be in tomorrow.'

Bea pressed her lips together, then jumped to her feet. 'Why the hell won't you listen to me, Mum?' Her eyes sparked with anger. 'I'm just trying to look after you and keep you safe and you just throw it all back in my face.'

She stormed out of the house, slamming the door behind her.

CHAPTER THIRTY

By eight o'clock that evening, Steph had got a final draft of the application finished, all her figures added up, the appendices were attached with supporting evidence, and she was happy with her work. She just needed Bill to go over it in the morning, then it could be submitted.

She'd locked herself in the office, not answering the couple of knocks on the door, determined to get finished no matter what. She was fed up with other people deciding her fate – this was one thing she could control. One thing she could get right.

It was still light outside when she left the shelter, and she hurried to the bus stop, thinking she might just be in time for the next bus. A hand grabbed her shoulder and spun her round, making her gasp, heart jumping. Her hand tightened round her handbag, terrified she was going to be mugged.

Then she recognised her assailant.

'Noah! Get your hands off me.' She tried to back away, furious with him for the trouble he'd caused, but his hand held her tight. She glared at him. 'How dare you come near me after what you've done.'

He looked forlorn, his face red and blotchy. 'Steph, wait, please. Just listen. I need to explain.'

Fury erupted in her chest, her words bursting out in an angry rush. 'Oh no. I'm not having any more of your bloody nonsense. You took me for a fool, didn't you? Mistook kindness for weakness. Well, you've got me all wrong.'

'I'm sorry,' he pleaded, his hand tightening its grasp on her shoulder. 'I had to say the drugs were yours. I had no choice, it was—'

'Enough! I've had enough.' Steph's hands sliced the air as if she was throwing his excuses to the ground, ready to trample them into the dirt. 'Leave me alone.'

She peeled his fingers from her jacket and ran up the street, relieved to see her bus already at the bus stop. She jumped on, showing her pass to the driver before slumping into a seat, chest heaving with the exertion. She blinked, trying to rid her mind of Noah's face, the abject misery in his eyes. Her heart was torn. *There are two sides to every story.* Perhaps she should have heard him out. Perhaps he did have a good excuse.

Listen to yourself! He set you up with the police, remember. The lad's a conman. A criminal. It's all play-acting and you fall for it every time.

She wriggled in her seat, letting her gaze roam across the shopfronts as they headed out of town. But thoughts of Noah wouldn't leave her. How had she got him so wrong? He came from a respectable family by the sounds of it, just a relationship gone bad, which seemed quite common with the young men she came across at the shelter, especially if a parent had a new partner and they felt pushed out. It was natural, she supposed, when boys grew into men, for tensions to arise, everyone wanting to do things their way, be themselves without the confines of their childhood. *Is that what happened with Max?*

She remembered that the pressure in the house had been

building for a while. Max's digs at his sister, his constant under-mining, sabotaging things that she loved, had brought things to boiling point. The final straw seemed to be when Bea's art port-folio had gone missing, with all her GCSE work. It hadn't yet been marked and the morning she needed to submit it, Steph and Bea had turned the house upside down looking for it.

'This has got Max written all over it,' Bea sobbed as she looked again under all the beds. 'He hates me, Mum.'

'Of course he doesn't hate you.' She stopped her search, knowing that wherever Bea's artwork was, it wasn't anywhere in the house.

'I saw him in the back garden last night. I'm sure I did. I came down for a drink. I couldn't sleep because I was nervous about today, you know, doing the final piece. I think I heard him talking to someone. Laughing. I didn't take much notice, to be honest, just went back to bed.'

Steph frowned. Her son had become so distant, anything was possible, but she'd thought she heard him in his room late on, moving around. She didn't sleep very well these days, the constant sniping between her children creating a toxic atmosphere that frequently kept her awake.

She looked out of the back window. 'The only place we haven't looked is the shed. Maybe your Dad's tidied it away in there not realising what it was. He's like a flipping magpie, isn't he? Everything he doesn't know what to do with ends up in there.' She wiped the tears from Bea's face. 'You go and get ready for school, I'll go and have a look out there.'

The portfolio wasn't in the shed, but her eye was caught by a wisp of smoke, curling into the clear morning sky, coming from the compost heap between the shed and the back wall. She went to investigate, her hands flying to her mouth when she saw the charred remains. Paper curled to a crisp, the handle of Bea's portfolio case the only thing left intact.

Andy flew into a horrible rage when he learned what had happened. Max stood there, taking it all with a secret smile on his face while Steph's heart broke. He'd been such a sensitive boy when he was younger, so cuddly and affectionate and now he'd turned into a vindictive bully. Burning his sister's art portfolio, ruining her chances of getting a grade in the only subject she really excelled at, well that was heartless in the extreme.

'You finished?' Max had said when Andy ran out of steam. 'There's no point me saying anything because you won't want to believe me.' Then he'd calmly turned and walked into the hallway, picked up his college bag and walked out of the door, the three remaining members of his family staring after him.

'When he's finished college, he's got to move out,' Andy said, turning to Steph, fire in his eyes. 'It's not fair on Bea. You've got to see that?'

Steph had looked from her husband to her daughter, who was inconsolable, having lost all her work, and she knew in her heart that she should agree. But she couldn't. It was like asking her to choose between her children and which mother could do that? She resolved to talk to Max again and see if she could find out what had happened to make him do such a terrible thing.

Of course, she never had the chance, because that night he left. And she'd never discovered the truth. Not that it was the only incident she'd never got to the bottom of. It was the tip of the iceberg, really, a whole catalogue of misdemeanours spreading through Max's childhood. She'd always put it down to frustration, but she could be wrong. Would she ever know if she didn't find him? It dawned on her then that she had spent so much time nurturing Noah like a surrogate son, she'd done nothing to find her real son.

Her gaze drifted across the park, and she realised with a panicked jolt that she was at her stop. She lurched out of her seat and down the aisle, her regrets trailing behind her.

The house was quiet. She stopped and sniffed as she

entered. No smell of cigarette smoke. Her ears strained to hear sounds that shouldn't be there, but it was as quiet as a mausoleum. She kicked off her shoes and padded through to the kitchen, the hairs standing up on the back of her neck, trepidation stirring the contents of her stomach. *What's happened this time?* But it was all as she'd left it. Tidier than usual after Bea's efforts, the remnants of air freshener lingering in the air. She let out a long, slow breath, hardly able to believe that she might be allowed a little bit of normality, before the next disaster struck.

What was that? A muffled bump. Her heart skipped and she put her bag on the floor, ever so gently, so she wouldn't make a sound. She crept back into the hall and peered up the stairs. It was gloomy up there, no chance of seeing anything. She held her breath, the sound of her pulse whooshing in her ears. Nothing. She could hear nothing. She flicked on the light.

'Who's there?' she called, her hand on her phone in her back pocket. Not a sound.

You're imagining things.

She looked up the stairs again, dismissing her fears, then went back to the kitchen. She was tired and hungry. Exhausted after her turbulent day. Why did everything have to involve a conflict these days, when she'd spent her whole life avoiding just that? She hated bad feeling, but now she'd even managed to create it between herself and Bea and Andy.

Why was it so wrong to want to be on her own? Everyone was so used to her being part of a couple, half of a whole, but she felt she had to get out of her comfort zone and prove to herself that she could actually function as a single woman. Even if that wasn't her natural choice, the longing for how things used to be always lurking at the back of her mind, this was her future and she had to learn to embrace it. Enjoy a different kind of life.

Meal for one? No problem.

The fridge stood in front of her, and she hesitated before opening it, wondering what she might find inside. *You're being stupid.* She yanked the door open, staring at the contents. Nothing out of place. Nothing in there that shouldn't be.

Another noise made her look to the ceiling. She was sure it had been above her. A footstep on that wobbly board in her bedroom.

CHAPTER THIRTY-ONE

Steph listened, her heart hammering in her chest. All was quiet. *It's your imagination running riot.* She stood at the bottom of the stairs, looking up, ears straining. Nothing. *Go and check.* Feeling more confident, she crept up the stairs, peeked into all of the rooms. *Of course there's nobody here, you silly woman.* She nodded, agreeing with herself and went back down to the kitchen, turned on the radio and opened the freezer, started shuffling through the ready meals. *Fisherman's pie?* The thought of it made her stomach curdle and she threw it back inside, slamming the freezer door. She slid her phone out of her back pocket and rang the Indian takeaway.

I deserve a treat after the day I've had.

She rubbed at her shoulders, easing out the knots of tension, pulled a bottle of wine from the rack on the worktop and poured herself a glass. She rarely drank on her own, knowing that one glass would lead to another and then the whole bottle would be gone. Alcohol crept up on you like that. But this bottle had been a present from Bea, her favourite Rioja, and the fact it was a present made her feel a little less alone.

She sighed. Poor Bea, she'd run off all upset and Steph

hadn't heard from her since. That was never a good sign. She took the bottle and her glass into the lounge. The gloom outside made a mirror image on the glass, and suddenly she felt all nervous again – the idea that someone might be watching her making her pull the curtains tight. She switched on the TV for a bit of background noise while she waited for her food to arrive, gulping her first glass of wine down far too quickly. She savoured her second glass, as her mood mellowed, her anxiety rubbed smooth.

She settled back on her new sofa and admired the soft grey of the leather, the pleasing contrast with the cushions. It was the first bit of furnishings she'd bought on her own in her entire life, always seeking Andy's opinion in the past before she made a final choice, and she could honestly say she was pleased with her decision. Perhaps she could make a go of this single thing after all.

An eighties band was playing on the TV, a power ballad that had defined her youth. She sang along, allowing herself to bellow out the words, nobody there to hear. It gave her a lovely sense of freedom and when it was finished, she laughed until her head filled with images of her and Andy dancing to the same song when they were dating, when everything had seemed possible. Her laughter soured into sobs, tears rolling down her cheeks, arms wrapped round her chest as she tried to rock the pain away.

The ring of the doorbell made her jerk to attention, remembering her takeaway. She swiped the tears from her cheeks, blew her nose and took a few deep breaths before answering.

But it was Andy who stood on the doorstep.

'I need a set of keys.' His face was locked in that familiar frown that seemed to be his perpetual expression these days, his voice hard. 'You can't lock me out of my own house, you know.'

Back to reality, she thought, wondering why she'd been crying over this idiot of a man only a minute ago. 'You don't live here anymore, though. And after everything that's happened, I don't want to give anyone else the keys.' She thought then about Noah, how he had a set. Then remembered she'd picked them up off the floor, put them in her pocket. She felt in her pocket, glad to find they were still there.

'What?' Andy leaned towards her, studying her face, his hand on the door casing.

Steph edged back. 'Nothing, I just remembered something.'

'You put the phone down on me.'

'Yeah, I did because you were being a dick.'

He gave a frustrated grunt. 'Calling me names isn't going to get us anywhere, is it?' Another grunt. He looked a bit uncomfortable, shifting position, his hand brushing over his hair. His voice softened, his eyes finding hers. 'Look, I meant what I said, you know. I want us to try again. A new start.'

She folded her arms across her chest, her body blocking the doorway. If he thought she was going to be won over that easily, he had seriously misjudged her current state of mind. She took a deep breath.

'I don't think that's going to be possible after everything that's happened.'

He gazed at her, his voice tinged with emotion when he spoke. 'But what *has* actually happened? That's the thing I realised today. It just hit me after you hung up on me. All this is about me thinking you were having an affair and you thinking I was having an affair...'

'You're living with bloody Charlie,' she snapped, spotting the Indian takeaway's delivery scooter pulling up at the kerb. 'I'm not living with another man, am I?'

A door banged upstairs. She almost jumped out of her skin and they both turned and looked.

'That lodger isn't still here, is he?' Andy's expression had clouded, his hands curling into fists. 'After what he did?'

'How do you know what he did?'

'Bea rang me, really upset that you wouldn't see sense and go and stay with her for a few days. She worries about you being on your own.'

Steph's hands gravitated to her hips. 'Oh, just go away, will you? I know your game. Once I'm out of the house, I won't be able to get back in again and you'll have sold it to your mate. I'm not stupid, you know.'

The delivery driver was standing in the drive, obviously uncertain about diving into the middle of a domestic. She beckoned to him to come closer, smiled her thanks as he handed her the bag.

'Sorry, Andy, I need to eat. See you around.' She tried to close the door, but Andy's foot was wedged in the way.

'I moved out,' Andy said, trying to squeeze his body through the gap, while she tried to push the door closed. 'I mean, I'm not staying with Charlie anymore. She got the wrong idea and I'm... I'm not interested. We were never having an affair, it was just somewhere to stay.'

'You expect me to believe that?' She grunted as she pushed against the door.

'I want to come home.'

That took her by surprise and for a moment she was distracted enough for her weight to shift and Andy managed to push his way in. She gave a growl of dismay and stepped away from him, sending him a furious glare so there could be no doubt that she wasn't happy with his intrusion. There was no way she could physically remove him, so she'd just have to let him say his piece, then ask him to leave.

But what if he doesn't?

She could feel her hackles rising, preparing her for a blazing row.

'Is he bothering you?' Noah stood on the stairs, a feral expression on his face that she'd seen the last time he and Andy had met. He was holding a skateboard, swinging it to and fro, looking like he might just fling it at Andy's head.

Before she'd had time to respond, Noah was down the stairs, the door wrenched open. 'I think Steph would like you to leave.' He jabbed the skateboard at Andy, catching him in the ribs, making him double over, yelping in pain. Noah took his opportunity and barged him out of the house, dead-locking the door behind him. He turned with a satisfied grin on his face. 'Sorted him out.'

'What the hell are you doing here?' Steph spluttered, backing away from him, a knot of fear in her chest.

CHAPTER THIRTY-TWO

Noah's smile slid from his face and he put the skateboard down, then held up his hands, just to show he meant her no harm.

'Get away from me,' she hissed, backing down the hallway towards the kitchen where she knew she could arm herself if need be.

He followed her, keeping eye contact, his voice apologetic. 'I know we had a problem today, but if you'll let me explain then I'm hoping you'll understand.' He put his hands together. 'Please, Steph. I'm here to apologise.'

'I don't want your apology,' she snapped. 'I want you to go. Now.' He didn't move. She pointed at the door, her finger waving in the air, betraying the shaking of her body. 'Right now.'

'I will go,' he said, advancing towards her. 'Once you've heard me out. Okay?'

Steph glared at him and marched into the kitchen, the smell of her food making her stomach rumble. She was so hungry she could no longer think, but the idea of eating had little appeal either, her stomach tying itself in knots.

How am I going to get rid of him? Will Andy call the police?

Noah followed her, standing behind her like a shadow, sending a chill through her body. She put the takeaway bag on the worktop and turned to face him.

'Just back off, will you?'

He did as he was told, took a couple of retreating steps, and she had to admit he looked thoroughly dejected. Not like someone who was going to do her harm. *You're doing it again. Wise up, will you?* She thought about the trauma of the day, the nightmare of repeated police questioning, and fire sparked through her body.

'How dare you come in here after what you did to me today?' Her blood was just below boiling point, her voice trembling with rage. 'Telling the police I'm a drug dealer, for Christ's sake? How could you do that to me when all I've done is shown you kindness?'

He gave a big sigh, went and sat at the table, sinking into a chair like his legs had lost all their strength. She stayed standing, the knife block behind her should she feel the need for a weapon.

'Right, this is the God's honest truth, okay?' He made eye contact. 'I owe this guy some money. I told you, didn't I? He sort of conned me into borrowing off him when I was first on the street. Anyway, I was stupid, I fell for it and now I have this debt I can't ever seem to repay. Every time I think I've done the last favour, he turns up with something else.'

Steph watched his face, looking for signs that he was lying. She wasn't going to fall for a sob story. Not again. She had to be convinced he was telling her the truth.

'Anyway, once I settled in here, he started sending me those parcels. Then people were ringing me with orders for drugs and... honestly, Steph, I've never done drugs.' He was emphatic, banging the table to emphasise his point. Steph jumped, surprised by his sudden burst of emotion. 'Never. But I had to sell the bloody stuff. Because if I didn't, I'd get another beating.

And each time I've not done what he's asked, the beatings have got a little bit worse.' His voice cracked. 'And then when you said the police had done a search, I told him it was way too risky, but he said I had to carry on. If the police came round again, I had to tell them the gear belonged to you.'

'So you've no choice but to do what he told you?' Steph's voice was softer now. She'd heard this story before from quite a few people at the shelter, getting themselves trapped into an unpayable debt that turned them into unpaid workers for all sorts of criminal activity. Drug dealing was a common one and she reluctantly conceded that Noah's version of events could be the truth.

'Well, he half killed me last time I went against him. I couldn't not do what he asked, could I? You've got to see that?' His eyes pleaded with her. 'I had no choice.'

She could feel herself wavering. He sounded very convincing, but she caught herself and gave him a steely glare, needing more answers.

'What happened at the police station, then? I hope you told them the truth?' A flash of anger made her fists curl.

He closed his eyes for a moment and when he spoke, he sounded thoroughly defeated. 'I did eventually. But I don't think they believed me. They've let me out while they investigate.' He puffed out his cheeks, picked at a fingernail. 'I was ever so careful getting here. Came round all the back alleys. He doesn't know I'm here. And I came over the back gate so nobody would see me.' His eyes met hers. 'He's pretty scary and... well... I wanted to warn you.'

Goosebumps raised the hairs on her arms. This was all sounding serious now. 'Who is this guy?'

He shrugged. 'I told you, I don't know his name. Nobody seems to. He's ex-forces, all buffed up, you know, works out, likes to throw his weight around. Thing is, he can be so easy to talk to but he's nice one minute, gnarly the next. You just don't know where you are with him. And that's how he likes it.'

'But what if he comes looking for you?' Steph's voice became a terrified squeak as she understood the implications. 'We're both in danger. Don't you see that?'

'I know. I know what you're saying but I think you're missing the point. What I couldn't work out is why he wanted me to point the finger at you? Set you up like that.' He frowned. 'It seemed personal, and it made me wonder... Do you think you might know him?'

Steph leaned back against the worktop, feeling a weight in her chest like a hand had pushed her there. That was a very good question. Could it be... was it possible that the man was Max?

CHAPTER THIRTY-THREE

Everything else was forgotten except the identity of the man who seemed to be behind her troubles. Could all of it be him? Max had a motive, that's for sure.

Steph hurried into the lounge and came back with a photo album, putting it on the table in front of Noah. 'The only person I know in the military is my son, Max.' She flicked through the album to the most recent photos at the back. 'Have a look at some pictures and see if you think it might be him.'

'I should warn you I'm not great at faces,' Noah said, looking worried.

She opened the album on a page with end-of-year pictures from when Max was sixteen and had just finished his GCSEs. He was looking sullen, hating to have his picture taken. His hair was long, a fringe draped over half his face, and she'd have to admit it wasn't the best photo to look for a likeness.

Noah studied the pictures, pulled a face. 'It's hard to tell, really. I think he's got the same shaped face.' He glanced up at Steph, who was standing behind him, peering over his shoulder. 'How old would he be now?'

'Twenty-eight.' She flicked back through the pages to see if there was a better picture, her heart aching at the sight of her troubled young son, hiding from the camera in the same way that he hid from his family. 'I suppose he would have filled out a bit.'

'I'm honestly not sure,' Noah said after a while. 'This guy has his head shaved. Dark blond eyebrows, though, so his hair is probably the same colour. His face is a bit rounder, but like you say, he would have filled out.' He sighed. 'You know, if you looked at pictures of me when I was fifteen and compared them to how I am now, I think you'd have a hard time telling it was the same person.'

Steph closed the album and went to put it away in the lounge. Noah didn't feel like the enemy now. She still wasn't sure how much she wanted to trust him, but she did need to find out whether this man might be Max. There was no hiding from the fact that whoever it was, they were out for revenge and who knew what they might do next.

She went back into the kitchen. 'I think I need to tell the police. That would be the safest thing.'

'They already know. Honestly, I told them everything. I mean, when they catch him, they won't say it's come from me.'

Steph narrowed her eyes, a question popping into her head that had been puzzling her. 'Did you do a deal then? Because I can't see why they'd let you out.'

Noah shrugged but wouldn't look her in the eye. 'You never know... The police might have picked him up by now.'

Steph gazed at him, not sure she could really trust anything he'd said. Cara's warning about Noah bringing trouble to her door loomed large in her thoughts. *Why didn't I listen?* If she talked to the police, they'd help her, wouldn't they?

'Look, I'm pleased you came and told me what's been going on, but I really think... I'm sorry, but I think it would be best if you leave now.'

He nodded, eyes on the floor as he went into the hall and

picked up his skateboard. 'I could keep watch tonight,' he said, a hopeful note to his voice. 'There's a good view from the attic window.'

She steeled herself, determined not to be taken in by him again, however apologetic and doleful he looked. 'You keep breaking into my house, Noah. That is completely out of order. And you've brought so much trouble back here with you, turned my life upside down. I can't let you stay.'

He bowed his head. 'I'll go out the back,' he said, traipsing through the utility room and letting himself out of the back door. She locked it behind him and watched as he climbed over the back gate, reminding herself that she needed to nail her window shut if she was going to be certain he couldn't get back in. He and whoever else wanted to enter her house. A chill ran down her spine, the thought of strangers in her bedroom, but now she was safely locked inside, she didn't want to go out to the shed for the toolbox just yet. She'd wait until she was sure Noah had gone.

She sat at the table, ran a hand through her hair. Had this mystery man been behind everything that had happened to her? Had he been in her house, sat on her bed? She checked the time. It was almost ten. *Too late to ring Bea and ask her to come and pick me up? To tell her she was right?*

Echoes of her daughter's final words before she stomped out reverberated in her head and she grimaced. Maybe the offer of going to stay wasn't there anymore. She pulled out her phone, dialled her number anyway but it went straight to voicemail.

She's still angry with me.

She rang the police. The detectives working her case would be in tomorrow morning, she was told, and they'd be round to take a full statement. In the meantime, it seemed Noah was telling the truth and had told them about the bully he'd mentioned. She was assured they would take her situation seriously and would have a patrol car check by her house at regular intervals during the night.

She sighed as she put down the phone. Did that make her feel better? *Not really*. Her body was shaking, her stomach griping through lack of food; her takeaway gone cold, still in its plastic bag on the worktop. The thought of being in the house on her own brought a flutter of panic to her chest. *It's okay. The police are watching out for you. It'll be fine.* But no amount of reassurance was going to make her feel better.

She rang Bea again, left a long rambling message asking her to call back. Then she heated up her takeaway, just for something to do, rather than really feeling like eating something. There was no chance of sleep while she was in such an agitated state, no point going to bed.

A little while later, the doorbell rang and two officers stood on the doorstep, checking she was okay, telling her to ring if she had any worries at all. They'd be round every hour or so, which was a relief. It was the best she could hope for.

There was no choice but to stay put for tonight and then make peace with Bea in the morning and ask if her offer was still open. Even if Noah's story was nothing more than a fanciful invention, she didn't want to be in the house on her own.

It might be nice to stay with her daughter for a little while, she thought as she went round checking the doors were locked, turning the lights off. And as Bea had said, even when Mark returned, she didn't have to see much of him if she stayed in her suite of rooms.

It felt too dangerous to stay here now.

She woke with a start, coughing in the thick smoke that filled her room, a hand clawing at her shoulder. Someone calling her name. She was hot, sweating.

'Wake up, come on, we've got to get out of here. Come on, Steph. Please. Get up!'

Noah? She wasn't sure if she was dreaming, his muffled cries bouncing around her head.

'Steph, come on.' His hand closed round her arm and he dragged her out of bed, the floor so hot, she could hardly bear for her feet to be on it. 'There's a fire downstairs.' His voice was shrill with fear. 'A fire. We've got to get out.'

She couldn't speak, not quite awake, still wondering if this was a nightmare. Then Noah picked her up and carried her to the door, his face covered with a bandana. She could hear the crackling of flames now, feel the heat surging up the stairs.

Noah struggled through the doorway with her in his arms, her legs banging against the door casing, making her cry out. She wriggled, aware of her thin night clothes. 'Put me down, Noah, I can walk.' Gently, he lowered her to the ground. The smoke curled up the stairs and into her lungs, setting off a coughing fit, her eyes watering so much she could hardly see.

'I think the stairs are still okay. Otherwise we'll have to jump out of the front window.' He glanced at her. 'Put something round your face.' He grabbed a towel from the bathroom, handing it to her.

'My phone.' Before he could stop her, she dashed back into the bedroom and grabbed her phone from the bedside table, the flesh of her feet singeing on the floorboards, like she was walking across hot coals. Thankfully, the landing was cooler and she jumped from foot to foot, while she coughed like she had smoked forty a day all her life.

Noah grabbed her hand, started pulling her down the stairs. 'I've rung the fire brigade,' he said as he tugged her downwards, so fast she struggled to keep her footing. She could see the glow of the fire in the kitchen doorway, the whole room alight. Black smoke billowed from the lounge doorway. The fire had spread in there too.

The hallway was a mass of swirling darkness, smoke stinging her eyes, the heat more intense down here. Their focus was the front door, Noah fumbling with the chain, turning the lock. Then a blast of cold air and the roar of the fire intensified behind her, like the war cry of a dragon catching up on their prey. He yanked her outside, while she coughed and spluttered, feeling like her lungs were going to burst.

The gravel of the pathway stuck to her feet, the pain almost too much to bear and still Noah pulled her forwards until they got to the pavement.

A siren in the distance and then the fire brigade were pulling up outside and she watched from her seat on the garden wall, with a detached curiosity, as they unrolled hoses and went about their business like a well-oiled machine.

Another siren and an ambulance drew up, the paramedics keen to take her and Noah to hospital for a thorough check-up.

She woke from a fitful sleep, drawn by the sound of a voice she recognised.

'Mum, thank God you're okay.' Bea gave her a hug, kissed her cheek, hugged her again. Her face was tear-stained, and she looked like she'd just thrown anything on in her rush to get out of the house. For once she wasn't colour-coordinated, but crumpled and mis-matched, her hair tied back from her face in a ponytail, no make-up. She looked so young and vulnerable.

'How did you know I was here?' Steph smiled, still drowsy with the sedatives she'd been given to help her sleep.

'The hospital rang. I'm down as your next of kin. Remember when you broke your ankle, you gave them my number.'

Emotion clogged Steph's throat. Never had she been more relieved to see her daughter. She held up her arms for another hug and Bea lay next to her on the bed, mother and daughter, cheek to cheek.

'Are you okay?' Bea asked. 'I haven't been able to speak to anyone yet.'

'Just smoke inhalation and some burns to my feet.' She tried to swallow, a searing pain making her wince, every breath making her feel there was a fire still burning in her chest. 'Nothing major.'

'That sounds painful.' Bea hugged her a little tighter. 'Christ, I was so scared when they rang me. A fire. I couldn't believe it, after everything else that's happened.' She kissed her cheek, stroked her hair, tucking it behind her ears. 'You'll have to rest up now, won't you?'

'We could have died,' Steph mumbled. 'I can't understand how it happened. It looked like it started in the kitchen but I didn't even cook anything last night. I had an Indian takeaway after Noah had gone.'

Bea sat up, a look of incredulity shaping her face. 'What? I can't believe you let him back in the house after everything with the police. Mum, what the hell were you thinking?' She gave a gasp, a hand covering her mouth. 'I bet this was his doing. I bet it was. Getting the munchies in the middle of the night and leaving the oven on, or the grill, or a chip pan.'

'No, he wasn't...' She frowned, wondering suddenly how Noah had been there. Then she remembered she hadn't nailed the window shut, had forgotten all about it after her conversation with the police. She remembered falling asleep on the sofa after they'd gone, stumbling up to bed when something on the TV woke her up. Had he been keeping watch outside even though she'd sent him away?

'He saved my life. Another few minutes and we wouldn't have been able to get down the stairs. As it was, the bedroom floor was starting to smoulder. I don't think it would have been long before it went up in flames.'

Bea gave a derisive huff. 'Just because he saved your life, doesn't mean it wasn't his fault.' She leaned forwards, frowning. 'Is he here?'

Before Steph had a chance to answer, Bea jumped off the bed and disappeared. Steph closed her eyes, too exhausted to call her back.

It wasn't Noah's fault, was it?

It hadn't even occurred to her that it might have been, but now Bea had planted that doubt in her mind, she had to consider it. Had the man told him to set the place on fire? Was that why he was so keen to warn her that she was in danger? Given everything that had gone before it seemed entirely possible.

Bea came back looking disgruntled and she sat on the chair next to the bed, her movements sharp, her expression annoyed. 'He's gone, apparently. They dressed a burn on his arm and he discharged himself.'

Steph hadn't the energy to reply. She wondered where he would go now, whether he'd have to go into hiding from the man who'd made him sell the drugs. Then the connection made itself again and it was too strong to ignore.

'Noah told me something...' Bea's eyes held hers and she told her everything she knew and how she thought it might be Max behind all her troubles. How this was revenge for something she'd done, or didn't do all those years ago. 'I never stood up for him. Your brother. I just spent my time trying to placate other parents, apologising for the things he'd done to their child.'

'And me, Mum. Don't forget he made my life a complete misery all the time I was growing up.' Her jaw hardened. 'Years and years.'

Steph sighed. *Where did I go wrong?* One child who was too good to be true and the other the opposite.

'Thank God for daughters,' she said, smiling at Bea, who reached out and held her hand, smiling back.

'Well, I'm going to take you home,' Bea said. 'Once they've got your meds together. Apparently, there are some dressings and a district nurse will come and keep an eye on things for the next week or so, make sure everything's healing. I told them you'd be staying with me because, well, you haven't really got anywhere else to go now your house has burned down.'

Steph really hadn't thought about that. *Now it's me who's homeless.* The irony didn't escape her, reinforcing the fact that trying to help Noah had spectacularly backfired. *Is there anything of the house left?* Horror grabbed her brain and squeezed. She realised now that she'd been so fixated on being independent she hadn't been able to see sense.

'What would I do without you?' she said, squeezing Bea's hand, sure she'd be safe in her gated house, with its high walls, electric fence, and state of the art security system. Nobody would be getting in there in a hurry. And being safe was currently top of Steph's list of priorities.

CHAPTER THIRTY-FOUR

Steph blinked, staring at the ceiling for a moment, unsure where she was. Then she remembered. *I'm at Bea's.* In her very own suite, no less, which Bea had just had redecorated. She couldn't believe it when she'd seen 'The Stephanie Suite' hand-painted on the door, with curlicues and hummingbirds surrounding it. A living room, bedroom and bathroom all to herself and bifold doors opening onto a private patio.

'Mum, you're awake.' Bea's voice made her turn her head to see her daughter in the doorway, holding a tray. 'Perfect timing. I've made you breakfast.'

She heaved herself up to a sitting position, so that Bea could set up the tray on the bed, folding out its little legs so it sat sturdily on top of the covers. Bea took her bowl of cereal and mug of coffee and settled herself in the velvet chair which sat next to the bed, curling her feet under her as she snuggled into the cushions. One with 'Mum' embroidered on it in gold, the other with 'Bea'. A matching pair.

Steph shuffled in the bed, bleary-eyed and not quite awake, trying to focus on the contents of the tray.

'I didn't know where I was for a moment.' She winced. 'Ow, my feet are sore.'

'You poor thing. You have burns on the soles.' She put her breakfast on the set of drawers next to her and jumped up. 'I'll just go and get your painkillers.' She adjusted the tray, beamed at her mum. 'Here you go, all your favourite things for breakfast.'

Steph smiled at her, trying to hide the fact that the smell of food was making her feel nauseous. 'That's a lovely thought, sweetheart, but I hope you won't be offended if I don't eat it all? My stomach's feeling a bit weird this morning.'

She glanced up at Bea, saw disappointment in her face.

'It looks delicious, though. So thoughtful of you.' Steph's eyes scanned the room, sliding past the new sofa, on towards the curtains and back again. She frowned. 'That sofa's just like mine. And the cushions. Oh, and the curtains too.'

Bea laughed. 'I know. I thought it would make you feel at home. Once I finally persuaded you to come and visit your daughter.' She patted her leg. 'Anyway, you tuck in while it's hot and I'll go and get those painkillers.'

Steph picked up her fork and speared a mushroom, giving it a dubious look before popping it into her mouth, not sure if she was going to be able to swallow anything. Her throat felt like it had been sandpapered. It was juicy, succulent and very tasty.

Bea nodded her encouragement. 'Nice?'

'Lovely.' She licked her lips, eating another one before picking up her knife and cutting off a sliver of bacon.

Bea waited. 'It's local bacon, oak-smoked from hand-reared organic pigs. As succulent as you like.'

Steph chewed. Bea was right. 'Very tasty, but I thought this was a vegetarian household?'

'Oh, you know Mark is, and I am when he's here, but when he's away I can eat what I like.' She giggled. 'Don't tell him, will you?' Then her expression changed, her smile fading, and she hurried out of the room.

Steph gave a sigh of relief and spat the bacon out into a tissue, thoughtfully provided in a box by the bed. Her throat was so sore she just couldn't seem to swallow it. She tried some beans, but they stung like crazy. The scrambled eggs went down okay, though, and she finished the rest of the mushrooms, but that was all she could manage. She pushed the tray away, most of the food left uneaten, and nursed her mug of coffee against her chest, the warmth of it soothing her singed lungs.

A little while later, Bea came back in, with a glass of water. She glanced at the uneaten food. 'Oh no. You didn't like it?' The look of disappointment was replaced a second later with a bright smile. 'Never mind. I suppose you've had a nasty shock. And all that smoke inhalation won't have helped.'

'It was a lovely thought and I really do appreciate it, but my throat is ever so sore,' Steph said, apologetically. 'I ate all the squishy things that didn't sting.'

She noticed Bea's bottom lip trembling, saw how she nipped it with her teeth, making Steph feel really bad for not managing more of the meal.

'How's the coffee?'

'Oh, this is lovely.' Steph took a sip. 'Just what I needed.'

'It's from Betty's. You know, the coffee shop we go to in Harrogate. You always choose this blend, so I knew you'd like it.'

Bea handed her a couple of tablets with a glass of water. 'These will take the pain away.'

Steph frowned. 'To be honest, I'm not really in too much pain. I mean, my feet are sore, but I'm sure they'll be fine.' She put the medication and water on the tray, picked up her coffee again. 'You know I'm not one for taking painkillers. Not unless I really have to.'

'The nurse said it would get worse before it got better.' Bea pulled a sympathetic face. She picked up the medication and handed it back to Steph, cocked her head to one side. 'Be a good patient.'

Steph clutched her mug a little tighter. 'You know I don't really trust medication. Not after your nan died. I'm sure all the medication she was taking reacted to each other.'

'You don't know that,' Bea pointed out, patiently. 'It's just a theory. Your theory.'

'I researched it,' Steph said, firmly, determined she wasn't taking any tablets unless she absolutely had to. At the moment the pain was bearable. Just a dull throbbing.

Bea shrugged. 'Okay. No problem, but they're there if you need them.' She smiled and sat on the chair next to the bed with her own mug of coffee, and they enjoyed a few minutes of companiable silence. She reached for Steph's hand and held it in her own. 'I'll look after you, Mum. Don't you worry.'

'I'm sure you will, sweetheart, but I've so much to sort out. I can't really be here for too long.' She let go of Bea's hand and tried to throw back the covers. 'There's the insurance to ring, and I have to tell Bill at work what's going on and—'

'Mum, stop it.' Bea grabbed her hand and put the covers back in place. 'You've no need to worry about anything.' She gave her hand a reassuring pat before letting go. 'I've already done all that while you've been asleep. Honestly, Bill says to rest and recuperate. No rush to get back to work until you're ready. And the insurance company are sending a claim form.'

Steph allowed herself to relax back on her pillows, closed her eyes while Bea tidied away the tray, relieved that at least those jobs had been done.

'You have a lovely rest, Mum, and I'll be back soon.'

She opened her eyes, caught Bea's gaze. There was a glow about her, a little satisfied smile playing on her lips, and it made Steph wonder how everything could be good in Bea's world, while hers was falling apart.

CHAPTER THIRTY-FIVE

Steph dozed off, blinking awake a while later, no idea what time it was. Even though Bea had sorted out some of her problems, there were things still preying on her mind. Like how did the fire start? Although she knew she was safe now and Bea was taking care of everything, she felt distinctly uneasy.

There was a lingering smell of smoke in her hair and on her skin. It had been the early hours of the morning when they'd arrived at Bea's and she'd been so exhausted, she'd just crawled into bed. Now the acrid aroma kept taking her thoughts back to the horrifying events of the night before. The crackling of the fire, the overpowering heat, her heart hammering so fast she thought it might stop.

Noah saved my life.

She needed to find him, make sure he was okay. Talk to the police about this shadowy character he'd mentioned, his theory that this man was behind everything. Then there was the awful possibility that man might be her son. Her heart ached at the thought, but she couldn't shake it. How terrible would that be, if Max had been the one who'd set the house on fire? Because somebody had. She was sure of it.

Does Andy know? She wasn't sure if Bea had told him, or if the police would. Her head was full to bursting with things she should be doing, people she needed to speak to and she felt twitchy and restless in this pristine room.

Bea's got it all under control. She took a few deep breaths, tried to calm down. *There's nothing to worry about. You're creating problems where there aren't any.*

She tried to make herself relax but lying in bed had never been her thing. She was a morning person, up and about as soon as she woke up. Even if she had been through a traumatic time of it, she couldn't lie in bed. There were people she needed to speak to, things to organise. She looked round for her phone, but couldn't see it anywhere. Then realised Bea must have it because she knew she'd taken it with her to the hospital.

She decided to get up and go and find her daughter, knowing that she'd feel better if she was busy doing something useful, getting rid of at least some of the worries on her list.

Her feet were throbbing a bit, but not too bad. She swung them onto the floor, bent and undid the bandages so she could inspect the damage. The soles were a livid red but there were no blisters, so that was good. At least she'd be able to walk. She rested her feet on the tiled floor, revelling in the coolness, wriggling her toes. That actually felt lovely.

The door opened and Bea walked in, a bowl in her hand. 'I brought you some yoghurt. I thought it would be nice and cooling for your throat.' She frowned. 'What are you doing? Come on, get back in bed.' She came over and started fussing with the covers. 'Rest is what you need.'

'I was going to the loo.'

'Oh right, of course.' Bea put the bowl on the bedside table. 'Can I help you?' Before she could answer, Bea had heaved her upright, an arm round her waist for support.

Steph laughed. 'I'm not an invalid, you know. And my feet

aren't as bad as I'd feared. I'm sure they'll feel much better by tomorrow. And I'm not one to stay in bed, am I?'

'Apparently singed skin can tear very easily, then go septic,' Bea said, her matter-of-fact tone making Steph take note. *Septic?* She hadn't thought about that.

'Well, I'll make sure I'm careful then.' She headed towards the en suite.

'The nurse told me all about it,' Bea continued, concern in her voice. 'She said I had to keep you in bed for at least a couple of days.' She sounded very officious, like she wasn't going to go against medical advice in a hurry and Steph's heart sank.

'Okay, love, I'm sure you're right. I promise I'll do lots of sitting down, okay? But I can't stay in bed. Really, I can't.' She looked longingly at the bathroom door. 'And right now, I really need to get to the toilet.'

Bea walked her into the en suite and stood with her while Steph looked at the loo. 'Do you need any help?'

'No!' Steph knew she sounded horrified, softened her tone. 'I'll be fine, love.' She shooed her away.

'I'll be right here if you need me,' Bea called, standing on the other side of the door.

Steph turned the lock, the idea of her daughter helping her to toilet too embarrassing to contemplate. She wasn't quite at that stage yet. The en suite had a walk-in shower and she turned it on while she had a pee, sure that Bea was listening.

'I'm going to have a shower,' she called, pulling off the pyjamas Bea had given her to wear. She realised then that they were a replica of a pair she had at home. The door handle turned, the fitting rattled. 'I'm absolutely fine,' she called, hoping Bea wasn't going to somehow find her way in.

The shower was amazing, a stainless-steel rainfall fitting that bathed her in steaming water; the organic shower gel smelled of honeysuckle, her favourite, and the shampoo was the same. Hopefully, she'd feel a bit more relaxed once the awful smell had gone and she felt clean again.

Ten minutes later, she emerged wrapped in the luxurious bath sheet, feeling thoroughly cleansed, as she shuffled over the tiled floor. Given the soreness of her feet, she wouldn't be doing much walking today, but she'd no intention of staying in bed as Bea had suggested. Her daughter was sitting in the chair by the bed, which had been tidied. Laid on top of the covers was an outfit. Bea was looking very pleased with herself and Steph did a double take. She hadn't thought about what she was going to wear, forgetting that she'd gone to hospital in pyjamas. 'Oh, new clothes! How on earth...?'

'I bought them for you a couple of weeks ago and forgot to give them to you,' Bea smiled. 'Saw them in Superdry and I know their stuff fits you so well. Just your colours too.'

She was right, it was exactly what Steph would have chosen for lounging about the house – comfy joggers and a pretty top. In fact, she thought she might already own a similar outfit.

'And underwear.'

'In the sale.' Bea grinned. 'I was buying some for myself.'

'Since when have you worn M&S bras and knickers?'

Bea shrugged. 'Doesn't everyone?'

Steph laughed, wondering why that uneasy feeling had settled in her stomach again. She took the clothes into the bathroom and dressed quickly. No socks, she noticed. Or shoes for that matter. But she was sure Bea would have something she could use for now, as their feet were the same size.

When she emerged, Bea held up some fluffy slippers. 'I got these for you too. They'll be lovely and soft on your poor feet.'

Steph's smile froze on her face. *Is this just a little too much?* And it seemed a strange coincidence that she had a whole new set of clothes for her. *Bea thinks ahead.* That was true. *She's always been that sort of person.* Reassured, she put the slippers on.

Bea leaned over and held up the bowl she'd brought in. 'Come and eat the yoghurt,' she said.

Steph looked at the gloop in the bowl and her stomach lurched. She shook her head. 'I'm fine for now, honestly I'm really not that hungry and I did have some eggs and mushrooms before, so...' She watched Bea's smile slide from her face and felt a pang of guilt. Bea was trying so hard. She took the bowl from her outstretched hand. 'But my throat feels like it's been sandblasted and you're right, it might help.'

She sat on the bed, taking tiny spoonfuls, forcing herself to swallow. The texture was a bit gritty, making her feel like she might gag and after she'd managed half a bowl, she put it back on the tray.

'Lovely, thank you.'

Bea frowned. 'You haven't eaten it all. Didn't you like it?' She sounded so disappointed Steph almost picked up the bowl again, but the thought of it made her feel sick, and she knew she couldn't eat another mouthful. 'I could put some fruit in or—'

'Honestly, love. I'm feeling nauseous. I can't face any more.' She gave a feeble smile. 'Maybe later?'

Bea sighed and nodded. 'Okay. Just doing my best to look after you.'

'You're doing a wonderful job,' Steph gushed, 'and I really appreciate it.'

Bea nodded, her eyes glistening like she might burst into tears. Steph looked at the bowl again but knew that she couldn't physically eat any more. Hopefully Bea would forget about it. Her list of things to do marched into her head and she looked around for her bag, then realised she'd left it in the house.

'I need to ring your dad, love. I don't suppose you know where I put my phone, do you?' Her gaze travelled round all the flat surfaces in the room, just in case she'd overlooked it, but she couldn't see it anywhere.

Bea frowned. 'Your phone? I don't think you had it with

you. When I picked you up, you were in your pyjamas and that was it. Do you think you left it in the house?'

Steph shook her head. 'I definitely had it with me. In fact, I burned my feet going back to pick it up.'

Bea shrugged. 'Maybe you left it in hospital? Shall I ring for you?' She was up and out of the room before Steph could stop her, the door closing behind her with a loud clunk.

The silence was welcome, and Steph gazed around the room while her mind took her back to the night before. Flames licking the kitchen doorway, black smoke billowing from the lounge, Noah's hand grasping hers so tightly, pulling her to safety. That blast of cold air when he'd finally opened the front door, the roar of the fire chasing them outside. She tasted salt, only then realising that tears were rolling down her cheeks.

She didn't want to be on her own with her thoughts, that terrifying feeling that she could have been burned alive. She hobbled to the door, staring at it when she worked out there was no door handle. Nothing to push or pull that she could see. *How on earth do you get out of here?* She tutted, cursing Mark and his fascination with all things electronic. This house had a mind of its own, regulating air quality and temperature, responding to commands to switch things on and off. It wasn't her cup of tea at all. There seemed to be what looked like a control panel to the side of the door, but she had no idea how it was supposed to work.

Her eyelids were heavy now, and she felt a little woozy, like she might fall over. She staggered back to the bed and sat down just as her knees buckled. *How strange*. She blinked, fighting to stay awake, but she was too tired, exhaustion pulling her down onto the bed. Her body toppled backwards onto the covers and her world faded to black.

CHAPTER THIRTY-SIX

After leaving the hospital and checking what was happening at the house, Noah had spent the rest of the night in the park, hiding in the bushes. He didn't think anyone would find him there.

He'd spent hours going over and over what had happened in his head, but it still made no sense. Even though Steph had asked him to leave, he couldn't in all conscience do that. He felt a responsibility towards her, knew it was his fault that she'd been put in such a difficult position with the police. All she'd ever done was be nice to him, compassionate, and he wanted to repay that kindness in some way. Or at least atone for the trouble he'd caused.

He decided he'd keep watch from outside, do his own mini patrols, not trusting the police to come by often enough to stop any trouble. Mind you, he wasn't sure what he'd do if the guy turned up. The boss, that's what the other lads called him and in truth that's exactly what he was. He was definitely the boss of Noah at the moment. Or he had been. But all that was going to change. His plan was to take pictures for evidence and call the police. He'd have no chance of squaring up to him by himself.

He'd found a good spot behind the hedge in the garden next door, hidden from sight by the wheelie bin. At some point, though, he'd nodded off, waking when he heard the crash of the kitchen window blowing out. He'd been instantly awake, the smell of smoke drifting into his nostrils and he'd dashed round to find the kitchen on fire. He'd been able to get through the broken window, although his arm had been singed by the flames. He didn't really notice it at the time, his focus on getting Steph out of harm's way. No smoke alarm had gone off, which puzzled him now because they were dotted all over the house. Surely the batteries couldn't have run out in all of them?

Once he was at the top of the stairs, he rang the emergency services to ask for the fire brigade, but apparently they'd already been notified. Another puzzle. Although it could have been a neighbour.

When he'd pushed Steph outside, from the corner of his eye, he'd noticed a car pull away from the kerb. A car he thought he recognised. It had been there before, outside the house, but he couldn't quite work out who it belonged to. Was it Steph's husband? He remembered the first time he'd been to the house. The husband and daughter had turned up. The car belonged to one of them, he was sure of it. So why would it drive off? Or was he making two and two add up to five?

His head was aching now and he couldn't think about it any longer. He looked round for his bag, then remembered he'd left it in the attic bedroom, no time to grab it when Steph told him she wanted him to go.

He made his way to the house, skirting round bushes and trees, constantly checking over his shoulder to ensure that he wasn't being followed. The fire was completely out now, although the acrid smell of smoke still hung in the air. The lounge window had gone, and he could see inside, the blackened tatters of curtains flapping in the breeze, nothing in there but the charred skeleton of a room, the metal frame of the sofa.

Three men huddled by the front door, high-vis jackets stating they were fire investigators. He walked over to them, stopping when he was challenged. 'You can't come any closer.' A man walked towards him, his hand out in front of him as if that would be enough to stop Noah getting past if he wanted to. 'This is an investigation scene.'

'I live here,' Noah said. 'In the attic room.'

'Oh, okay, right. What's your name, lad?'

'Jason Bourne.' It came out before he could think about it. His go-to alias.

The man started writing it in his notebook, then looked up, frowning. 'Yeah, right. You taking the piss?'

Noah shook his head, tried to look innocent, like he didn't know what the man was implying. He hadn't meant to give a false name, but it was force of habit with people in authority. A bad mistake. He wanted information and starting with a lie wasn't going to help.

'My mum was a big fan of the films.' He shrugged, toughing it out. 'I get that all the time.'

The man stared at him for a moment, then finished writing.

'How long have you lived here?'

'Just a few weeks.'

'Can you tell me what happened?'

Noah took a deep breath, and decided he really needed to tell the truth now. Lies wouldn't help Steph, wouldn't help the authorities sort out exactly what had happened and who was to blame. He told the investigator everything he remembered about the previous evening. Being asked to leave. Waking up and smelling smoke, the sound of breaking glass, knowing something was wrong.

'I got my landlady out. Then the fire brigade turned up and

we went to hospital in the ambulance.' He held up his hands. 'That's it. That's all I know.'

The man looked him up and down, Noah conscious of his singed clothes, his face blackened with soot, the bandage on his arm. 'And now you're back here. Nowhere else to go?'

He shook his head, the weight of his situation pressing down on him. 'I was homeless before my landlady took me in. She works at the homeless shelter.' He sighed. 'Looks like I'm back on the streets again.'

'I'm sorry to hear that.' The man looked at his notebook, clearly unsure what to say.

'I wanted to see what caused the fire.' Noah frowned. 'It seemed to have started in the kitchen.'

'You're not wrong. You weren't cooking chips, were you?'

'My landlady had a takeaway. I didn't eat. As far as I'm aware, nobody was cooking anything.'

The man nodded, looked thoughtful. 'Will you just wait there for a moment please?'

He went and spoke to the other fire investigators while Noah went and sat on the wall. He felt grubby and sore, the burn on his arm throbbing. The only thing he'd managed to save was his phone, which lived in his back pocket. Not that it was much use to him without any credit. He had no idea what to do next, no idea at all.

The men came over as a group to talk to him and he went through his story again while they asked questions about timings and exactly what he'd seen and heard.

'Did somebody do this? Was it arson?' he asked eventually.

Nobody answered, the men looking at each other. 'We believe it started with a chip pan,' the investigator said. 'But I can't tell you any more than that, except to say that the police will be involved.' He looked around the group, then back at Noah, wagged a finger at him. 'And you didn't hear that from me.'

Noah nodded and stood up, ready to leave.

'Can we give you a lift somewhere?' the man who'd been taking notes said. 'We're just about finished here.' His eyes were full of concern. 'I'm really sorry you've lost your place to stay, but I'll take you wherever you need to go.' He shrugged. 'The homeless shelter? A friend's house?'

Noah thought for a moment.

'I don't suppose you could help me find my landlady, could you? I want to make sure she's okay.'

The man smiled. 'No problem. I need to speak to her anyway. She's not answering her phone, so she's probably still at the hospital. I couldn't get an answer from the switchboard. Probably easier to just turn up then they have to deal with you.' He went and had a word with his work colleagues, then led Noah to his car. 'We'll go and get something to eat first, shall we?'

Noah hesitated before getting in. Should he just leave now? Leave all this behind him, move on to somewhere new, where nobody knew him. He bit his lip, torn now about what to do.

'In you get,' the man said, holding the door open.

Noah lowered himself into the passenger seat, sweat beading on his brow. Was he walking himself into trouble?

It's the right thing to do. And it was time he made some big changes to his life. Time he fought back against the boss, who'd conned him into trouble, who'd made him a criminal. He had to know Steph was okay, had to apologise, because at the back of his mind was the idea that this was all his fault.

CHAPTER THIRTY-SEVEN

Steph woke to find Bea sitting in the chair by the bed, gazing at her. She groaned, a foul taste in her mouth, her head feeling like it was being squeezed in a vice.

'Hello, sleepyhead,' Bea said. 'I thought you were never going to wake up.'

'What time is it?' Steph yawned, her body feeling like it didn't quite belong to her.

'Well, you've missed lunch and it's nearly teatime.'

Steph struggled to a sitting position, rubbing at her eyes. 'But there's so much I've got to do.' She frowned, remembering getting dressed and then what? How did she end up back on the bed? 'I was coming to look for you earlier but... I couldn't get out of the damned room. Honestly, Bea, don't you think Mark has taken this high-tech stuff a bit too far?'

Bea smiled. 'You don't really need to go anywhere today, though. The doctor said to rest, remember?'

'Yes, I know, but...' Steph picked up the glass of water by the bed and took a sip, wincing when she swallowed, her throat feeling raw. 'Anyway, did you find my phone?'

Bea held up her hands, gave her an apologetic look. 'I'm

sorry, but no. It's not in the house, or in the car. I rang the hospital, and they had a look, but it's not there either.' She raised an eyebrow. 'Are you sure you brought it out of the house? Might it have fallen into the fire?'

Steph considered that. It was possible, she supposed. But then she had an image of it on the top of the cabinet next to the hospital bed and could picture herself picking it up. 'I brought it here. I definitely did.' She gave a frustrated huff. 'I've got to ring—'

Bea put a hand on her arm. 'No, Mum, you don't have to ring anyone. I've done it all for you while you were asleep. Dad was very relieved. Cara sends her best wishes and the insurance company emailed a claim form, which I filled in and sent back.' She smiled. 'I hope you don't mind. I thought there would be less things for you to worry about if I just got on and did it.'

Steph closed her eyes, relaxed back on her pillows. Bea was so efficient it put her to shame. But it was nice not to have to worry. Maybe she should just let go a little and allow Bea to look after her for today. Tomorrow would be different, she was sure. Tomorrow she could decide what she was going to do next, sort out all those other problems which she couldn't quite remember now.

The next morning she woke late, feeling groggy, a headache throbbing at her temples. She'd slept like the dead, which she hadn't done for years. Her eyes blinked open, but the lids were so heavy with sleep it was quite a struggle to keep herself awake.

She turned on her side, startled when she saw Bea sitting in the same chair, watching her.

He heart skipped. 'Christ, you nearly gave me a heart attack.'

Bea laughed. 'Just checking you're okay. You had a fever last night and I was worried you might have an infection. In your lungs or something. Smoke inhalation can do crazy things to your body.' She pulled a face. 'I made the mistake of googling it.'

Steph put a hand to her forehead, satisfied that she didn't have a fever now. Today would not be spent in bed and she sat up, swinging her legs to the floor. What she needed to do was find out who had set her house on fire. Speak to the police, the fire service, find out what they'd discovered. Tell them about the man who'd set her up as a drug dealer, the one who had Noah in his pay. Her heart started to race, panic fluttering in her chest. *You're safe here.* She took a deep breath, telling herself to calm down.

'Can we have breakfast in that lovely conservatory of yours?' she asked, determined not to be stuck in her room again. 'I love the way you've designed it.' Then she'd have access to the house phone. There'd be no excuses, no fobbing her off.

Bea beamed at her. 'What a lovely idea.'

Steph pushed her feet into her new slippers, wincing a little and stood up, feeling a little wobbly. 'I'm starving.' And she was, after hardly eating anything the day before, except the bowls of cooling yoghurt, with that mystery gritty ingredient – probably some weird health food. Bea's cupboards were full of stuff she'd never heard of, with supposedly magical health-giving properties. Mark was very keen on all that, he even had his own nutritionist to do meal plans for them.

Bea linked her arm through Steph's and guided her out of the bedroom like she was a geriatric, but to be fair, she was hobbling along like she was ninety and needed a hip replacement. Walking was more painful than she'd thought it would be, even with the padding of the slippers. By the time they reached the conservatory, which extended into the garden from the kitchen, she was more than ready to sit down.

She sank into a leather recliner, Bea pressing a hidden button, so her feet were up, tucking a fleecy blanket over her. She beamed. 'Comfy?'

Steph returned the smile, nodded. 'Thanks, love. What a gorgeous garden you have. So private with the walls.' She frowned. 'In fact, is that wire fence round the top new? I don't remember it.'

Bea flapped a hand. 'Personally, I think it's a bit ugly, but Mark insisted after someone managed to get over the wall and stole all the koi carp from the pond.' She sighed. 'Can you believe that? Honestly, him and his fish. He was daft about them. Can't see the attraction myself but he used to go out and talk to the bloody things. Anyway, his security advisor recommended an electric fence, so that's what we've got.' She laughed. 'You'd be fried if you tried getting over that.' She scanned the garden. 'Thankfully nobody has given it a go yet.'

Steph swallowed. It seemed extreme, in this country setting, but Mark did have a lot of money and she supposed that in itself would attract criminals.

'When did you say Mark would be back?' she asked, hardly believing that she was actually hoping he might return sooner rather than later. 'He's been away for a lot longer than normal this time, hasn't he?' Once he was home, Bea's attention would be divided and not quite so oppressive. She just felt that her daughter was watching her the whole time and it was... unnerving. Too much. She'd always been a bit like that, even as a child, very intense in one-to-one situations. Of course with two children, and Max being a troubled soul, Steph had often had other things to deal with. Andy had been the one to take Bea out and entertain her.

Bea's face went blank for a moment, her gaze fixed on the garden, the lily pond where she supposed the fish used to be. 'Well, these negotiations take a while, you know. He's not sure exactly when he'll get home.'

She started banging the coffee grounds out of her fancy Italian machine with more force than was strictly necessary. Steph winced, the sound jarring. There was something weird going on. *Have they had a falling-out?* There'd been no mention of discord, apart from the issue with Bea wanting a baby and Mark never being home. Surely Bea would have said something if there was a problem? But then Steph had been consumed by her own broken marriage and would have to admit that she hadn't really been focused on her daughter.

She felt guilty about that now.

'I'm sorry to hear that. I know you miss him. Hopefully he'll be back soon.'

Bea laughed, high pitched and brittle. 'Oh, I very much doubt it.' Steph watched her daughter as she measured out the coffee grounds, set the machine going, pouring milk into a metal jug, making it frothy, just like an expert barista. She was definitely a little off kilter today, her response suggesting that there was something amiss between her and Mark.

Bea brought the coffee over along with some croissants and a bowl of yoghurt for breakfast.

'Tuck in,' she said, watching intently as Steph picked up the yoghurt, then put it down again, in favour of a croissant.

She grimaced. 'You know, I'm not a big yoghurt fan. I think I'll give that a miss.' She bit into a croissant, all soft and buttery and warm. She smiled at Bea. 'Delicious.'

Bea scowled. 'Yoghurt's very healing for burns to the throat. That's why I've been giving it to you.' She pushed the bowl towards Steph, gave a tight smile. 'Think of it as medicine.'

Steph shook her head. 'I'm sorry, love. Just the thought of it is making me feel sick and anyway, my throat is feeling a lot better today.'

'Well, that's good.' Bea didn't sound like she thought it was good at all. Then her eyes lit up. 'I know, I'll make you a smoothie. You really enjoyed that last time you were here, didn't you?' She was on her feet before Steph could reply, pulling ingredients out of the fridge. 'My super healing mix. You'll love it.'

Steph watched as she emptied fruit and seeds and goodness knows what else into her blender. She gave an involuntary shudder, wondering if the gritty yoghurt would have been a better option. Last time, Bea had put all sorts of seeds into the mix, and she'd been picking them out of her teeth for hours afterwards, a sour taste in her mouth that had lasted all day. She had felt energised, though. *Treat it like medicine.*

Bea handed her a purple frothy mix and Steph closed her eyes, downed it in one, managing to suppress the grimace at the end. She smiled at Bea, handed her the glass. 'Thank you, love. Let's hope it works. I'm feeling so sluggish today, I don't know what's got into me.'

Bea sat back down, took Steph's hand and started inspecting her nails. 'I can give you a manicure if you like. Put some acrylics on. You've been biting your nails again, haven't you?'

Steph slid her hand back from her daughter's grasp, and picked up the remains of her her croissant. 'Maybe later.' She took a bite, glad to have the buttery taste to take away the sour flavour of the smoothie. It was time to change the subject, otherwise she'd have her daughter giving her a full makeover, like she was some sort of toy to play with. She wondered again about Bea's earlier response to her question about her husband.

'So tell me... Has something happened with you and Mark? Is there... a problem?'

Bea's eyes gleamed with a sheen of tears. 'He's gone. And, well...' She sighed, her voice no more than a whisper, 'he's not coming back.'

CHAPTER THIRTY-EIGHT

Steph choked on her croissant, eyes watering as she fought for breath.

Bea jumped up and started thumping her on the back. 'Christ, Mum, we can't have you dying on a bloody pastry. Not when I've got your full attention for the first time in my life.'

Finally, the piece of pastry dislodged, and Steph sank back into her seat, chest heaving, her brain reeling from this new revelation.

'Mark's left you?' She opened her mouth, closed it again, lost for words. Something so big, so momentous and she hadn't known. 'Oh, love, and you've been so supportive of me and your dad since we split up and here you are dealing with the same thing all on your own.' She reached over and rubbed Bea's shoulder. 'When did he go?'

Bea pursed her lips, looked out at the garden again. 'Oh, it was a few days ago.'

'I can't believe you didn't tell me.'

'Well, there's been so much going on in your life, I really didn't want to burden you with my problems as well.' She lifted a shoulder in a half-hearted shrug, her face drawn down by sadness. 'I didn't think you'd be interested.'

Steph gasped, appalled that her daughter would think such a thing. 'But of course I'm interested! Oh, love, you poor thing, this is terrible.'

Bea wiped a tear from her cheek, gave a watery smile. 'Not that terrible. We got married too young and I don't think I shaped up to be the woman he wanted me to be.' She gave another sigh and dabbed at the crumbs on her plate with her index finger, popped them in her mouth. 'I always felt like I was a disappointment, really. I couldn't measure up to the people he wanted to socialise with.' Her voice had an edge of bitterness. 'I mean, those people live in another universe compared to me.' Another shrug. 'We wanted different things.' She smoothed the baby blue joggers she was wearing and gave a wry smile, the tears gone now. 'Every cloud has a silver lining. At least I don't have to deal with them now. Or him.' Her smile warmed and she reached over and caught her mum's hand. 'You can stay here with me. You and me, Mum, making new lives together. At least we have each other.' Her smile widened. 'It'll be fun, won't it?'

Bea's eyes were lit with a fervent gleam.

Does she mean she wants me to live here permanently? The idea struck horror into Steph's heart. She wanted to say something that would make Bea feel better, but a future living with her daughter would never work. They were so different, and Bea could be very intense, demanding her full attention.

It was something Steph had always struggled with because she liked her own space, enjoyed a bit of quiet time. Bea was wonderful in short, finite doses, but sharing a house, well... that had been a tricky balancing act when she was young, let alone a confident adult. Steph felt she would disappear, all the progress she'd made learning to be herself, living on her own, would be lost. Her life wouldn't belong to her anymore, it would be Bea's.

'We can go on holidays. You don't even need to work, Mum. Not anymore. Mark's loaded.'

Steph blew out her cheeks, panicking, her heart starting to race. 'Honestly, love, I'm really finding this hard to get my head around. I mean, if you don't mind talking about it... What exactly happened?'

'He decided he liked Europe better than living here and I didn't want to go. He came back home, told me his plans, we had a major row and he left for good. He said he was going up to Scotland first to clear his head, then he had a villa sorted out in Spain.' Bea's face changed then, and Steph didn't think she could probe any further. Perhaps she'd get more out of her later, but now she sensed the conversation needed to move on. It didn't really matter how they broke up. What mattered was that it was over and there were things that had to be sorted out.

'So... you're getting divorced?'

'Oh, we're not going to bother with that. Can't be wasting all that money on legal fees.'

'But what about the house? And sharing out money? You'll need legal support to get a proper agreement, won't you?' She winced when she'd said it, wondering if she was being insensitive, but her practical brain had formed the words before she could think about it.

'You don't have to worry about any of that. I get to keep everything we have in the UK. It's simple that way.' She beamed at Steph. 'I'm bloody loaded, Mum. Fancy that, eh? Like I said, no need to work. We can spend our time enjoying ourselves. Travelling the world. I've always wanted to go to Australia, see kangaroos in the wild, explore the Great Barrier Reef. So many things that Mark didn't want to do.' She clapped her hands together, excited. 'He can't stop me now, can he?'

Steph took a sip of her coffee, avoiding her daughter's eye. Something about this seemed a bit off. Sudden. *Is she traumatised? In shock?* It felt like she hadn't really come to terms with the reality of her husband's abandonment. 'No, love,' she said, deciding she'd explore the difficult terrain of Bea's emotions another time. 'I don't suppose he can.'

Bea chattered on about all the things she could do, how she was going to invest her fortune. The cottage she had rented in Cornwall where they could spend the rest of the summer, the assumption being that her mum was going to be permanently at her side.

Steph started to feel a little woozy, her head spinning.

'Shall we go and sit outside?' she suggested, the early greyness having cleared into beautiful sunshine. Before Bea could answer, she got up and went to the conservatory doors, which opened out onto a patio. She seemed to remember the whole pane of glass slid into the wall, with some opening mechanism she couldn't work out. Frustrated, she turned to Bea. 'How the hell do you open doors in this flippin' house?'

Bea tapped her watch. 'You need one of these.' She walked over and swiped her watch over a glass tile by the door and it slid open. 'Abracadabra! Cool or what?'

'Very cool,' Steph said, hoping Bea could detect the note of concern in her voice. If she didn't have one of those watches, did that mean she couldn't get in or out on her own? The house, with its high walls and electric fence and electronic door locks, was beginning to feel as oppressive as her daughter's plans for their future.

They sat on the patio, Bea continuing to chatter about her plans while Steph wondered how on earth she was ever going to leave and live her own life, rather than the one her daughter had lined up for her. She had no phone, had been unable to see a landline anywhere and couldn't even get out of the house without Bea being with her.

I feel like a prisoner.

The thought made her catch her breath. She told herself off for thinking like that. Surely this was a temporary situation, just a few days while she recovered and then the insurance company would provide temporary accommodation while her own house was sorted out. She let out a deep breath, wondering how on earth she was going to break it to her daughter that she wanted to leave. That Bea's future wasn't her future. Knowing that she was coping with the sudden breakdown of her marriage did shine a different light on the situation though, making it so much harder. She'd have to wait for the right moment.

'We'll always be together now. So much lost time to make up for.' Bea folded her arms across her chest, looking serious. 'I know we've had this conversation many times, but you spent way too much time fussing over Max when we were kids and completely ignoring me. Even though I got the best grades at school, was captain of the netball team, head girl, all of that and you really didn't seem to take much notice.'

Steph groaned inwardly, wondering how their conversation had come to this old chestnut. Not sure she was up to it. 'Oh, Bea. Of course I noticed, you know I did. When did I ever miss a parents' evening or a sports day, or any event at school, for that matter? And you know why I had to focus so much energy on Max. He really struggled.'

'He was a bully.'

Steph couldn't stand that term being applied to her son, remembering the sweet child he used to be before things started to change. 'I don't think he was deep down.'

'You *know* he bullied me.' Bea was clearly frustrated. 'How much evidence did you need?'

Steph's heart sank. She was in no mood for an argument, feeling sleepy again, her lids heavy.

'I love you both. Equally,' she said.

'You loved him more.'

There was something of the truth in that statement, a truth no parent would ever acknowledge out loud. But Steph was all for the underdog, helping the underachiever, wanting the best for her child. For both her children. 'No, I didn't.'

'You spent way more time with him than with me.'

'I don't... I don't think I did.'

'I *know* you did.' Bea was emphatic, her gaze too uncomfortable to meet.

Steph's eyes closed again, her head resting on the back of the sun lounger.

'It's all right, Mum, I've forgiven you,' Bea said, her voice gentle now, seeming to come from far away. 'You've got the rest of your life to make it up to me.' She laughed then, a weird, strangled sound, although Steph couldn't work out why it was funny, her fuzzy brain drifting off into sleep.

CHAPTER THIRTY-NINE

Noah followed Chris, the fire investigator, into the hospital, stopping behind him at reception in the queue of people waiting to be attended to. Three people were behind the desk dealing with queries. Finally, it was their turn and Chris asked if Steph was still there.

The receptionist scrolled through her screen, tapped a few buttons.

'Let me see... She was discharged in the early hours of this morning.'

'Okay, thank you.' Chris smiled his thanks and started walking away.

Noah followed him outside, and grabbed his arm. 'Wait. Is that it? I thought you were going to help me find out where she is?'

'I'm sorry, but I just investigate the fire. We can't ask for contact details.' He gave a helpless shrug. 'Data protection. There's nothing more I can do, I'm afraid. But at least you know she's okay, or they wouldn't have discharged her.'

Noah frowned, his mouth working out his next question. 'Just to be clear... You think it was arson?'

Chris nodded, his lips pursed, his eyes troubled. 'I don't think we can draw any other conclusion, to be honest. An accelerant was used to lead the fire through the house, you see. That's why it took hold so quickly.' A shadow crossed his face. 'Don't tell anyone I told you that.'

Noah wondered who he thought he was going to tell. 'So... the police will be involved?'

'Yes. That's the next step. They'll take it from here.'

'And they'll try and find Steph?'

'I'm sure they will.' Chris put a hand on Noah's shoulder. 'Don't worry yourself, mate. I'm sure she's fine. They wouldn't have discharged her if she wasn't okay. A relative must have come and picked her up.' He checked his watch. 'Look, I've got to dash, good luck with everything.' He pulled out his wallet, took out a couple of twenty-pound notes and passed them to Noah. 'Hope this helps.'

With a wave of the hand he was gone, Noah watching him disappear into the car park while he stood outside the hospital entrance wondering where to go next, the money clutched tightly in his fist. Unease sat at the back of his neck. If it was arson, who was responsible? That's what he was worried about. The urge to hide overtook him and he sneaked away to a quiet corner at the back of the building, exhausted by the events of the previous night and overwhelmed by the need to sleep.

The next day, he woke with a clear mind and a guilty conscience. He wanted to see Steph for himself, see with his own eyes that she was safe.

He went back inside the hospital, joined the queue at the reception desk.

'I've come to see my mum. Stephanie Baker,' he said to the receptionist, a different woman from the previous day.

The woman's eyes flicked up and she gave him a sympathetic smile. 'Let's have a look...' She scrolled then nodded to herself. 'Here she is. Says she was discharged.'

Noah looked puzzled. 'That's weird. She rang me and I said I'd pick her up.'

'Oh dear, looks like there was a change of plan.'

He gave the woman a hesitant smile. 'I'm just wondering where she is, that's the problem. Her phone isn't working, you see, and I'm desperate to see her.' He hoped she could see the concern in his eyes. That was real even if his story wasn't. 'Our house burned down. I was out working and... well, I'm basically homeless now.' His eyes met hers and he could see she felt sorry for him. Could he get more information out of her? 'Was it my dad who picked her up?'

The woman looked at the screen, fingers pressed to her lips, her eyes glancing from side to side, checking what her colleagues were doing. She lowered her voice, leaned forwards so nobody else could hear. 'I can't actually tell you details. But I can tell you it wasn't your dad. It was a woman. Her address is in Dewsbury.' She gave him a smile, patted his hand. 'Hope that helps.'

She looked past him to the next person in the queue and he shuffled away, not sure what to do next. He went outside and sat on a bench, with no place to go, nowhere to call home and the knowledge that the man he still owed a debt to was probably after him. The main thing that was bothering him, though, was Steph. Someone had tried to kill her. Why else would they set the house on fire with her in it?

He remembered the car speeding away from the kerb when they'd stumbled out of the house. A car he'd seen before. It was his only lead and he had to check out his hunch that it belonged to her husband.

Steph had told him about the apartment block where he lived. Then he remembered how aggressive Andy had been when they'd last met. How he refused to listen, had wanted Noah out of the house, sure he was trouble. Well, he'd been right about that.

The apartments were down by the station, and he'd have to be careful not to be seen. He slipped into a charity shop and bought himself a beanie hat, grey joggers and hoodie. He even found trainers, a bit big, but they would do. He was glad to dump his clothes – blackened and stinking of fire – and checked himself in the mirror, quite pleased with the result. He didn't look like himself, way too clean, but that was the point. Was he still identifiable, though? He bought a pair of reading glasses, just to make sure.

Outside the apartment block, he tried to remember the name of the person he was looking for. Charlie? It sounded familiar. Hadn't he overheard Steph and her husband arguing about that? The fact that Charlie was a woman? He went into the foyer, saw there was an office in the corner, a concierge service in operation.

'Hello?' a woman's voice called out to him. 'Can I help you?'

He walked over, unsure. She was dressed in a business suit, hair all sleek and shiny, big glasses. 'I'm... um. I'm looking for a man called Andy Baker.'

The woman frowned. 'Hmm, I'm not sure I recognise that as the name of one of our tenants. Just let me check.'

'Oh, he's not a tenant, I don't think. Not formally. He was staying with a woman called Charlie, I think?'

The woman thought for a moment, then she held up a finger as she remembered, a satisfied smile on her face. 'That could be Charlotte Watts. Let me ring for you, see if Mr Baker is here.'

She disappeared into her office and came back looking a little startled. 'Well, I wasn't expecting that response. She says he's not there and if you see him to tell him to come and get his stuff before she throws it out.'

Clearly, they'd had a disagreement. It also meant that Andy wasn't here the night of the fire, so it could have been him. Was it a way of forcing Steph to move out? Or a way of getting rid of her completely?

He walked outside and sat by the river, needing a moment to think things through.

There was only one course of action open to him. The one he least wanted to take.

CHAPTER FORTY

Steph woke up with a splitting headache again. She frowned. There seemed to be a pattern to this. Every time she had something to eat, she fell asleep and woke up feeling terrible. Her eyes drifted across the garden to where Bea was busy, walking up and down with one of those little machines that scatters fertiliser on the lawn.

It was funny, her daughter had never been keen on gardening. That had been Mark's thing. He was always adding new things, like the pond and the Japanese garden in front of it, the little copse of acers which turned fantastic shades of red, gold and bronze in the autumn. The borders full of lavender which smelled wonderful when you walked past. Steph had to hand it to him, he had quite an eye for garden design. But maybe he just hadn't let Bea get involved?

Mark was surprisingly environmentally friendly for someone so materialistic. The house was carbon neutral, built to the highest standards. He'd even had a biomass boiler installed recently, burning woodchip from renewable sources. Steph remembered him showing her round last time she was here, regaling her with all the technical details and extremely proud of his new acquisition.

Steph drifted in and out of sleep, and every time she woke up, Bea was on another area of the vast lawn, engrossed in her job. But then if Mark was gone, it was her responsibility now to tend to the grounds and maybe it was something to do to take her mind off things. Poor Bea. After her own marital troubles, she could completely empathise. It was all so sudden, though. She usually rang Steph up whenever she and Mark had a row, looking for moral support, but this time, when it was really serious... nothing.

It doesn't feel right. In fact, nothing about Bea – or the way she was behaving – felt right.

She sat on the edge of the sun lounger, fully awake now. It was time to have a proper conversation with her daughter. Be a bit more assertive, although she always struggled with that where Bea was concerned. Still, it was the only way Steph was going to make it clear that she couldn't live here.

She walked over to where Bea was working, emptying a bucket of some powdery substance into the spreader machine, coughing as the dust blew into her face.

Bea turned, shocked by her sudden appearance. 'Mum, don't stand there, for God's sake. You don't want to be breathing that in. Just...' She put the bucket down and grabbed Steph's arm, guiding her back to the patio. 'It's not good for your lungs.'

'I wanted to talk to you, love.' She turned to face her daughter, took a deep breath. 'Look, I'm not sure you're thinking straight. Mark's leaving has obviously been a big shock and then the fire and everything. You've been through a traumatic time.' She sighed. 'The thing is, though, I need to go back to Leeds. I've got work to do and the insurance company will pay for accommodation until the house is fixed.'

Bea's mouth dropped open. 'No, Mum. No. You need to

rest, in fact, let me make you some lunch.' She looked at her watch. 'Well, it's more like tea now. You've been out for ages.'

Steph clenched her teeth, frustrated that her daughter wasn't listening. 'I'm really not hungry. But I do need to speak to the insurance company quite urgently and as my phone has gone missing, I was wondering if I could borrow yours.'

Bea flapped a hand, dismissing her request. 'I told you, I dealt with all that. Nothing to worry about.'

'I was wondering then... what did they say about hotel accommodation?'

Bea smiled and pulled her into a hug. 'Don't be daft. Why on earth would you want to go to a hotel when you can be here?' She turned and swept an arm across the magnificent gardens. 'It's paradise, isn't it?'

Steph pulled away, trying to be firm. 'Yes, of course it's beautiful. But the thing is... I need to go to work. I've got a few projects on the go and they won't happen without me pushing them on. And I've got things to chase up for clients, housing to sort out for them. Plus, I have to check that Noah is okay.'

Everything rushed back, all the things she should be doing, the people she should be looking after. It was important. And, as important as anything, was finding out if this mysterious character Noah had talked about was in fact Max. If he'd been the one causing her trouble. *Did he set the house on fire?* If nothing else, she needed to speak to the police.

Bea's bottom lip started to wobble, her voice all shaky when she spoke. 'You want to leave me. All on my own. When my husband's... gone?'

Steph bit her lip. *I can't, can I?*

'Tell you what?' She put a reassuring hand on Bea's shoulder. 'Why don't you come with me? We could get a nice room for both of us.'

Bea shook her head. 'No, you don't understand. I've booked us a holiday.'

'What?'

'That's right.' Bea smiled, that weird gleam in her eye again. 'I thought you could convalesce in Cornwall. I'm sure I told you. Bill said you could take as much time off as you needed.' She guided Steph back to the sun lounger, pulling her down so they were sitting side by side. 'Honestly, Mum, there's nothing to worry about. We're leaving tomorrow.'

Bea smelled of ash. That must have been what she was spreading on the lawn. Part of the routine with the biomass boiler, she supposed. The ash had to go somewhere. All part of the cycle, but it reminded her of the fire.

'But there are things to worry about. I need to speak to the police.' Quickly, she ran through everything that had been happening, what Noah had told her about the man he was in debt to, how he had been causing all the trouble. How on the night of the fire Noah had been sure something bad was going to happen. 'I didn't want to ring you so late at night and you hadn't been answering my calls, so I wasn't sure if I was going to be welcome. I was planning on ringing you in the morning to see if I could come and stay.'

Bea looked stunned for a moment, then laughed. 'You were going to come and stay anyway?'

'That's right, but then the house caught fire and – well, you know the rest.' Steph stared at her. She really was being very odd. 'Are you okay? Do you think, perhaps, this is all a bit much for you?'

'I've never felt better.' She patted Steph's leg, a satisfied smile on her face.

'The thing is, I'm wondering if Max is behind all this. If he set Noah up to pin the drug dealing on me. Maybe he started the fire?'

Bea's smile fell from her face. 'Oh, Mum, you've got this all wrong. That's not Max. I can one hundred per cent guarantee it.' She caught Steph's eye, frowning now, her voice sharp. 'You know, you're doing it again. Here I am bringing you somewhere safe, looking after you and all you can think about is bloody Max.' She tapped her head with her index finger, leaning towards Steph until she was inches from her face. 'Get it in here that Max is never coming home. Not ever. He went ten years ago and you really need to forget him. Then maybe you'd be able to think about me.'

Steph reared away from her daughter, alarmed by the venom in her voice. 'I know you two didn't get on, but as I've said many times before, you are both my children.'

Bea sneered. 'Wrong again. He *was* your child. I still am.' She gave a frustrated growl. 'I can't believe you're doing this. Ruining everything. Why can't we just have a nice time together? Why can't you be interested in me? Just me, here in front of you, your only bloody daughter. What the hell do I have to do to get a bit of parental approval, eh? A bit of love and affection?'

Steph could feel Bea's body trembling next to her, eyes shining, and knew she had to do something to neutralise the situation before Bea exploded.

'Oh, sweetheart, you know I love you. Of course I do. I was just looking at all the options. Noah said this man he owes money to was ex-forces and I was trying to think who'd want to frighten me out of my house and the only people I could think of were Max, your dad and his friend who wants to buy the property.' Bea glared at her, mouth clamped shut. 'It's nothing to do with not loving you. Nothing at all.' She grabbed Bea's hands and held them tight. The truth was she didn't know what to do with her when she was like this, and she was desperate to calm her down.

Bea snatched her hands away and stared at the house, lost in her thoughts for a moment. She stood. 'I'll... um, go and get us something to eat,' she said, walking away.

Steph lay back on the sun lounger, emotionally exhausted

and relieved to have a moment to herself to think. That had been quite some outburst, filled with so much pent-up rage. She hadn't realised how strongly Bea had felt about having her undivided attention.

It could be her.

The thought popped into her head, making her breath catch in her throat.

Is it possible?

Bea had plans for them. Lots of plans, which she'd clearly spent a fair amount of time thinking about. She wasn't behaving like Steph's presence was unexpected. She was behaving like it was all part of a natural progression. *Something she'd prepared for.* And she'd been pestering Steph to come and stay for a while now.

Is this a response to Mark's leaving? She doesn't want to be on her own? Or was it something more established? An unfulfilled need that went back into her childhood. On the surface, she didn't seem unduly concerned about Mark walking out on her, but deep down, was she in shock? *Would that explain her strange behaviour?* Whatever the reason for Bea's strangeness, if she was the one behind it all, she definitely had a warped view of the world.

As she struggled to find an alternative theory, Noah's comments wormed into her head. He was convinced the man he was in debt to had been out to get her. Could he be a gun for hire, as it were? Bea wasn't short of money. Hadn't she just said she was loaded? She'd be perfectly capable of paying someone to do her dirty work.

She shook the thoughts from her head, annoyed with herself for even entertaining such fantastical ideas. *You've been watching too many movies.* This was stupid thinking. Why couldn't she just believe that Bea was desperate for a bit of attention now that she was on her own? *It's natural, isn't it? All perfectly explainable.*

And Noah could have been shifting blame to protect himself. She hadn't thought about that one, had she? Why should she trust a word he said? He'd told the police she was a drug dealer, for God's sake. Who was she going to believe, her daughter or a virtual stranger? But the fire... He'd left the house before that had happened. Then she remembered her bedroom window, the way it didn't shut properly. She hadn't nailed it as Bea had suggested because she'd stormed out and... He could have come back in when she was asleep.

Her head felt like it might explode with her conflicting theories. Then Andy's face popped into her mind and she was more confused than ever. He'd been adamant he wasn't having an affair with Charlie, although Bea had hinted that he was. Mind you, Bea's strategy had always been divide and conquer where her parents were concerned, playing them off against each other. *Is she doing that now? Keeping us apart rather than letting us settle our differences?*

The more she thought about the last few months the more the evidence stacked up to suggest Bea had been behind the collapse of Steph's life as she knew it. Her heart was racing now, Bea's words ringing in her ears. 'We have our whole lives together.' Was that her plan? To keep Steph with her, make sure she could do nothing but give her the undivided attention she'd always desired.

Sweat gathered under her arms, making her hands clammy.

I've got to leave.

She'd never been more certain of anything in her life. Fear wrapped its tendrils round her chest, squeezing the air from her lungs, making it hard to breathe. She saw Bea come out of the kitchen, a tray in her hands with two green smoothies sitting on it. Steph's heart sank. It would be full of kale and spinach and God knows what else and Steph really couldn't stomach all the goodness. She had an old-fashioned palate, liked her meals to be solid rather than liquid. Her stomach churned at the thought of having to ingest the slime in a glass that was heading towards her.

She realised that since she'd been at Bea's, she hadn't really eaten a proper meal. She kept falling asleep and missing normal mealtimes. And then when she did get something, it was liquid, with a gritty texture. Something sparked in her brain. A pattern making itself clear.

She's drugging me.

Her pulse speeded up a little more. No way was she drinking that thing. She'd have to make an excuse. Her mind scrabbled to work out what to say as her daughter came closer.

Bea put the drinks on the table and passed one to Steph while she took the other. Steph's stomach lurched. She shook her head, put a hand up to stop Bea passing anything to her. 'I'm sorry, love. I'm feeling a bit nauseous.'

'This will settle your stomach.' Bea winked at her. 'Secret ingredients.'

Steph forced a smile. 'I'll give a try in a bit. Honestly... I can't drink it now.'

Bea held it out to her. 'Don't be a wuss, Mum. Just get it down you. Think of it as medicine.'

Hmm, she keeps saying that. Food as medicine. Was it a Freudian slip because there was real medicine in there? Some sort of sleeping tablet crushed in?

Steph took the glass and put it on the table, adamant she wouldn't be forced to drink it. She looked around wondering what she could use as a distraction, remembered the pool that Mark had built in the basement. 'I was wondering if we could have a swim. That would be relaxing, wouldn't it?' It would also mean Bea would have to take off her watch and Steph might have a chance to grab it and get out of the house. Even if she had to flag down a passing motorist.

'Oh, we haven't got time for that. We're going once we've had lunch. I've packed everything up.'

'Going? What do you mean?'

Bea downed her drink then stared at Steph, a deep frown creasing her brow. 'You're just incapable of hearing anything I say, aren't you? It's like I'm invisible.' Anger snapped through her words. She moved closer, picking up the drink and forcing it into Steph's hand. 'Drink this. Then we are going on holiday. I told you all about it if you'd bothered to listen.' She gave a determined smile. 'We're going to Cornwall.'

Bea's face was flushed, her pupils dilated. There was a scary look in her eye and Steph started to gabble. 'I'm sorry, I'm just not thinking straight. I remember now. Cornwall, how lovely. Of course I'll drink this but could I have some water to dilute the aftertaste?'

She took a sip, forced herself to swallow, pulled a face. 'Honestly, I'm not a big fan of these green smoothies.'

Bea huffed and stood up, stomped into the house and Steph tipped the contents of her class into the planter beside her, leaving a little bit in the bottom. When Bea reappeared and she was sure she was watching, she pretended to finish it off.

She gulped down the water Bea offered her and sat back on her lounger, only to be pulled to her feet by her daughter. 'Come on, you're not listening again. I said we're going.'

'What? Right now? Are you sure we can't have a swim first?'

'I don't think you'll be in a fit state for a swim. Can't have you drowning.' Bea laughed and linked her arm with Steph's pulling her towards the house. Steph tensed, thought about resisting, then decided it was better to go with the flow. Surely she'd have a better chance of escape on their journey rather than in the house with its invisible door locks.

Nobody will know where we are. Her heart flipped and she took some deep breaths, trying to calm down. *You'll be fine. You're an intelligent woman. You'll think of something.* For the first time in her life she'd have nobody to rely on except herself.

CHAPTER FORTY-ONE

Steph allowed herself to be led towards the underground car park. 'A holiday will be lovely, just what I need after the last few months.'

Bea's hand squeezed her arm and she beamed at her. 'I know! That's exactly what I thought. And nobody will bother us. It's a lovely little cottage, fully modernised, overlooking the Atlantic. There's a delivery service for everything we might need. Honestly, we don't need to be bothered by anyone.'

Steph's legs felt heavy, her brain telling her to resist, that she was going to be a virtual prisoner, she needed to run. Right now. But she held her nerve, because in this high-tech fortress there was nowhere to run to. 'Sounds idyllic,' she said, a note of hysteria in her voice. She swallowed her panic. *Stay calm. Stay calm. Stay calm.* There would be a chance. At some point, if she was patient, Bea would relax and she'd be able to get out. Until then, it wasn't so bad, was it? Spending time with her daughter.

She's drugging you.

Apart from that. She'd just have to be careful what she ate and drank. Maybe pretend to be drugged so Bea wouldn't notice something was wrong. Yes, that's what Bea was expecting, so that's what she needed to do.

She yawned and clung on to Bea's arm. 'I'm feeling a bit wobbly, actually. Honestly, I don't know what's wrong with me. I don't seem to want to do anything but sleep.'

Bea patted her hand. 'It's a natural reaction to shock and you've had a really terrible time, haven't you? You'll just have to relax and let me look after you for a while. Let all the fuss die down.'

'What fuss would that be?' Steph asked before she bit her lip, wishing she hadn't said anything.

'The fire, Mum. Your house burned down, remember?'

'Oh yes.' Steph giggled, which she hoped was a suitably doped up reaction. It was certainly the opposite of what she felt like doing.

Bea stopped by a sporty red Honda with roll bars and bucket seats. She opened the door. Steph frowned. 'What happened to your BMW?' She'd been hoping that Andy would realise she was missing and would know Bea picked her up, maybe come looking for her when he couldn't reach her on her phone. If Bea wasn't at home either – and this was a long shot – they might trace Bea's car from number plate recognition. That wouldn't happen now. She was literally going to disappear. Her heart thundered in her chest. *Think, think, think.* But her mind was blank, wiped clean by panic.

'This is Mark's. Mine now. Goes like the clappers. I thought it would be fun for a change.'

Steph didn't answer, just climbed in and closed her eyes, let Bea sort out the seat belt, pretending to be too sleepy to do it herself. Meanwhile, her brain started to throw ideas at her. Outlandish, stupid ideas until it came up with something that might be the solution. Something that was only possible now they were in a different car. It seemed like fate.

She'd pounced on the plan, clutching it to her. This was it.

Her one chance. It would go against all her instincts, she'd have to be brave and pick the right moment. As plans went, it wasn't without risk, but it really was her only chance.

Bea made sure they were both fastened in then turned on the radio, humming to herself as she exited the car park and negotiated the lanes out of the village. Steph kept one eye closed – the one Bea could see, the other just a little open, so she could judge the right moment. They turned onto the main road, a dual carriageway with grass embankments, quite busy at this time of day. Steph took a deep breath. *Do it now!* She yanked the handbrake on, tugged the steering wheel out of Bea's hands and turned it towards the side of the road.

The car skidded in a terrifying semi-circle, before jerking to a halt. The car behind went hurtling into them. Another massive jolt as the car behind that one slammed into them. A three-car pile-up. The airbags went off with a bang and she was thrown back in her seat, a sharp pain in her chest, Bea screaming.

A few moments later, her door was pulled open, a man's concerned face peering in. 'Bloody hell, what happened?' he said, his eyes wide with shock. 'Are you okay?'

'Bea. My daughter,' Steph gasped. 'She had a fit or something. Please help her.'

Steph clambered out of the vehicle and sank into a heap on the embankment at the side of the road while the chaos erupted in front of her.

Bea was yelling at the man that she was fine, to get his bloody hands of her. Running round the car and shouting at Steph to get back in.

'I'm not going,' she shouted back, looking around for people to stop Bea hauling her away. She started crawling up the embankment, her arms and legs refusing to co-ordinate. 'Please don't let her take me.'

Two men got hold of Bea and pulled her back. 'Look, love,

you've got to see that your car ain't going anywhere in that state. Not with the back and the bonnet caved in like that. And look at that wheel. It's not supposed to be at that angle, is it?' She wrenched her arms from their grasp and stormed up the embankment to where Steph had come to a halt, cowering in the grass, horrified by the expression on her daughter's face.

CHAPTER FORTY-TWO

Noah made the call, the number embedded in his mind.

'Hello.'

A familiar voice. He choked back a sob but couldn't speak.

'Hello? Who's this?'

Still he couldn't say anything, just listened to breathing on the other end of the line. He cleared his throat. 'George, it's me. Noah.'

Now it was his stepdad's turn to be speechless. He could hear his mum's voice in the background. 'Is it one of those prank calls?' The sound of sniffing. 'George, what's wrong?'

'Hello, who's this?' His mum's voice, shrill and annoyed.

Noah laughed through his tears. *Typical Mum, taking over.* 'It's me. Noah.'

A shriek, and then his stepdad came back on the line.

'Where are you, son? You're not in trouble. You've never been in trouble and I'm sorry if I ever did anything to make you feel like this wasn't your home.' He gave a big sniff. 'Your mum's been chewing my ear about that and I can see now that I could have been a bit more... inclusive. I've learned my lesson. Things will be different, I promise.' He could hear his mum in the background but couldn't make out what she was saying. 'We're coming to get you. Just tell me where you are.'

Noah's euphoria at hearing the voices of home fizzled like a wet firework. *Be brave, it's time to tell the truth.* If he wanted to climb out of this pit he'd got himself into, he had to face up to everything. 'Actually, I am in trouble. Big trouble.' He hesitated, pushed himself on. 'I need your help.'

'Oh, son, we thought you were dead. Nothing can be worse than that.' George's voice was thick with emotion. Noah had never heard him like this, never seen this soft side to him, but hope ignited in his heart. 'Just tell us where you are. We're coming. Right now, we're on our way.'

Noah gave them directions then he made the next call.

'Hello, Leeds Central Police Station.'

'Hello. I... um, well... I have some information for you. About the house fire in Headingley. I want to come and give you a statement but I...' He closed his eyes. Was this something he'd regret? Was he setting a ball rolling that he couldn't stop, that would leave him exposed? 'Thing is, I'm hiding. I don't... feel safe.' He hesitated, then powered on, fortified by his parents' reaction. *It's going to be okay.* 'I need someone to come and get me.'

The voice at the other end of the line started taking information, asking questions and a few minutes later he leaned back against the wall. That was it. Done. Ten minutes and he'd be safe. For now. Then everything would be out in the open, he'd tell the truth and face the consequences. Living in constant fear was no life. Living on the streets was harder than he'd ever imagined. Whatever happened to him now, at least he'd be able to look forwards. He was still young. He could rebuild his life and he knew that his parents would be there to help him find his way. His heart was racing, and he felt a bit light-headed. *I've done the right thing.*

Hopefully by giving a witness statement in relation to the

fire, it would lessen the impact of the other stuff he'd done. It might make him vulnerable, but he had to live with his conscience, own his mistakes.

He watched as a police car drew to the kerb and only then did he come out of his hiding place. This was it. The first steps to a better future.

A police officer got out of the front of the vehicle, surprised when Noah appeared behind him.

'I'm Noah Stratham,' he said, his voice shaking with nerves. 'I'm hoping you're here to pick me up.'

'That's right.' The officer looked him up and down, frowning. 'You've been in the wars, haven't you?'

Noah glanced behind him, feeling exposed and nervous. 'Can I get in?'

The officer opened the back door and Noah slid inside, relieved to be safe from harm at last. He leaned forwards before the driver could start the engine.

'This is urgent. I need to tell you about my landlady, I think she's in danger.'

The officers glanced at each other, clearly puzzled. 'What makes you think that?' the one in the driver's seat asked.

Noah inched forwards. 'Her house was set on fire last night and the fire investigators told me this morning that it was arson. If I hadn't been there to get her out, she could have died.'

The officer in the passenger seat got his notebook out of his pocket and started to write while the other officer spoke. 'Well, if the fire investigators are involved, there should be a report.'

'I don't think they will have written it yet. I was with them not so long ago. That's not everything, though. I went back to the hospital this morning to see how Steph, my landlady, was and she'd been discharged. They wouldn't give me the name of the person who picked her up. But they said it was a female relative who lived in Dewsbury.' Noah took a big breath, desperate to get his story out before he could be interrupted. 'I think it was her daughter. And that's why it's a problem. The thing is, I'm sure I saw her car last night, near my landlady's house. She drove off when we got outside. And she doesn't live in Dewsbury.

'So that's two things that don't add up. It's the false address that's bothering me, though. Why would she do that? The only reason I can think of is she doesn't want to be found. Which means there's something weird going on. And then—'

'Whoa, slow down,' the officer who was writing said. 'Let's just go through that again, a bit more slowly.'

'But there isn't time,' Noah insisted. 'I think Steph's in real trouble.'

'Do you know the daughter's name?'

'It's Bea. And she's married to an ex-footballer and his name is...' Noah stopped, his mouth still open, his brain frozen. 'Mark something.' He grunted with frustration as the name escaped him. 'Used to play for Leeds United, five or six years ago.' He squeezed his eyes shut, willing the name to come to him. 'Midfielder. I can picture him.'

'Oh, you mean Henderson? Mark Henderson?' the officer in the passenger seat said. 'I remember him.'

Noah gasped with relief. 'That's it. You're right. Henderson. And I'm sure my landlady said her daughter lived in Harrogate, not Dewsbury. So why would she give the hospital a false address? It doesn't make sense.' He stopped to draw breath. 'I think... well, I think she started the fire. She was there. Last night, she was there when we got out of the house. But instead of coming to help she drove away. Why would she do that?'

The police officers looked at each other again, and Noah wasn't sure if he was getting through to them how worried he was for Steph's safety.

'Please, you've got to check she's okay. And if it's a false alarm then I'm sorry. But I have this horrible feeling...'

'Okay, okay. Calm down,' the officer in the passenger seat

said. 'I'll ask them to run some checks while we're on our way back to the station and then we can take it from there.'

'I can remember the licence plate,' Noah added.

'Good, that'll help. We should be able to get an address from that.'

Noah was frantic now, remembering how long he'd had to wait when he was last at the station.

'Can't we just drive there and check she's okay? I thought someone had tried to kill her last night. But I was wrong. The intention was never to kill her. When I rang the emergency services from the house, they'd already been informed. And then I saw her daughter's car drive away when I got us both outside. Except I couldn't remember whose car it was last night, just that I'd seen it before. The intention was never for Steph to die. The intention was to make her homeless, so she would go and stay with her daughter. That's what she's been doing all along. Her daughter. A sane person wouldn't do that, would they?'

'That's quite some allegation.' The driver nodded to his colleague and they got out of the car and had a conversation before the one in the passenger seat started speaking into his radio. It seemed to be taking a very long time, but eventually they got back in.

'Okay, we're going to go via Harrogate,' the driver said. 'There's nobody else free to go and check. But we've got an address, so it shouldn't take long.'

Noah shuffled back into his seat, putting his seat belt on before they sped away, blue lights flashing, siren blaring and he knew he'd done the best he could. *Is it enough?*

CHAPTER FORTY-THREE

Bea had blood trickling from her nose, smeared across her cheeks like warpaint, fire in her eyes.

'Get back in that car,' she snarled from between clenched teeth, as angry as Steph had ever seen her. She grabbed Steph's arm and tried to yank her to her feet, but Steph resisted as much as she could.

'Leave her be,' a man said, who had been in one of the other cars and was waiting for emergency services to show up. A queue of traffic was building up along the carriageway and into the distance, the road reduced to a single lane after the crash.

Plenty of witnesses. Steph thought she might be safe now, her body so tense she thought she might break into little pieces. At least her plan had worked, even if she was a bit battered as a consequence. She had bruised ribs, damage to her neck, and some scrapes to her face, but thought she was otherwise okay.

Bea pulled away from the man she was arguing with and plonked herself next to Steph. She was silent for a little while, then got up and made a call, looking much brighter when she came back and sat down.

'It doesn't make any difference,' she said eventually. 'I have premium roadside assistance. They'll take us to Cornwall. We can hire a car when we get there.'

'I'm not getting in a car with you,' Steph said, quietly, not wanting the rest of the people waiting for assistance to be involved in the conversation. Bea turned and smiled at her, patted her arm like she'd made some silly comment.

'Of course you are. We're going on holiday, remember?'

'I don't want to go on holiday.'

Her mood changed like a switch had been flipped. 'There you go again, slapping me down. Every time I try and do something nice for you. Why is that? If I was Max you'd be off like a shot, wouldn't you?'

'No, that's not true. It's just I have a lot of things to sort out and—'

'I've sorted everything,' Bea snapped. 'I told you. All you have to do is relax and have a nice time. Why can't you understand that?'

Steph sighed, wondering how long the emergency services would be. 'Because it's not what I want.'

'Why not? Why don't you want to spend time with your daughter? Why?'

Steph chose her words carefully. 'You're not yourself, Bea. Honestly, I think you're in shock.' She tried to keep her voice calm while her stomach churned with nerves. 'I think Mark deserting you like that has turned your world upside down and you're looking to me for support. But with everything that's been going on I can't do it.'

'Of course you can.' Bea was getting increasingly irate now. 'No effort involved. All I want is for you to give me a bit of attention for once in your life.'

'I need a bit of time to myself, Bea.'

'You're so selfish, do you know that?' Bea hissed. 'You've never wanted to do anything for me, you were always bending over backwards to accommodate that stupid, pathetic brother of mine. Well, Max isn't here anymore. He'll never be here again.' Her face was inches away from Steph's. 'He's dead.' She stopped for a second to let that bombshell of information register. 'That's right, your precious son is dead.'

The thud of her heartbeat shook Steph's body as Bea confirmed her worst nightmare. 'He isn't,' she said, instinctively in denial.

Bea gave a satisfied sneer. 'I know for a fact that he is. One hundred per cent sure. I've already told you this, but again you won't listen.'

'But they would have told us.'

Bea's eyes bored into her, anchoring her to the ground. 'Who would have told you?'

She couldn't move, could hardly speak, her voice wavering, uncertain. 'The armed forces. We're his next of kin.'

'He disowned you. Us. He didn't tell anyone he had a family. So when he died there was nobody to tell.'

'How do you know this?' Tears pricked Steph's eyes. 'You're lying.'

Bea laughed. 'I may have lied about many things but not this. This is the God's honest truth. I met an old schoolfriend who joined up at the same time. Nick Scott, my first boyfriend. Remember him? They were in the same regiment. He told me.'

Steph couldn't speak, her world in free fall. She'd often wondered about his silence, wondered if it meant he'd died, but had hoped he was still alive somewhere, enjoying his life. 'How long have you known?' she whispered, hardly wanting to acknowledge it might be the truth.

'Years and years.'

'And you've let me wonder all that time, let me hope he was alive?'

Bea didn't answer for a moment, gave a sly smile, a triumphant look in her eye. 'It's harder when you don't know, isn't it?'

Steph felt a chill run through her. She knew then that Bea hadn't told her as a punishment, letting her agonise over whether he was alive or not. How had she not known her daughter had such a cruel streak hidden underneath her caring exterior?

'I don't know who you are anymore.' She backed away from her daughter. 'You've been torturing me, haven't you?'

Bea laughed, a sound infused with madness because nothing about the situation was funny. 'Oh, you don't know the half of it. I've been trying to get your attention for quite some time now. Trying to get you to come and stay with me, but you've just ignored all my efforts. I thought a little accident would do the trick and it did for a couple of weeks, but then you scampered back home, didn't you?' Her face darkened. 'After that I decided to try a different approach. Not me personally, of course. My friend, Nick, who has a whole network of minions ready to do whatever he asked.' She winked at Steph. 'Contacts, you see, Mum. I reckon a good network of contacts is the key to success, don't you think?'

Steph inched further up the banking, her heart thundering so hard her whole body was shaking. Bea didn't seem to notice, lost in her narrative.

'Even though I managed to scare you half to death, instead of coming to stay, what did you do? You got some homeless bum as a lodger.' Her fists pummelled the grass in frustration. 'Who does that rather than stay in a luxury mansion? It makes no sense. Once again, you just wouldn't listen to me, would you? I had to get those drugs planted so you'd get rid of him.'

She crawled up the embankment towards Steph, who'd reached the fence at the top and could go no further. Her eyes sparked with fury. 'You know the thing that bugs me most? It was supposed to be me who saved you from the fire. Me. I was supposed to be the heroine in that particular disaster. Then that loser beat me to it. Ruined it.'

Bea was at the top of the embankment now and Steph couldn't seem to function. She understood what it was like to be a rabbit caught in a car's headlights because that's exactly how she felt. She knew she was in danger but fear had consumed her, taken away her faculties. She couldn't even speak now she knew what her daughter was capable of. All of it had been her.

A road assistance van had managed to weave its way through the traffic and pulled up in front of the group on the embankment. A man jumped out. 'Bea Henderson?' He looked round at the little group gathered on the grass embankment.

Bea stood and yanked Steph to her feet, her fingers wrapped tightly round her arm as she dragged her down to the road. 'That's us. Come on, Mum.'

CHAPTER FORTY-FOUR

'There's been a crash,' the police driver said, listening to the radio. 'That's near where we're going, isn't it?'

His colleague was silent for a moment as he studied the satnav. 'I think you're right. But it's on the other carriageway. We should be okay. We've only got another mile before our turn-off.'

Noah gazed out of the window, willing the car to go faster, but instead of speeding up, they started to slow down. Even with their sirens blaring and lights flashing, people weren't getting out of the way. The road was blocked. There was nowhere for them to go.

'Looks like there's been a shunt up ahead,' the driver said. 'And there's the crash on the other side by the looks of it.'

'Probably people on this side gawping at what's going on over there, not concentrating on their driving that's caused the problem.' The officer tutted. 'How many times have we seen that happen?'

The driver shook his head. 'People. Can't resist having a look at a crash, can they?'

Noah's gaze tracked across the road to the other carriageway. He could see a rescue vehicle with its orange lights flashing on the roof. A man was standing by the cab having a heated conversation with a woman, her long blonde hair blowing in the wind, while his arms were gesticulating. And next to her was...

'Steph! That's her. On the other side of the road.' He tugged at the door but it wouldn't open. 'You've got to let me out. That's my landlady over there with her daughter.'

'We'll handle this,' the driver said, catching his eye in the mirror. 'You can stay here.' The officers got out of the car, weaving through the stationary traffic before hopping over the central barrier.

Noah pressed his face to the window, but it was hard to see what was happening. Other people were getting out of their cars, trying to see what was going on, but he was stuck and knew he'd just have to wait.

More police arrived on both sides of the road, along with a couple more rescue vehicles.

After what seemed like half a lifetime later, the officers came back with Steph and she slid into the back seat next to him.

'Am I pleased to see you,' he said, desperate to give her a hug, but knowing that he had to keep his distance. 'I've been so worried about Bea doing something terrible.'

Steph burst into tears, her body shaking as she sobbed and he reached for her hand, giving her the only comfort he could think of.

'I'm so sorry it came to this. I didn't know... didn't understand what was happening.' Her hand squeezed his and he knew he had to carry on or he'd never find the courage to be honest with her. 'I need to come clean and I hope you'll forgive me. I was the intruder. I was told to do it. That's how I knew how to get into the house.'

She sniffed back her tears. 'I know. I worked it out. And Bea told me the rest.' She bit her lip fighting back her tears. 'My daughter. How could she do those things to me?'

Noah didn't have an answer. Couldn't imagine what sort of twisted logic would make a person behave that way.

'You're safe now,' he said, wondering if he was forgiven.

She turned to him and gave him a watery smile, wrapped both her hands round his. 'And so are you.'

CHAPTER FORTY-FIVE

SIX MONTHS LATER

Steph looked round her ground-floor apartment, in a small development on the edge of Headingley, happy with the way it was looking. She'd only moved in a week ago but had already found places for everything.

The doorbell rang and she checked herself in the hall mirror before opening the door. Andy stood there holding a bunch of yellow roses. He looked hesitant and she smiled at him. 'Come in, see how it's shaping up.'

The animosity between them had faded and a new affection had started to blossom. She even believed that he hadn't been having an affair with Charlie after she'd bumped into her in town and asked her directly. She'd admitted that she'd had a major crush on Andy, but he hadn't been interested no matter how hard she'd tried.

She couldn't say if their relationship was built on friendship or love, but they enjoyed spending time together and had slipped into an easy routine of meeting up a couple of times a week for walks and meals, trips out to the Dales, or taking in a movie. They did more together now than they ever had when they were living in the same house, but Steph enjoyed having her own space and being able to make her own choices.

He had moved to Wakefield, having started a new job there, but Steph had wanted to stay in Leeds. This was her home-town. Her job at the homeless shelter had ended when the grant funding finished, their new application being unsuccessful. She did volunteer there though, going in on a Saturday morning every week to help people with their finances, which gave her an opportunity to meet up with Cara for lunch. Every now and again, she helped in the kitchen when Phil needed time off. She still found him a little creepy, but he'd been exonerated from any wrongdoing and she'd felt bad for suspecting him.

Now she worked as an administrator in a small distribution business, just five of them in the office and she was enjoying it immensely. A new start, new friends, and she was good at her job. It had been a real confidence boost. So much so that she'd plucked up courage to go back to the choir.

Noah had gone back home and they chatted regularly on Messenger. He was applying for jobs but hadn't managed to secure a permanent post as yet. In the meantime, he was volun-teering at the local library, which he seemed to be enjoying.

Steph and Andy's divorce was on hold for the time being, both of them unwilling to take the final step when there were so many other things to process in relation to their family. They had to deal with what had happened to Max and Bea. She had been charged with arson, attempted murder, breaking and entering, and causing criminal damage. With Noah's help, the police had tracked down and arrested her sidekick, Nick, and with his evidence, conviction was a certainty. Thankfully she'd pleaded guilty, making sure to reduce her sentence by co-oper-ating, but also sparing them the ordeal of a trial. Sentencing would be happening once psychiatric assessments had been completed.

Steph had been to see Bea at the secure hospital where she

was currently on remand. She'd seemed quite happy in a drugged-up, dreamy sort of way. The psychiatrist was still making her assessment, but it appeared she thought she had a personality disorder with psychopathic tendencies. Born that way, seemed to be the verdict, a child who wanted to monopolise her mother's affection and resented her brother having any attention. Steph had tried to press her about Max but she'd refused to speak about him.

Still, she'd found a box that had belonged to her son, one of the few things that had survived the house fire. It was a lockable metal box that had belonged to her own dad and been passed on to Max as a present when he was a boy. It contained all his treasured items. His favourite little superhero figures, photos, pictures he'd drawn which he'd been particularly proud of and half a dozen notebooks full of sketches and doodles.

Looking through them, she'd begun to understand for the first time the real dynamics of their family. Dark drawings documenting his despair at not being believed by his parents. Cartoon strips depicting incidents. His sister bullying him, tormenting him at school, causing trouble with teachers by stealing his homework, playing practical jokes and pointing the finger at him. Doing the same at home, destroying her own toys and saying he'd done it. Bea had been the bully, not him. All those years and Steph had never suspected that she was looking at everything the wrong way round. No wonder he'd left home and not been in touch. He must have been furious with his parents for not seeing it. Believing Bea instead of him.

It broke her heart that she'd been manipulated so completely by her daughter at the expense of her son.

'We're going to be late,' Andy said, tapping his watch.

She grabbed her coat, nerves fluttering in her stomach. She checked herself in the mirror again, rubbed her teeth to remove a smudge of lipstick. Andy grabbed her hand and pulled her out of the door, closing it behind them. 'You look lovely. Come on.'

They didn't speak on the way to the station, nor as they rushed through the car park. Steph checked the arrivals board when they got to the concourse. 'Platform eight,' she said, dashing ahead of her husband.

'There,' Andy shouted, pointing to a tall young man, and a dark-haired woman, a little boy between them holding each of their hands.

'Max,' she shouted. 'Max!'

The man turned at the sound of her voice, his eyes scanning the sea of people until they alighted on her and his face split into a wide grin. He waved, pulling his family towards them.

She ran, launching herself at him, feeling his arms close round her, his tears on her face. She couldn't speak, neither could he. Andy joined them, throwing his arms round his wife and son. 'Bloody hell,' he said. And that, thought Steph just about summed it up.

She hadn't believed Bea. Couldn't believe that Max was dead, had to find out for herself. Andy had felt the same and between them they had started searching, both of them horribly aware that they should have done it sooner. Because if they had, none of the recent horrors would have happened.

He had joined the army, but only served three years. By then he was trained as an engineer and had found a job in North Wales where they made parts for Boeing. He had met his wife there and they had married five years ago. Their son, Cai, was four.

Apparently, he'd thought about getting in touch many times, but he was always stopped by the shadow of Bea and her threats. She said she'd kill him if he ever came home and he'd believed her – even if his parents couldn't see the evil in her, he'd experienced it for most of his life. He couldn't let himself be anywhere near her or her influence. Then the longer he stayed away, the harder it became to make the first move. He was still angry about what had happened, but Steph was hopeful they could work their way through it.

It was funny, but she was almost glad for the traumatic events from six months ago. If Bea hadn't engineered the end of her life as she knew it, she wouldn't have the life she had now. And she had to admit, she was happier than she'd been for a very long time.

Every cloud has a silver lining.

And being reunited with Max, meeting his family, having a new daughter and grandson. Well, that was one heck of a result.

CHAPTER FORTY-SIX

Bea sat in the meeting room waiting for the psychiatrist. She looked forward to these sessions. Dr Anderson was the one person who actually listened, who was interested in Bea and asked proper questions. In fact, she was really lovely and considerate and in return, Bea would feed her little nuggets of information. Sometimes it was the truth and sometimes it wasn't. She was pretty sure the lovely doctor couldn't tell the difference.

She enjoyed making things up, flipping reality on its head. She was bullied at home. Her brother was horrible to her. She was emotionally scarred from a terrible childhood. Was it surprising she had wanted some attention from her mother, when she went to extreme lengths to get noticed?

She hadn't mentioned Mark. Not at all. Pretended that she hadn't a clue she'd even been married.

Nobody would find out the truth about that one. Not when he'd been burned to ashes in their biomass boiler and his remains spread over the garden. Not a scrap of evidence left, she was sure of that. It was his fault for picking a fight about koi carp. After all, who even cares about fish? He was ignoring her. Refusing to listen. Again. She just flipped, pushed him in the stupid fishpond, then waded in and held him under. It was only when she let go and he bobbed to the surface, eyes wide open, glassy, that she realised what she'd done. He deserved it. Thank God she'd had his phone to text messages to his friends, saying he was going to Scotland for a bit of a break. He needed some time on his own to catch his thoughts. People got lost in the mountains all the time, didn't they? Who would know?

It had been tricky getting his car up to the Highlands, but she'd organised a hire car for her to pick up at a hotel in Oban, at the end of the train line, so it looked like that's how she arrived. Nobody would know. She left his car at the start of a well-known walk up a local Monroe, so it looked like he'd gone out and got lost somewhere. Pretty bloody clever even if she did say so herself.

For the crimes the system knew about, she'd only get a few years and then she'd be out. Her solicitor thought she'd spend the time in the secure unit, and she was pretty happy about that. In all honesty, life here wasn't too bad at all. And the meds, well they were rather lovely too. What was so terrible about daydreaming the day away?

Then once she was out, she'd be free to do what she wanted. Track her stupid mother down and make her pay the price for her betrayal. Oh yes, when she was out, she'd definitely make her mother pay attention.

'Bea, are you listening?' Dr Anderson said, startling her out of her thoughts.

She blinked, turned to look at her. 'Sorry, I was miles away.'

The doctor gave one of her benign smiles, like a nun, Bea thought. 'I was saying that the police are here to interview you. They've found some new evidence.'

Bea was definitely listening now. She'd been sure she was finished with the police. They hadn't been for weeks. Maybe months. She frowned, unease stabbing at her chest. 'What do you mean, new evidence?'

The doctor stood, her notebook clasped to her chest. 'I'm sure they'll explain it all. We'll have another chat tomorrow, shall we?'

Dr Anderson closed the door, happy to hear the clunk of the lock engaging. The prison officer, who always accompanied her on these interviews, peeked through the glass panel before joining her to walk back down the corridor.

'Talk about deluded,' the prison officer said, shaking her head. 'She's no idea, has she? I heard her talking to her solicitor the other day, insisting that she had no real crimes to answer for and would be out in a couple of years tops.'

Dr Anderson laughed. 'Dream on, Bea. Let me assure you, she's going to be our guest for a very long time.'

A LETTER FROM RONA

I want to say a huge thank you for choosing to read *The Guest Room*. If you enjoyed it and want to keep up to date with all my latest releases, just sign up at the following link. Your email address will never be shared, and you can unsubscribe at any time.

www.bookouture.com/rona-halsall

It always amazes me how a book evolves from the initial spark of an idea to the finished story. This one started when I was reading an article about homelessness among young men. Some of their tales were truly chilling – that's when Noah and his predicament began to take shape. And as I thought about homes and what they meant to different people, other characters began to emerge, telling me their stories. Homelessness is such a big issue in these times, so many people living on the edge, often hidden from view. The point I wanted to make is that anyone can find themselves homeless. It just takes a bad series of events to tip our worlds upside down. We can't judge others, can we? We haven't lived their lives. I hope you understood Steph's actions came from a place of compassion and kindness.

I also wanted to explore the subject of sibling rivalry, this being a relationship unique to many families and something everyone can relate to. Even if they have no siblings of their own, they will have experienced the way their friends relate to theirs.

I hope you loved *The Guest Room*; if you did, I would be very grateful if you could write a review. I'd love to hear what you think, and it makes such a difference helping new readers to discover one of my books for the first time.

I love hearing from my readers – you can get in touch on my Facebook page, and through Twitter, Instagram or Goodreads. I also have a new website if you fancy having a look!

Many thanks,

Rona Halsall

https://ronahalsall.com

facebook.com/RonaHalsallAuthor
twitter.com/RonaHalsallAuth
instagram.com/ronahalsall
goodreads.com/18051355.Rona_Halsall

ACKNOWLEDGEMENTS

As usual I have a long list of people to thank who have been involved in the writing and production of this book. It was written while my husband was seriously ill and then going through recovery and rehab, so it's needed a lot of patience and messing about with deadlines.

Big thanks to my agent, Hayley Steed of Madeleine Milburn Literary, Film and TV Agency, for adding the voice of reason to my initial plot ideas, which can be a little crazy until she calms me down.

Also thanks to my lovely editor, Isobel Akenhead, for her endless enthusiasm and helping to make my stories so much better.

Bookouture are a wonderful publisher, who have been so kind and patient with me. So thank you to everyone who's played a part in making this book and the audio version as good as it can be and getting it out into the world. Special thanks to the publicity team of Kim, Noelle and Sarah for their efforts.

I have a little band of beta readers: Kerry-Ann, Gill, Sandra, Chloe, Wendy, Mark and Dee, who give me valuable feedback on early drafts, so thank you lovely people – the book wouldn't be what it is without your comments.

I also need to thank bloggers and reviewers who read early copies and post their reviews all over the place. I'm so grateful for the time and trouble you take.

Big thanks also to fellow authors for moral support in hard times!

Last, but not least, thanks to my husband, David, for being such a warrior and my family and friends for all their love and support.

Printed in Great Britain
by Amazon

77916222R00166